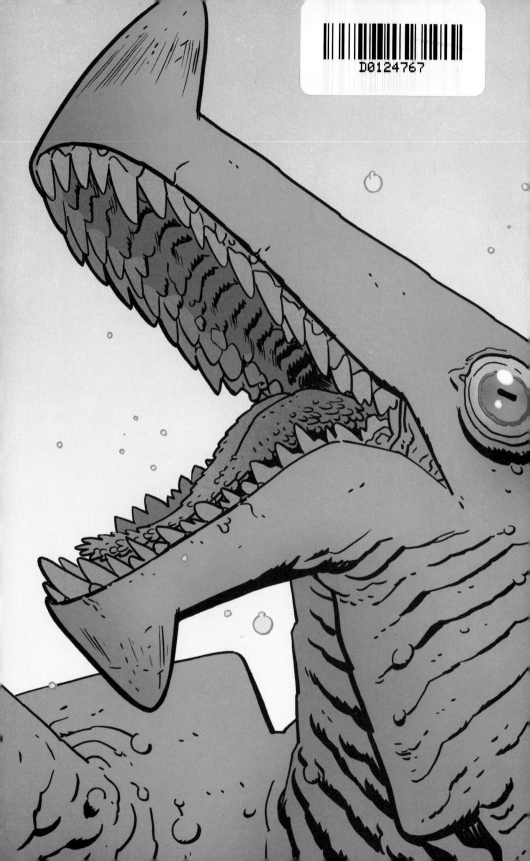

Logo Design by RICKY DELUCCO
Book Design by SONJA SYNAK
Edited by ROBIN HERRERA & ZACK SOTO

Published by Oni-Lion Forge Publishing Group, LLC

James Lucas Jones, president & publisher • Sarah Gaydos, editor in chief • Charlie Chu, e.v.p. of creative & business development • Brad Rooks, director of operations Amber O'Neill, special projects manager • Margot Wood, director of marketing & sales • Devin Funches, sales & marketing manager • Katie Sainz, marketing manager Tara Lehmann, publicist • Holly Aitchison, consumer marketing manager • Troy Look, director of design & production • Kate Z. Stone, senior graphic designer • Sonja Synak, graphic designer • Hilary Thompson, graphic designer • Sarah Rockwell, graphic designer • Angie Knowles, digital prepress lead • Vincent Kukua, digital prepress technician • Jasmine Amiri, senior editor • Shawna Gore, senior editor • Amanda Meadows, senior editor • Robert Meyers, senior editor, licensing • Desiree Rodriguez, editor • Grace Scheipeter, editor • Zack Soto, editor • Chris Cerasi, editorial coordinator • Steve Ellis, vice president of games • Ben Eisner, game developer Michelle Nguyen, executive assistant • Jung Lee, logistics coordinator

Joe Nozemack, publisher emeritus

onipress.com   lionforge.com

@ChrisSamnee | @COLORnMATT | @ccrank
@chrissamnee | @colornmatt | @ccrank

First Edition: August 2021

ISBN 978-1-62010-784-3
eISBN 978-1-62010-805-5

Printed in Canada.

Library of Congress Control Number: 2020947317

1 2 3 4 5 6 7 8 9 10

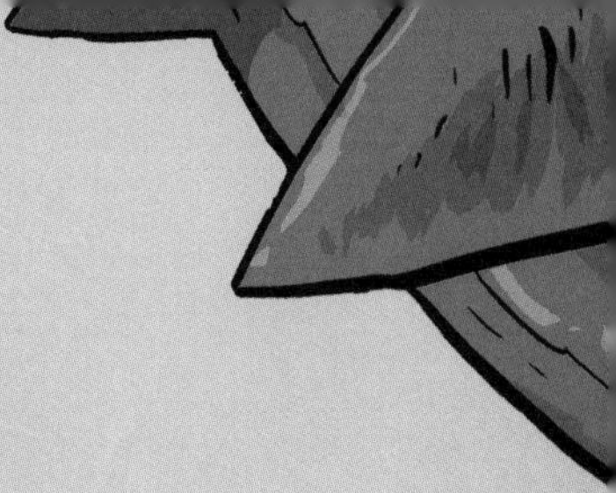

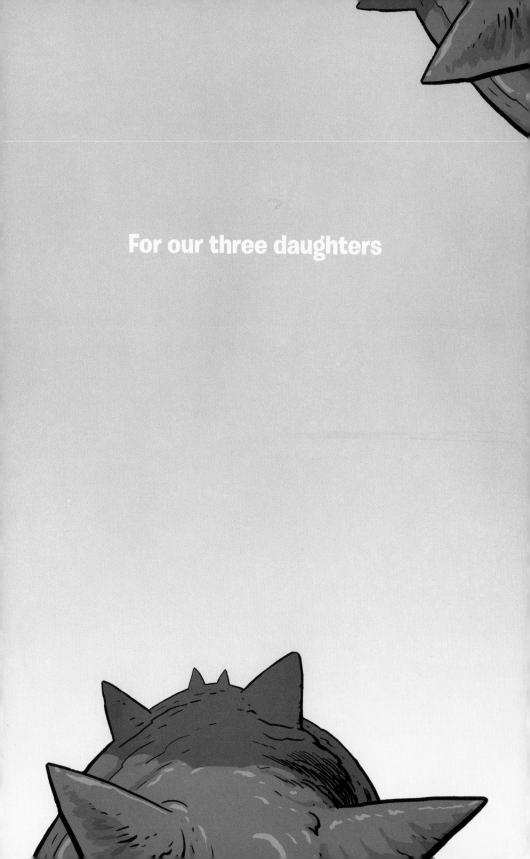

For our three daughters

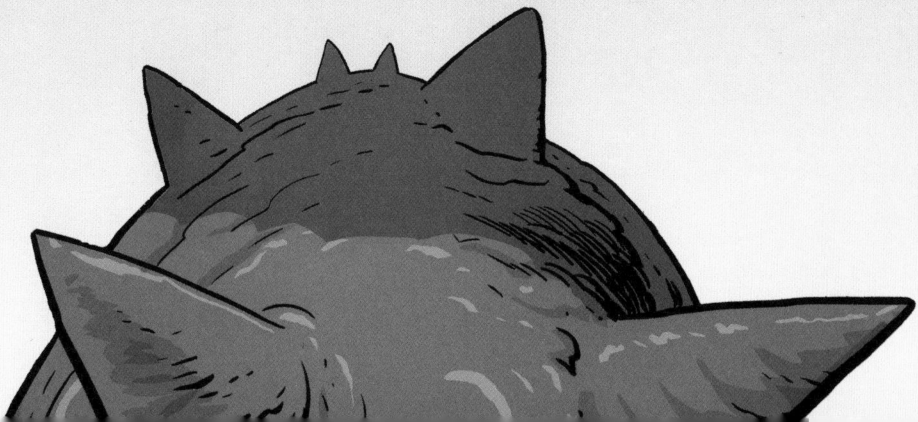

CHAPTER 1

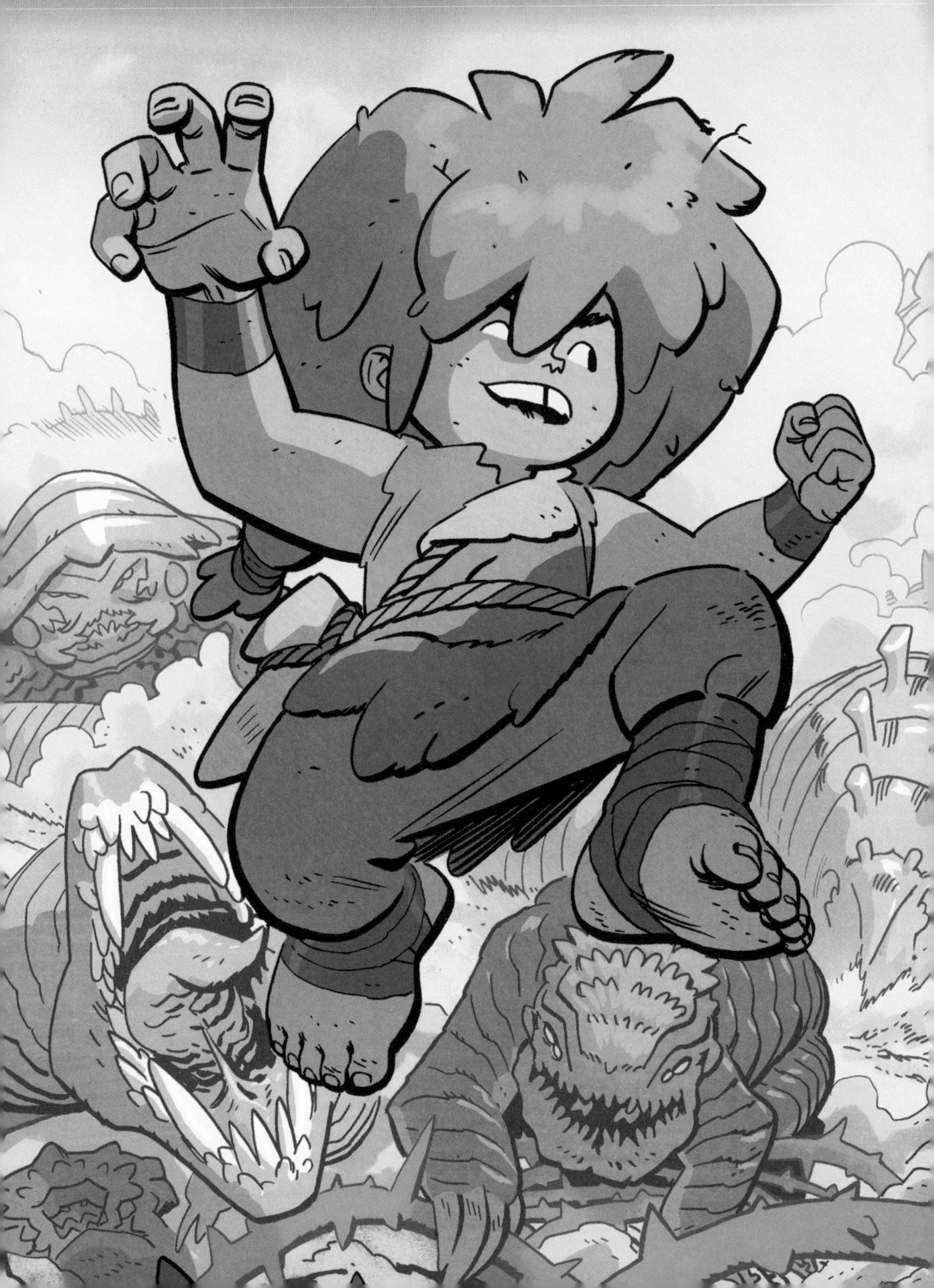

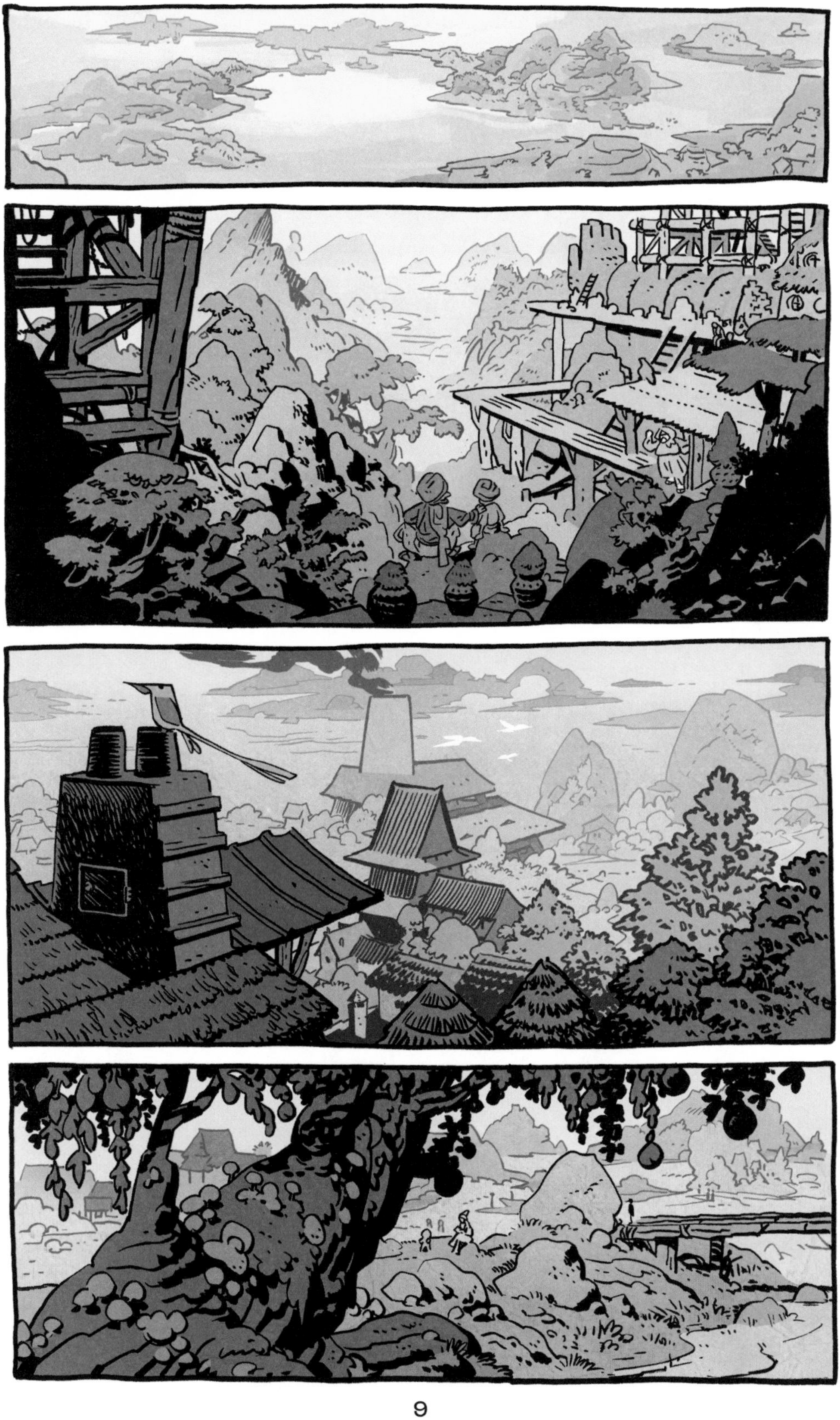

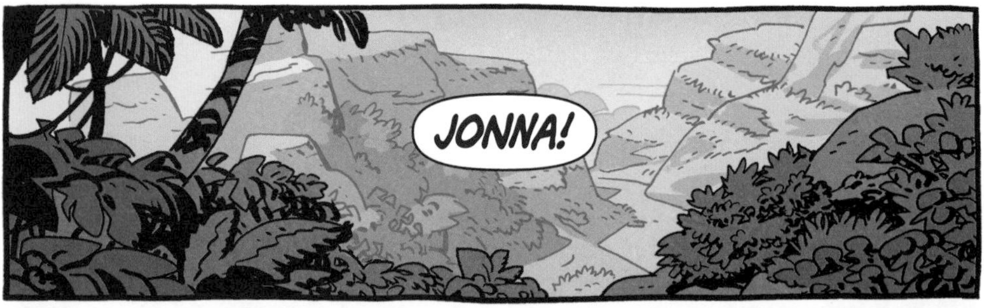
JONNA!

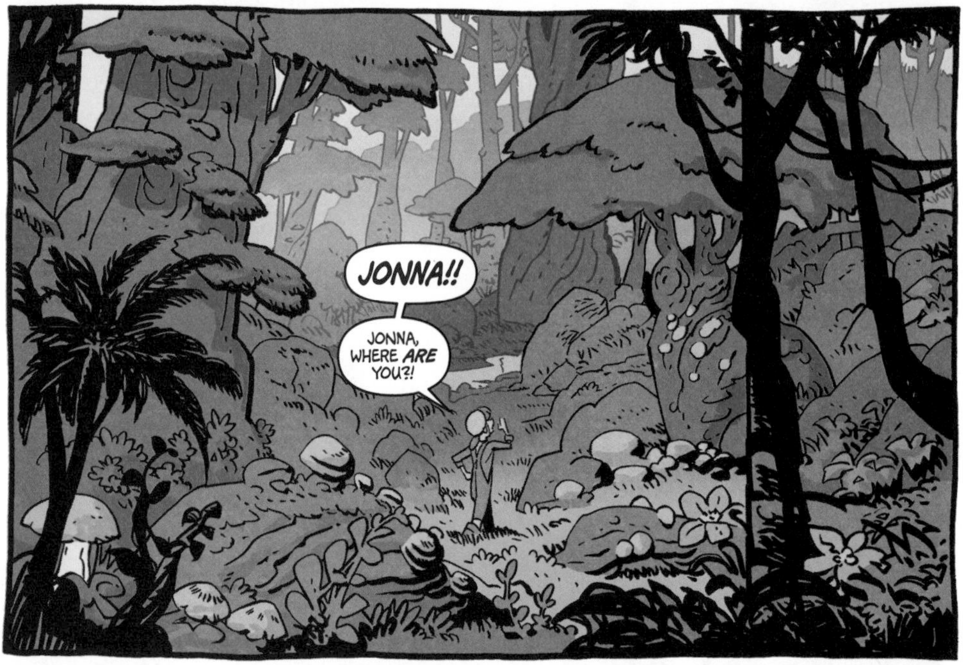
JONNA!!
JONNA, WHERE ARE YOU?!

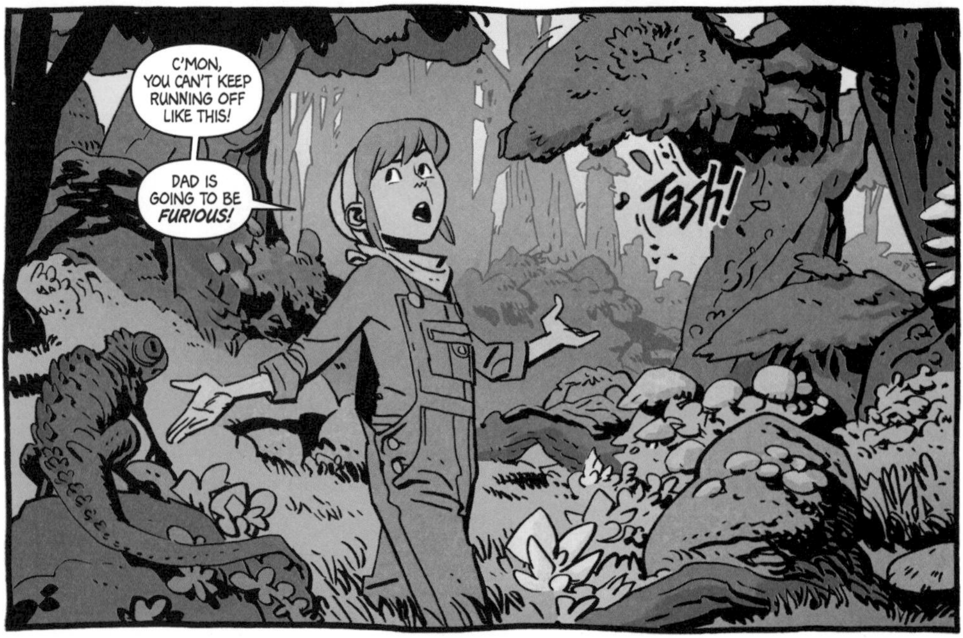
C'MON, YOU CAN'T KEEP RUNNING OFF LIKE THIS!
DAD IS GOING TO BE FURIOUS!
TASH!

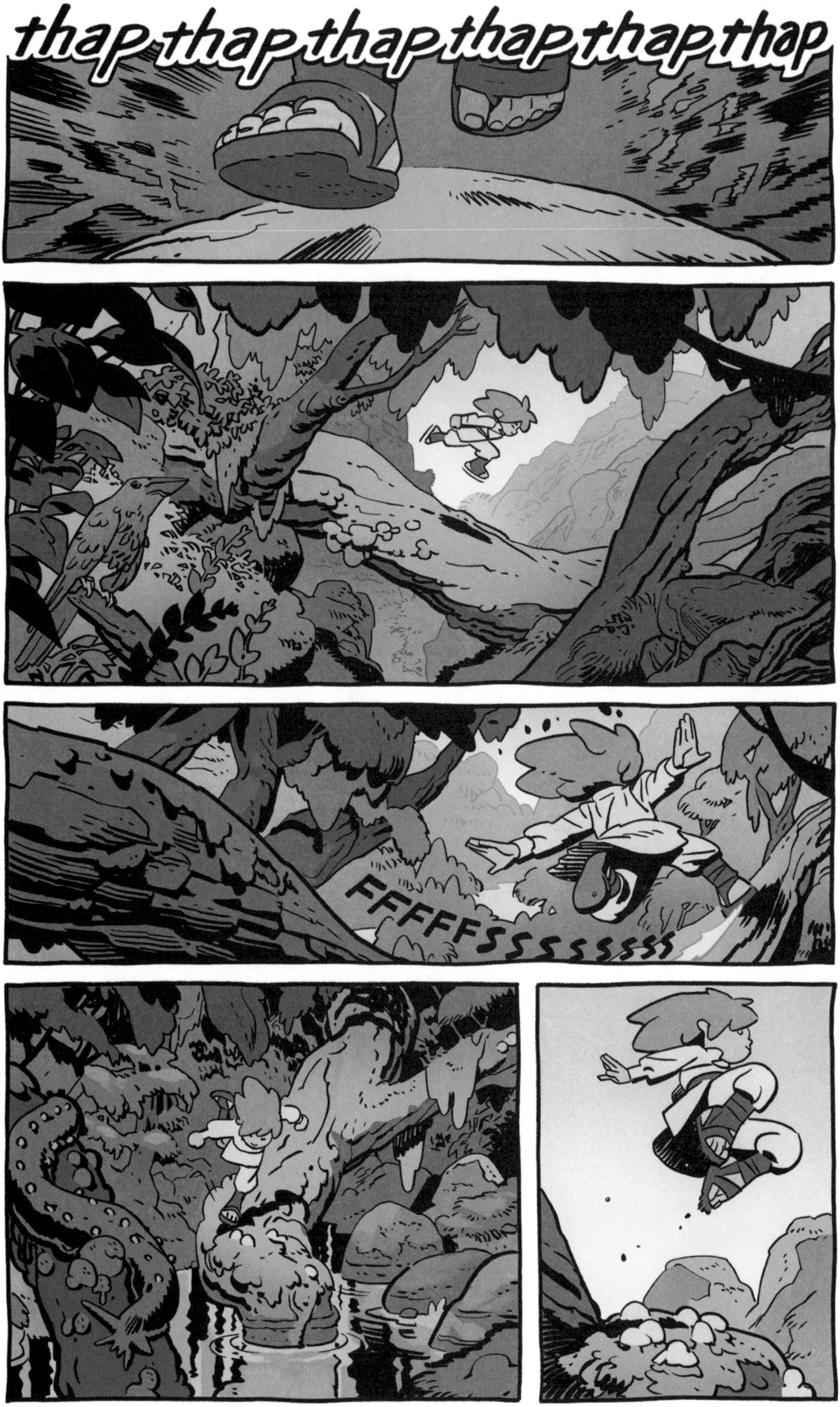
thap thap thap thap thap thap
FFFFFSSSSSSSSS

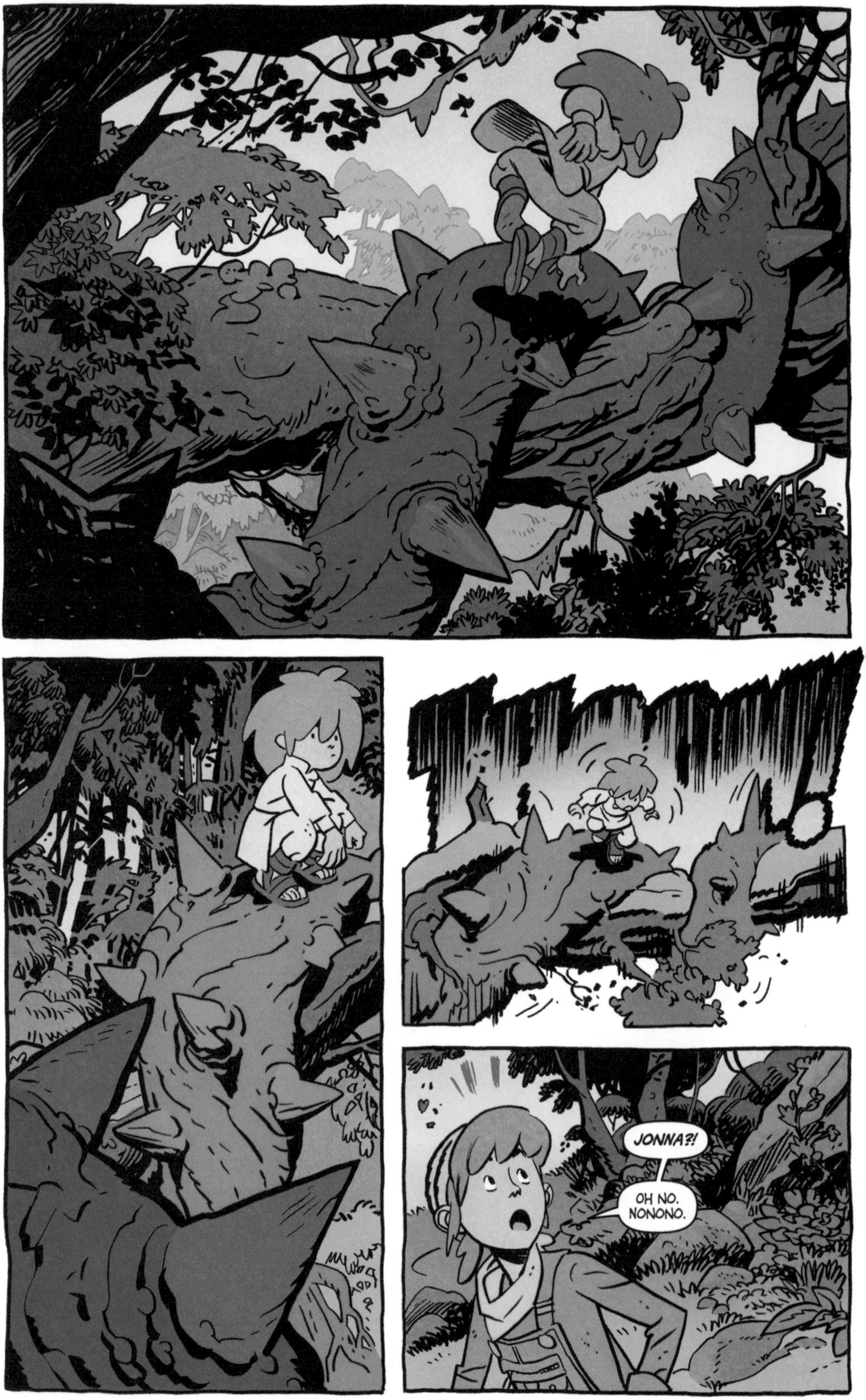
JONNA?!
OH NO. NONONO.

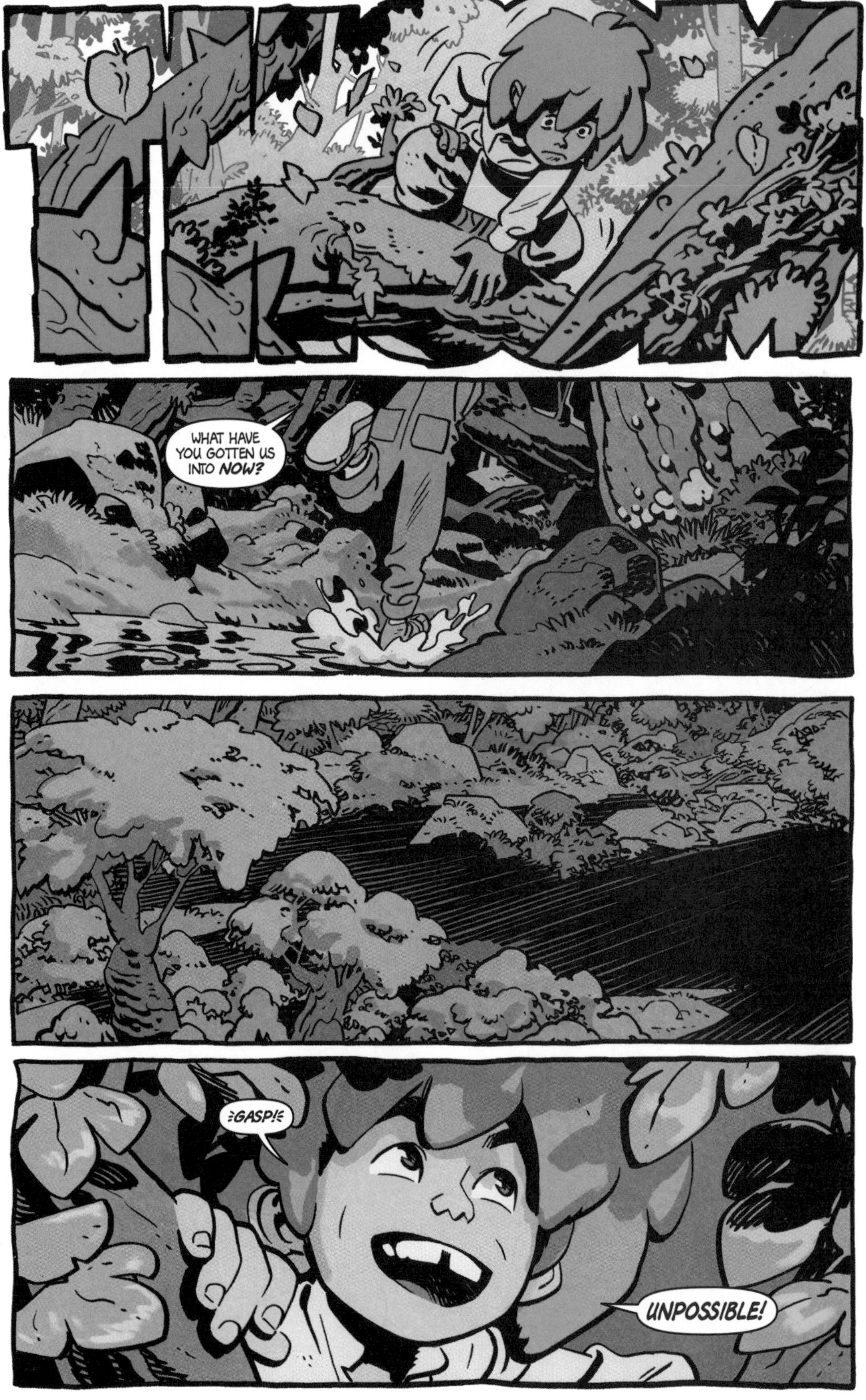
WHAT HAVE YOU GOTTEN US INTO NOW?
GASP!
UNPOSSIBLE!

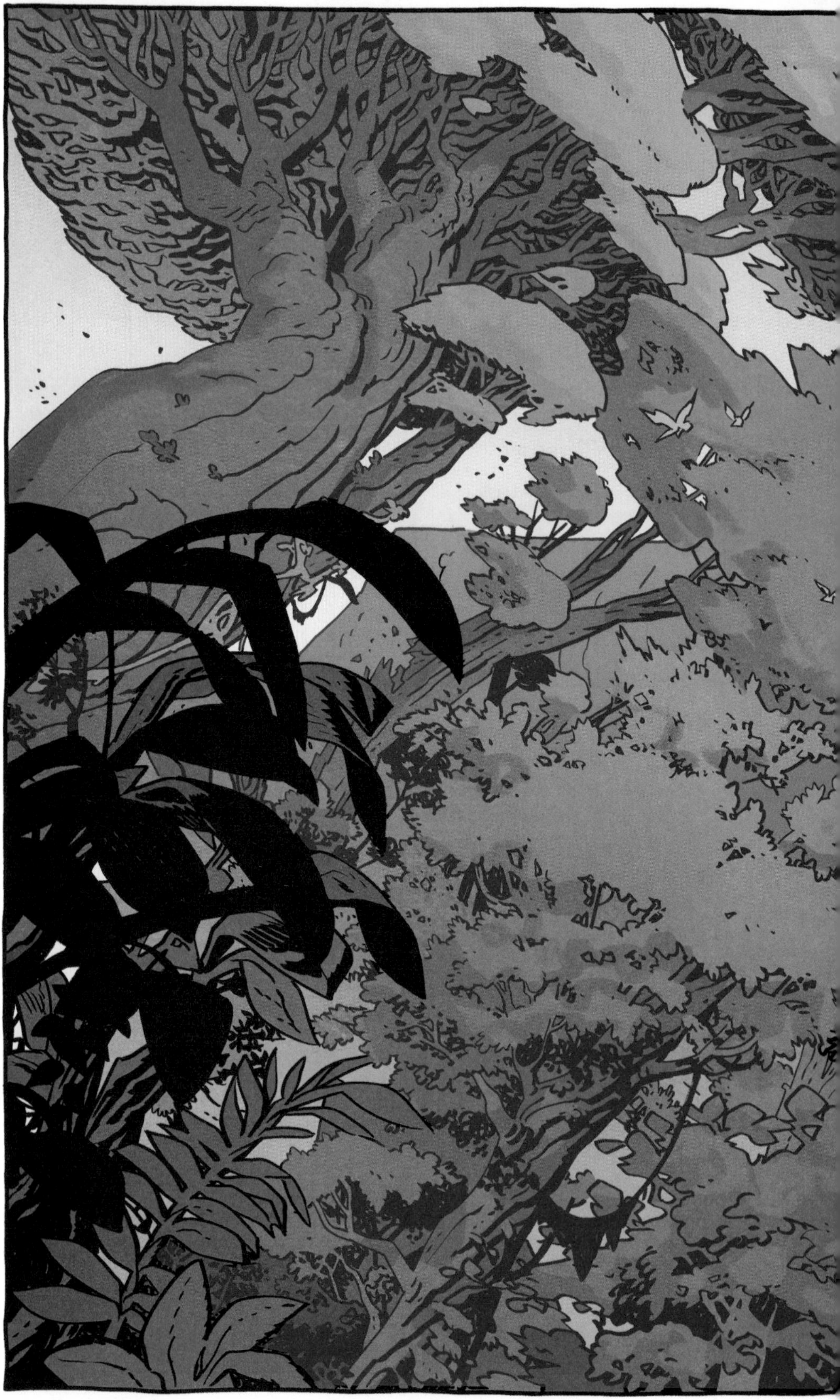

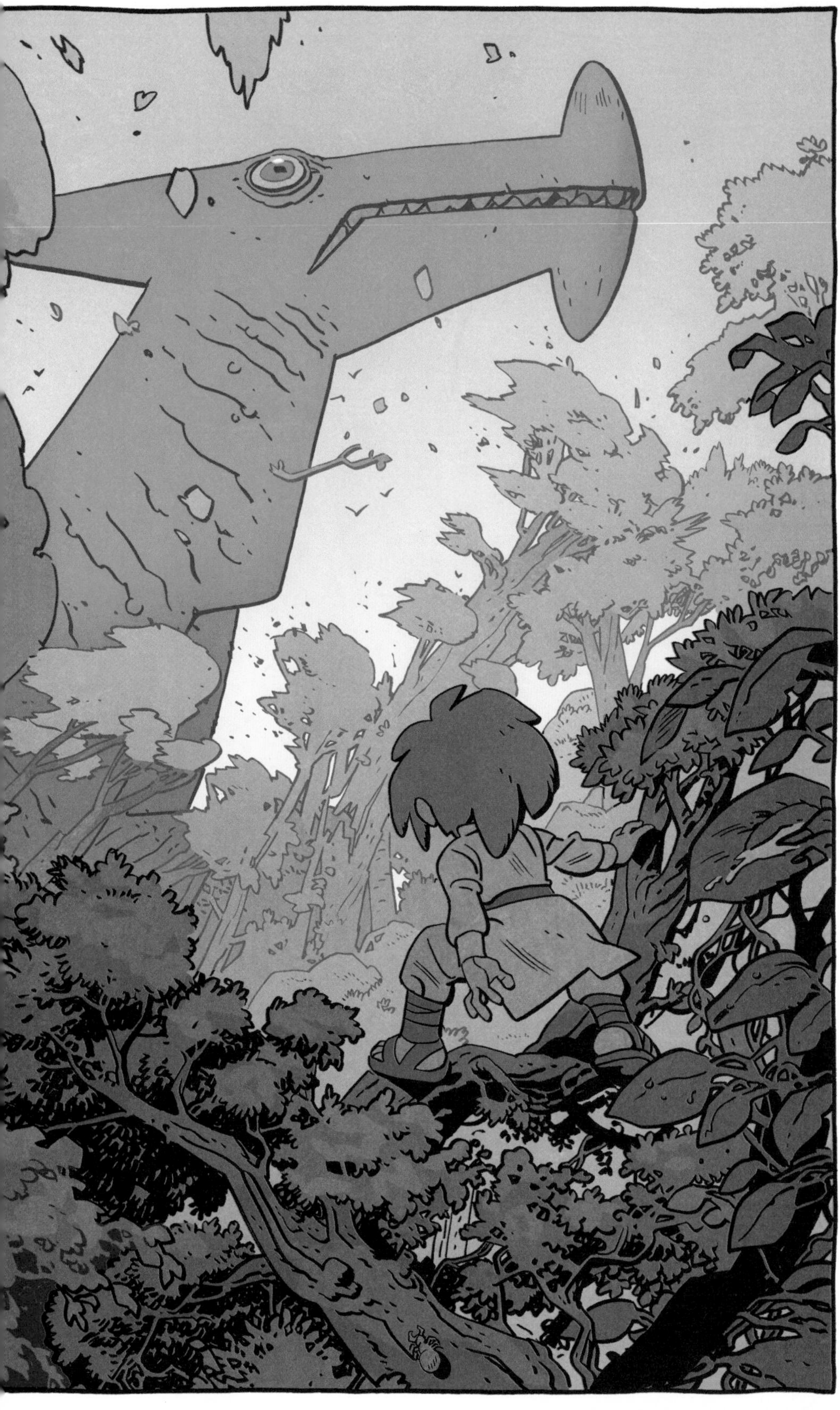

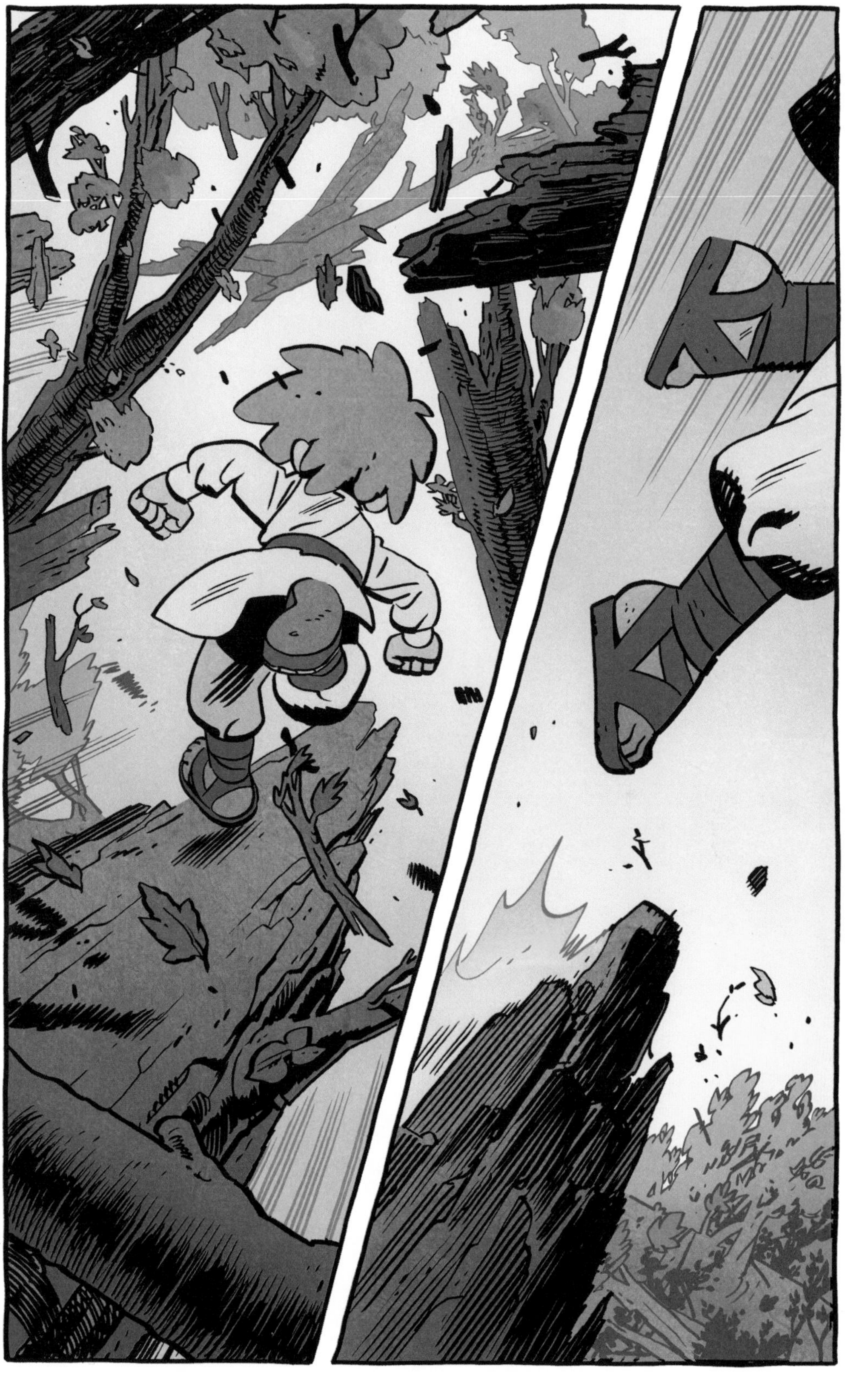

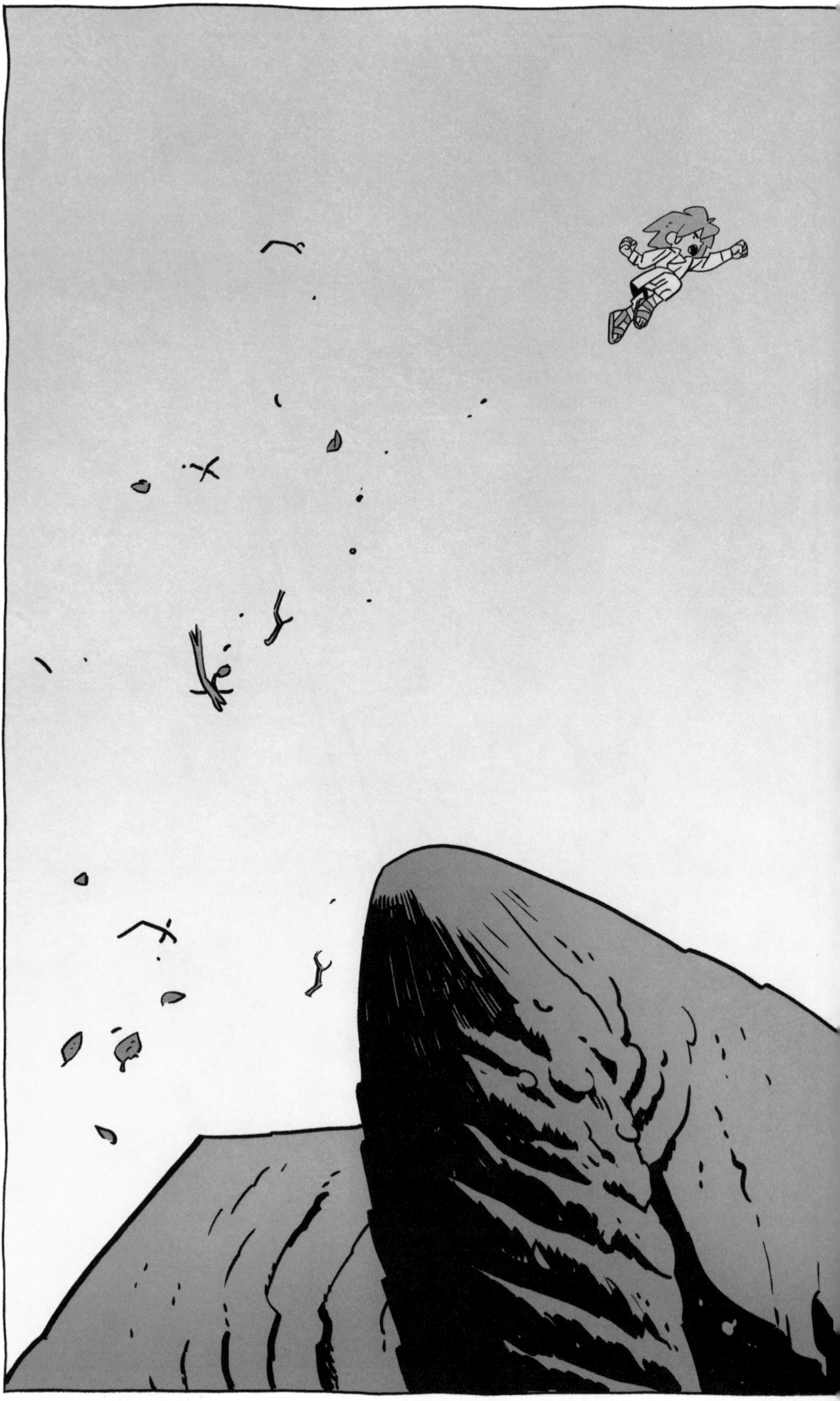

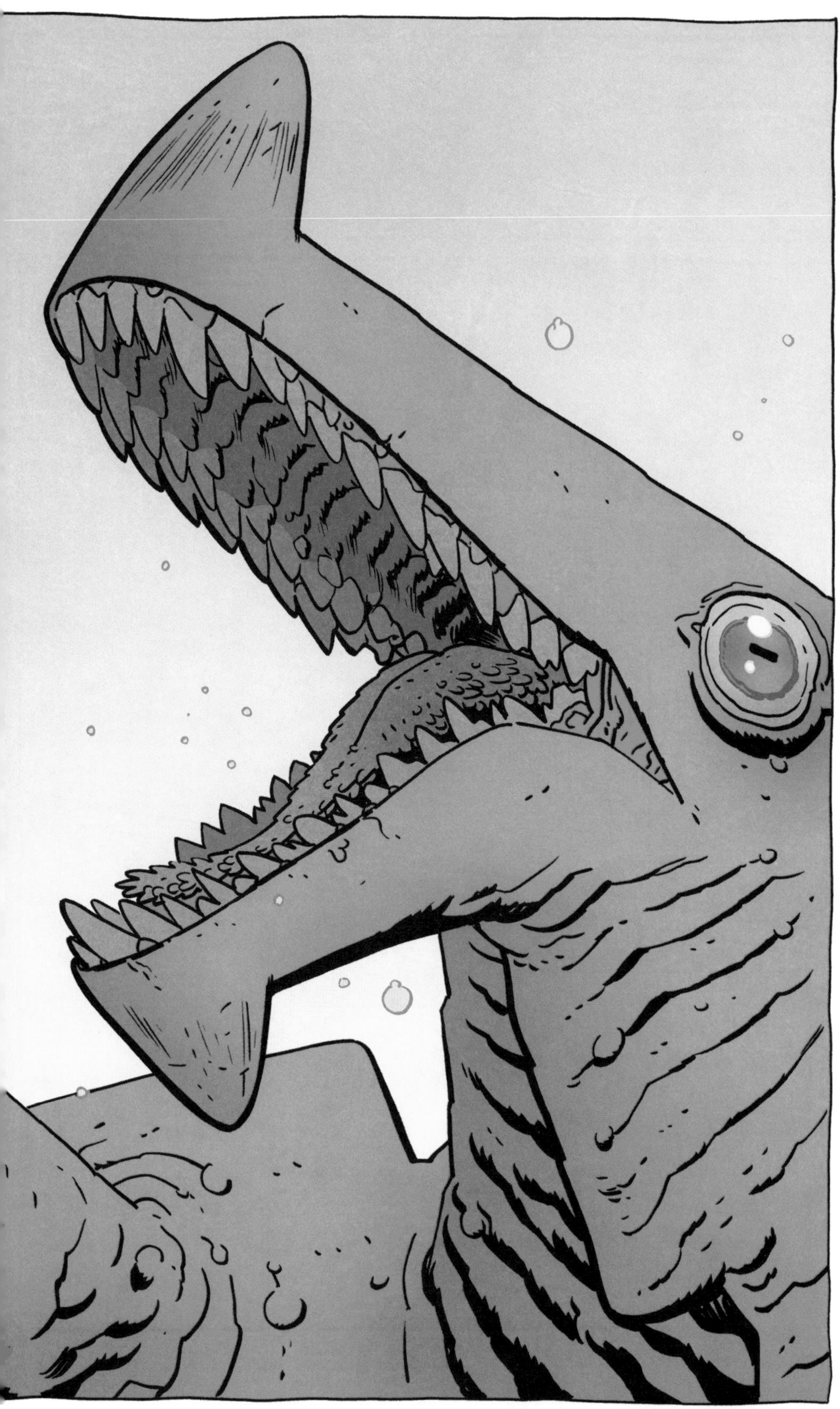

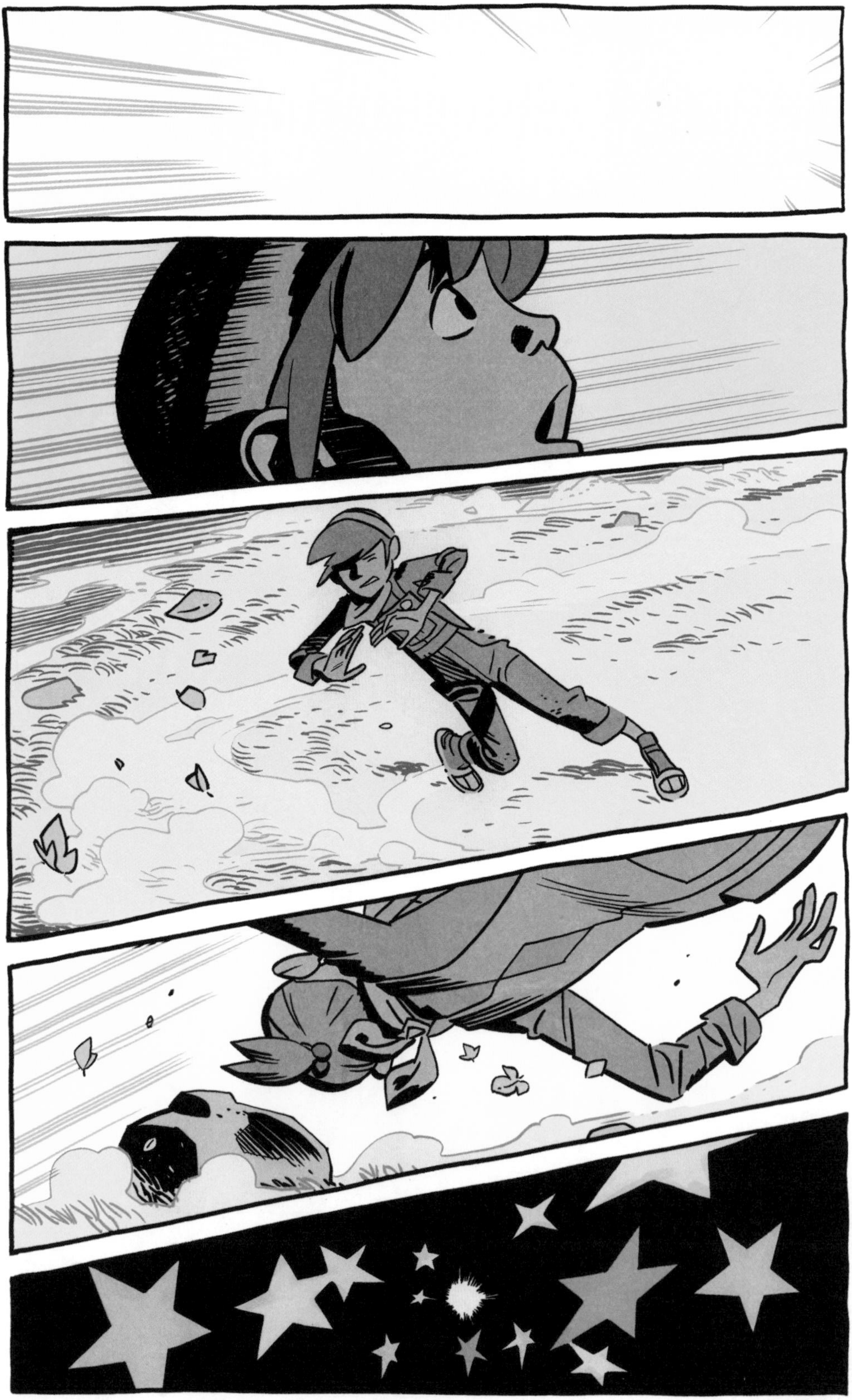

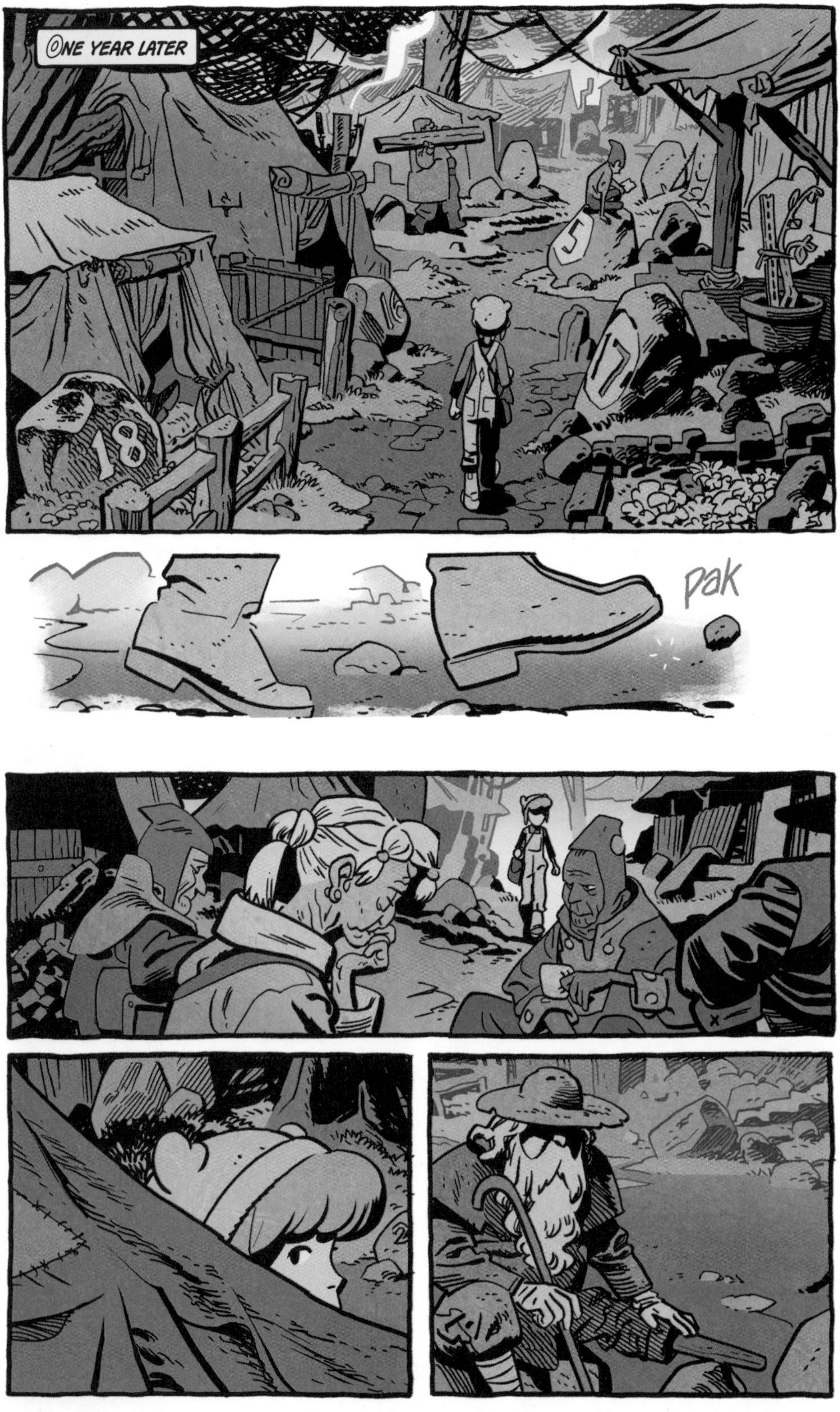
One year later
pak

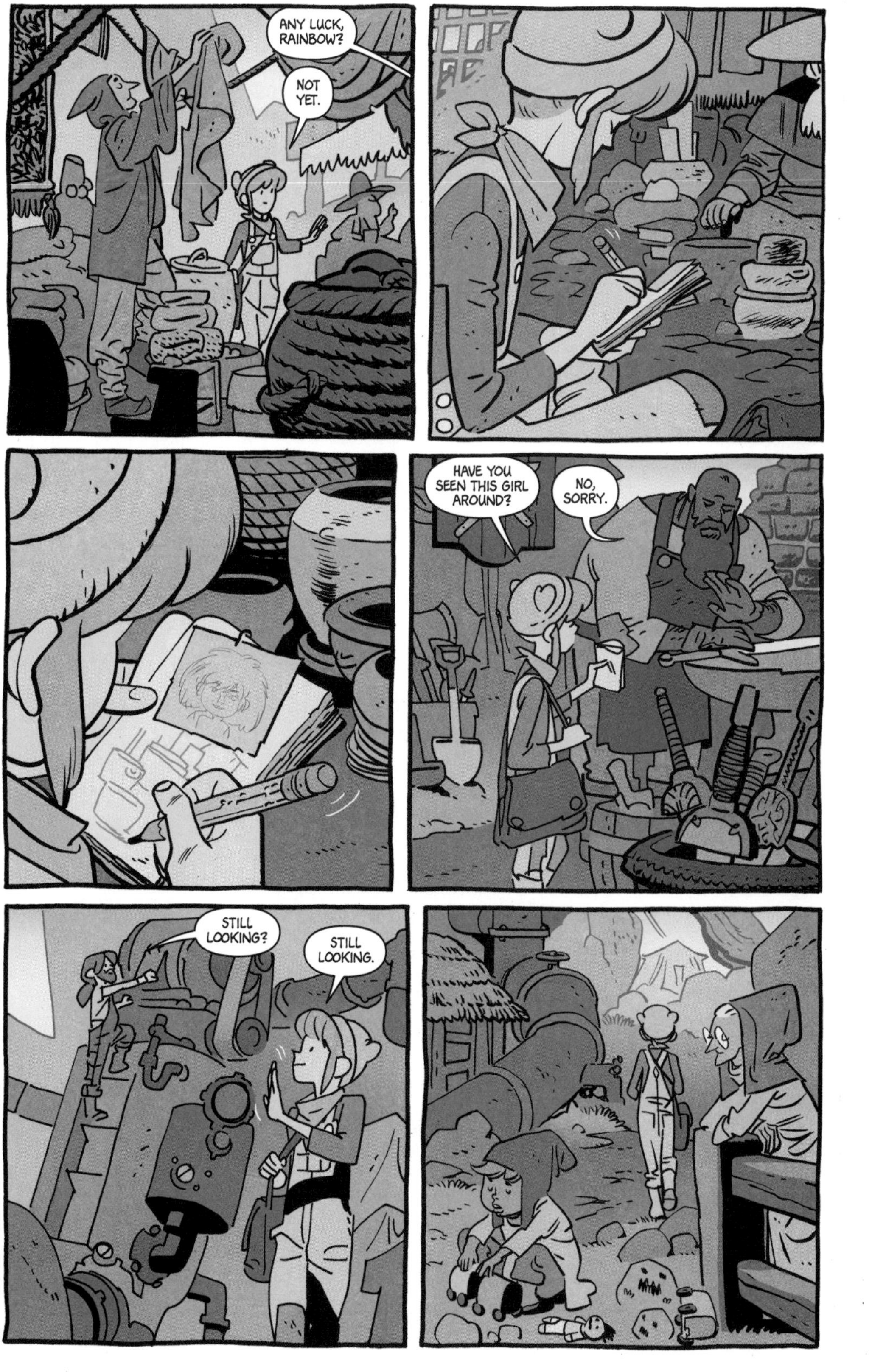
ANY LUCK, RAINBOW?
NOT YET.
HAVE YOU SEEN THIS GIRL AROUND?
NO, SORRY.
STILL LOOKING?
STILL LOOKING.

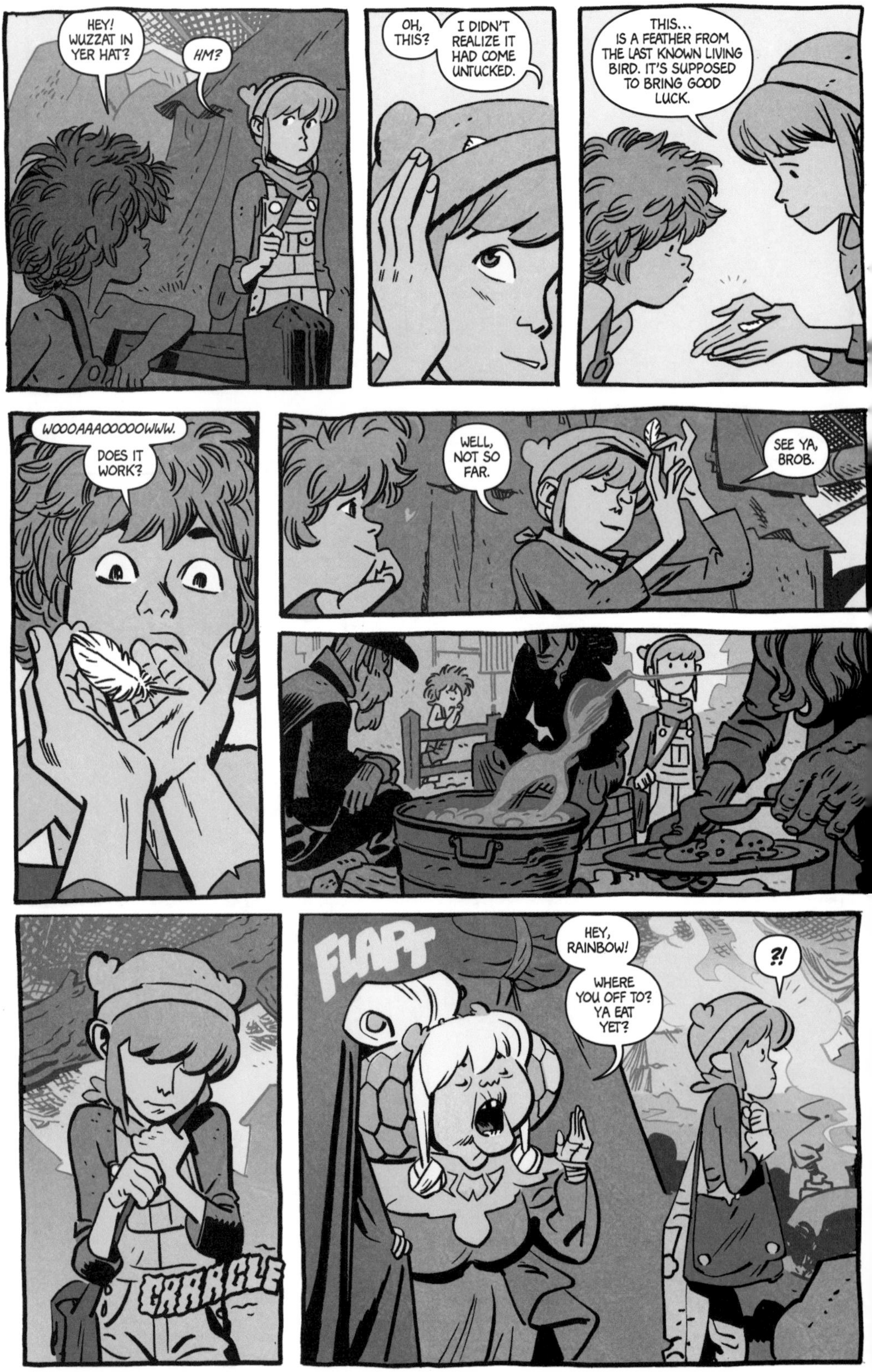
HEY! WUZZAT IN YER HAT?
HM?
OH, THIS?
I DIDN'T REALIZE IT HAD COME UNTUCKED.
THIS... IS A FEATHER FROM THE LAST KNOWN LIVING BIRD. IT'S SUPPOSED TO BRING GOOD LUCK.
WOOOAAAOOOOOWWW.
DOES IT WORK?
WELL, NOT SO FAR.
SEE YA, BROB.
CRRRCLE
FLAP
HEY, RAINBOW!
WHERE YOU OFF TO? YA EAT YET?
?!

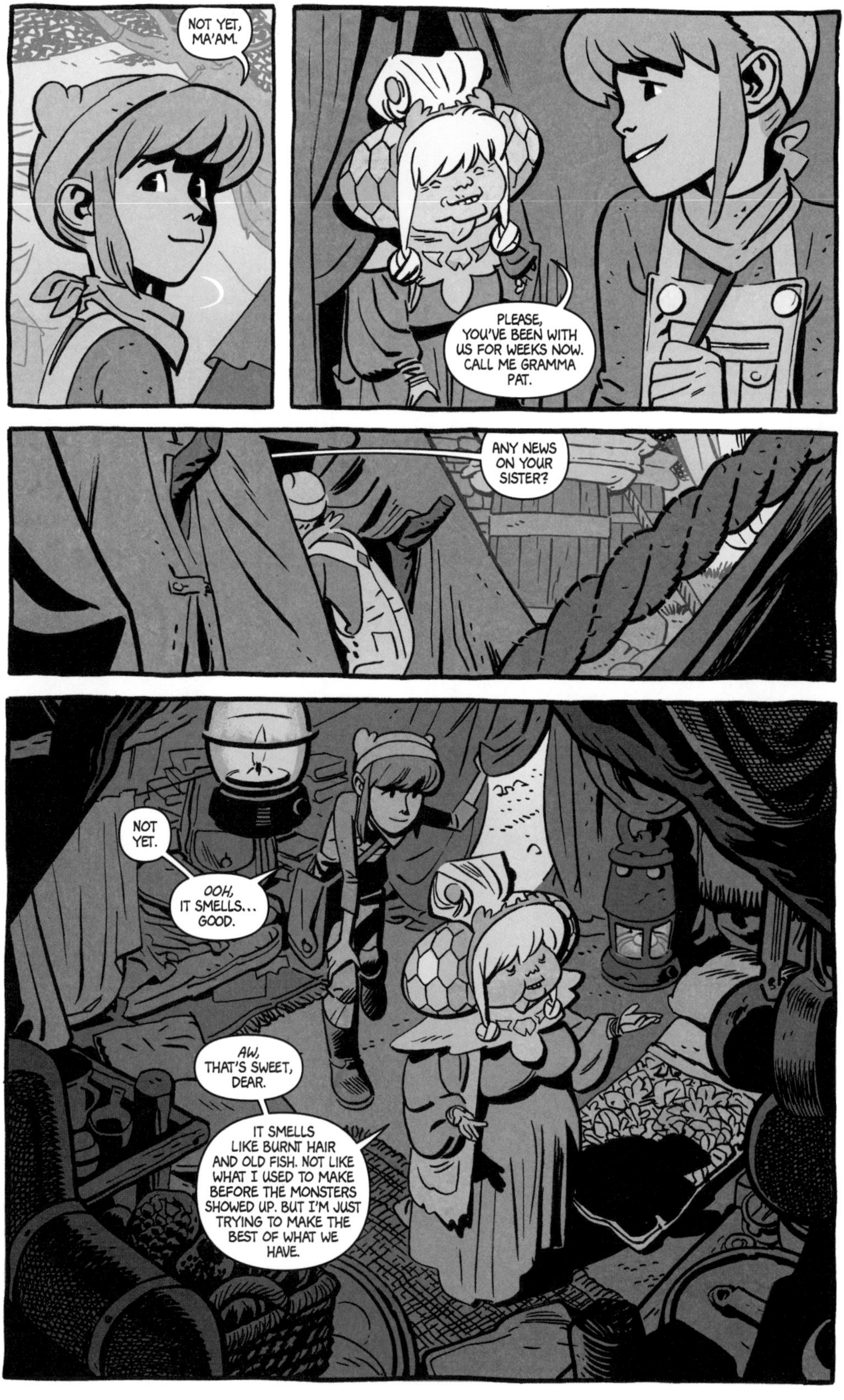
NOT YET, MA'AM.
PLEASE, YOU'VE BEEN WITH US FOR WEEKS NOW. CALL ME GRAMMA PAT.
ANY NEWS ON YOUR SISTER?
NOT YET.
OOH, IT SMELLS... GOOD.
AW, THAT'S SWEET, DEAR.
IT SMELLS LIKE BURNT HAIR AND OLD FISH. NOT LIKE WHAT I USED TO MAKE BEFORE THE MONSTERS SHOWED UP. BUT I'M JUST TRYING TO MAKE THE BEST OF WHAT WE HAVE.

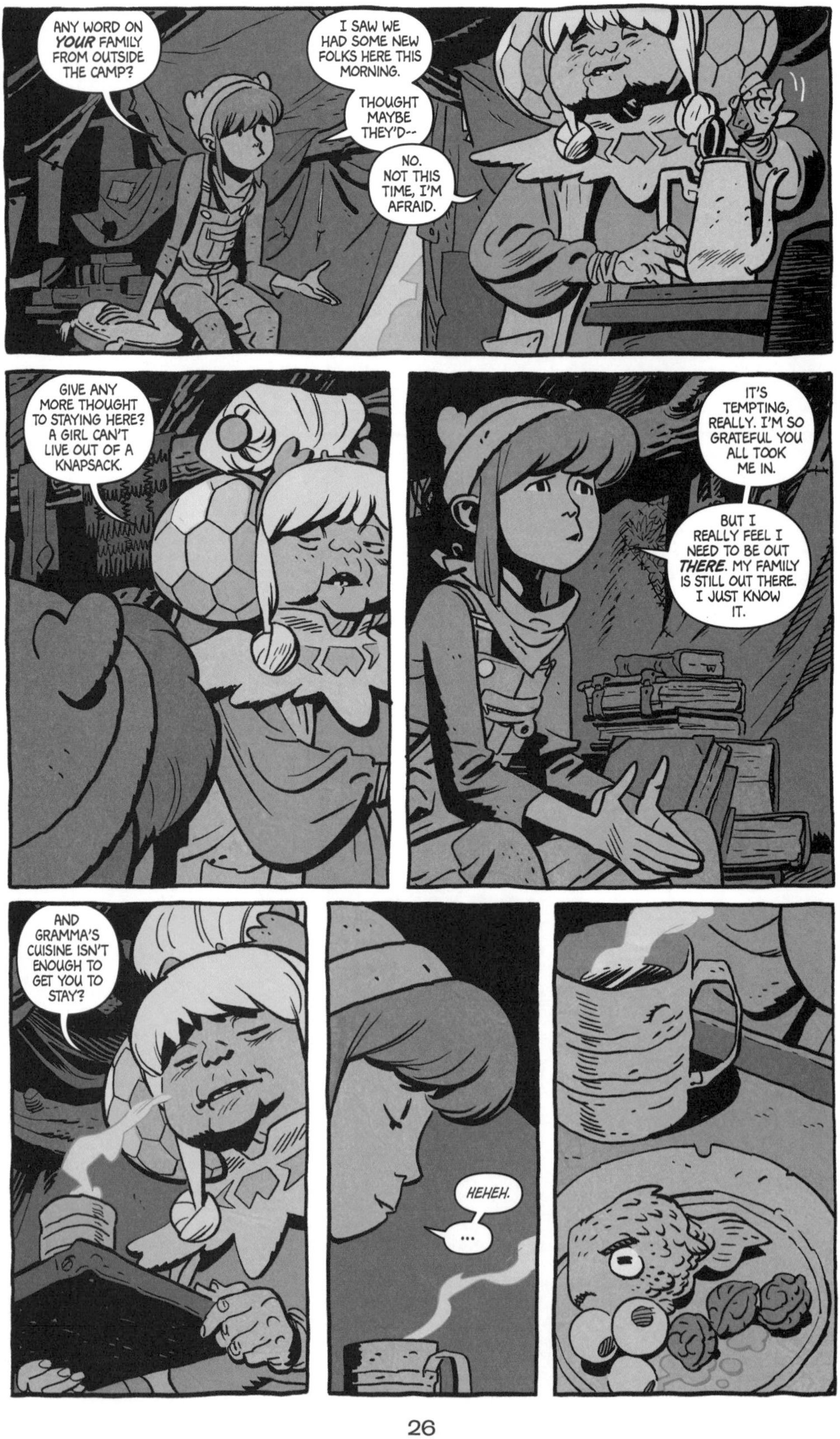
ANY WORD ON *YOUR* FAMILY FROM OUTSIDE THE CAMP?
I SAW WE HAD SOME NEW FOLKS HERE THIS MORNING.
THOUGHT MAYBE THEY'D--
NO. NOT THIS TIME, I'M AFRAID.
GIVE ANY MORE THOUGHT TO STAYING HERE? A GIRL CAN'T LIVE OUT OF A KNAPSACK.
IT'S TEMPTING, REALLY. I'M SO GRATEFUL YOU ALL TOOK ME IN.
BUT I REALLY FEEL I NEED TO BE OUT *THERE*. MY FAMILY IS STILL OUT THERE. I JUST KNOW IT.
AND GRAMMA'S CUISINE ISN'T ENOUGH TO GET YOU TO STAY?
HEHEH.
...

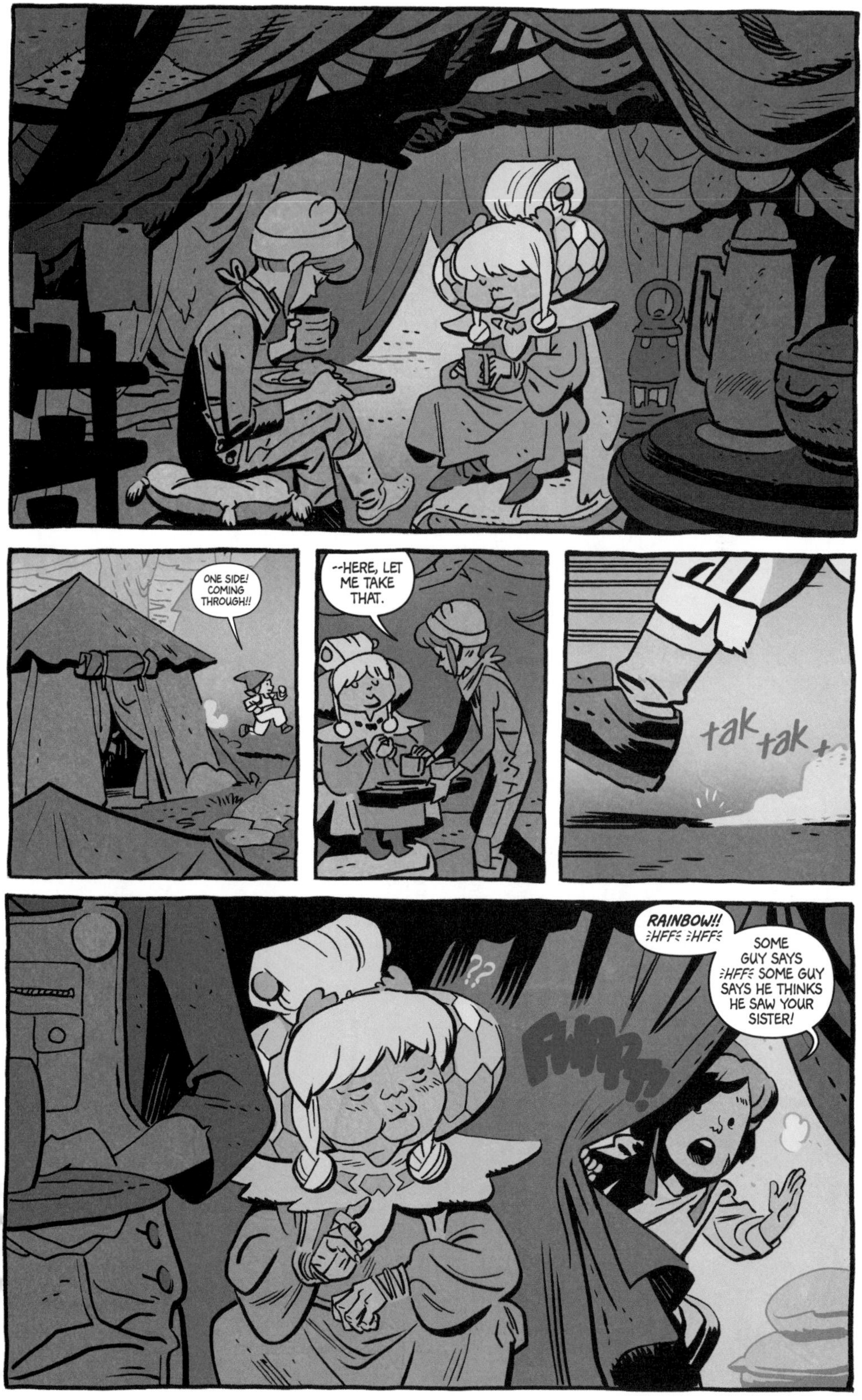
ONE SIDE! COMING THROUGH!!
--HERE, LET ME TAKE THAT.
tak tak t
RAINBOW!! HFF HFF
??
FWAP
SOME GUY SAYS HFF SOME GUY SAYS HE THINKS HE SAW YOUR SISTER!

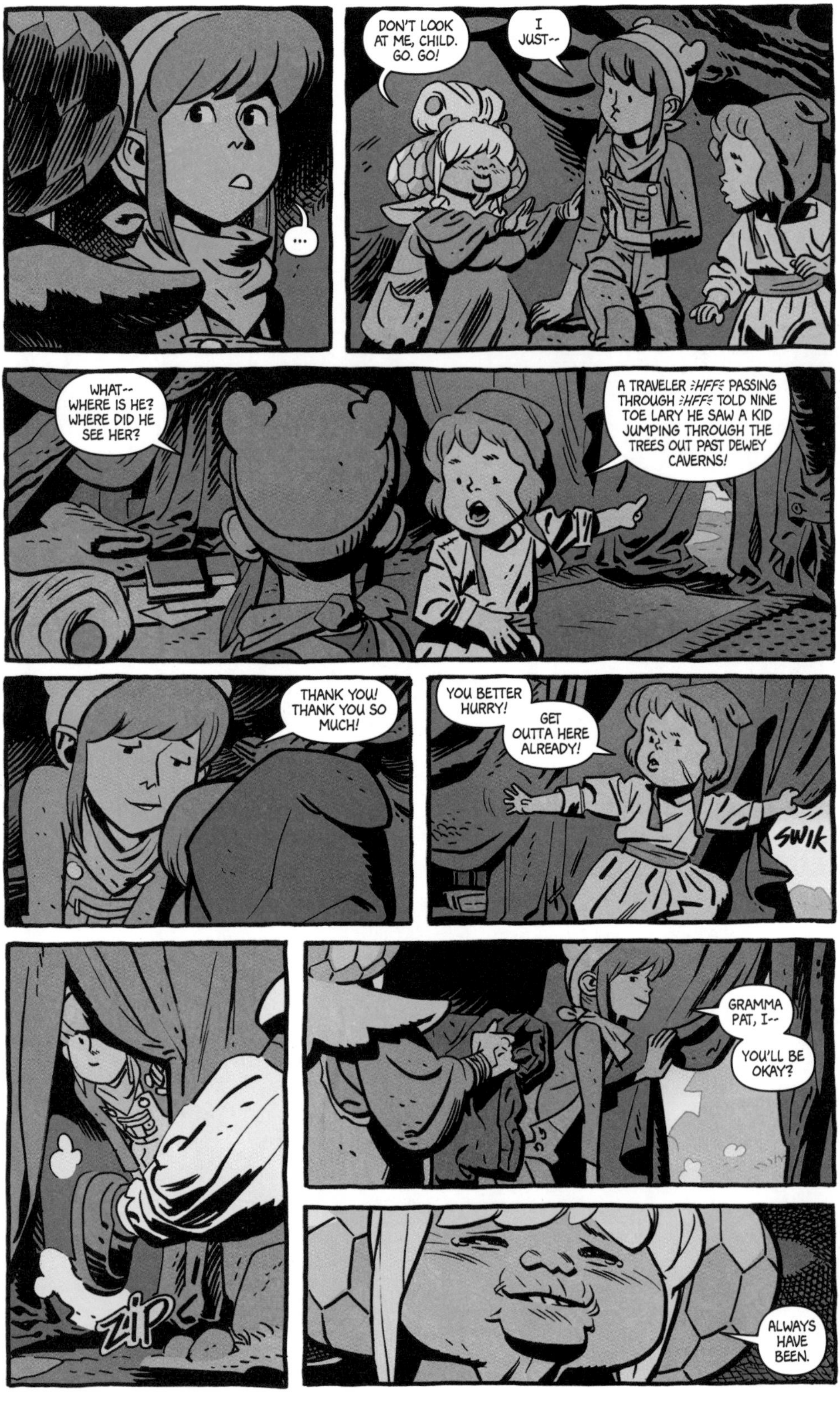
...
DON'T LOOK AT ME, CHILD. GO. GO!
I JUST--
WHAT-- WHERE IS HE? WHERE DID HE SEE HER?
A TRAVELER ≷HFF≶ PASSING THROUGH ≷HFF≶ TOLD NINE TOE LARY HE SAW A KID JUMPING THROUGH THE TREES OUT PAST DEWEY CAVERNS!
THANK YOU! THANK YOU SO MUCH!
YOU BETTER HURRY!
GET OUTTA HERE ALREADY!
SWIK
ZIP
GRAMMA PAT, I--
YOU'LL BE OKAY?
ALWAYS HAVE BEEN.

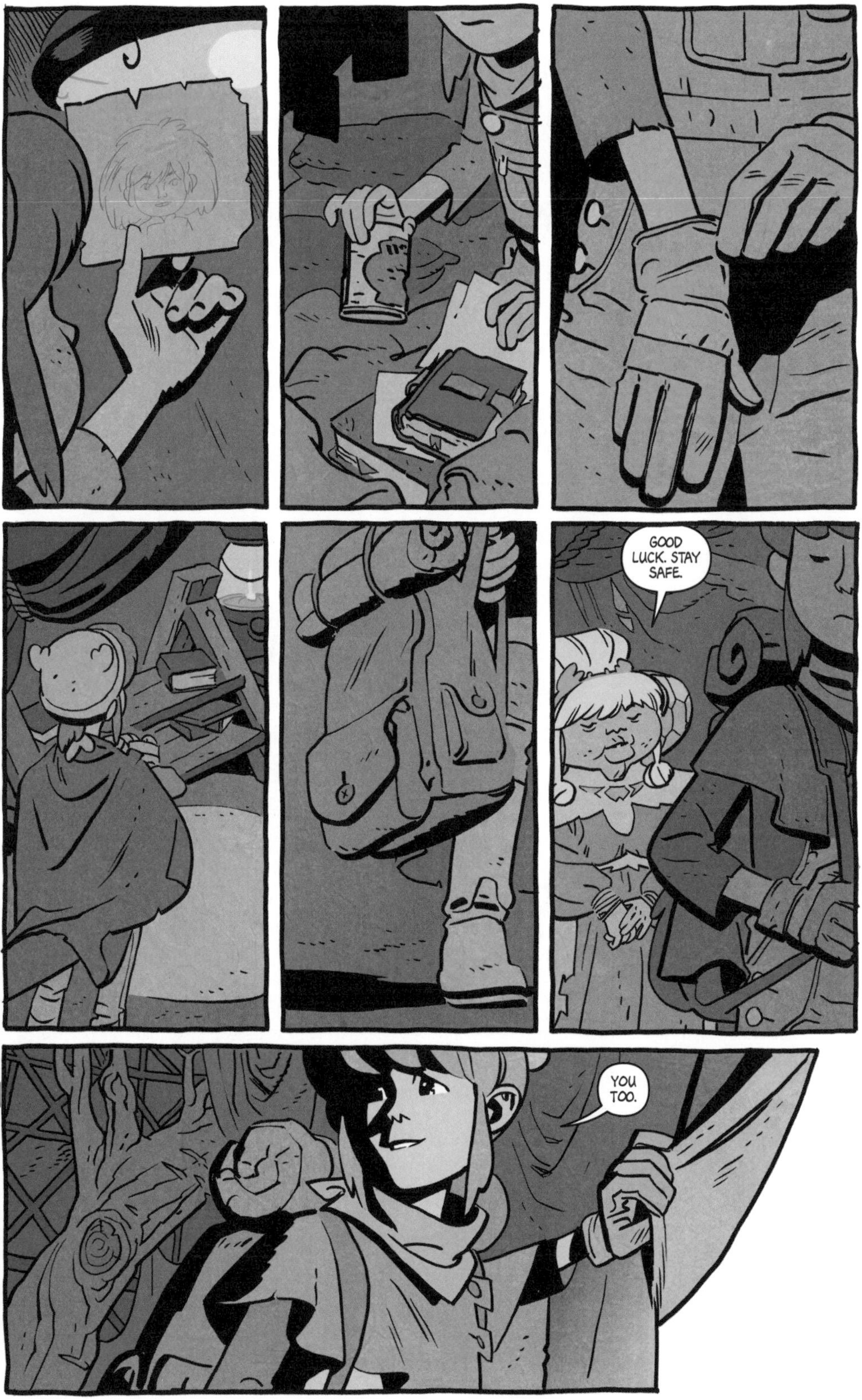
GOOD LUCK. STAY SAFE.
YOU TOO.

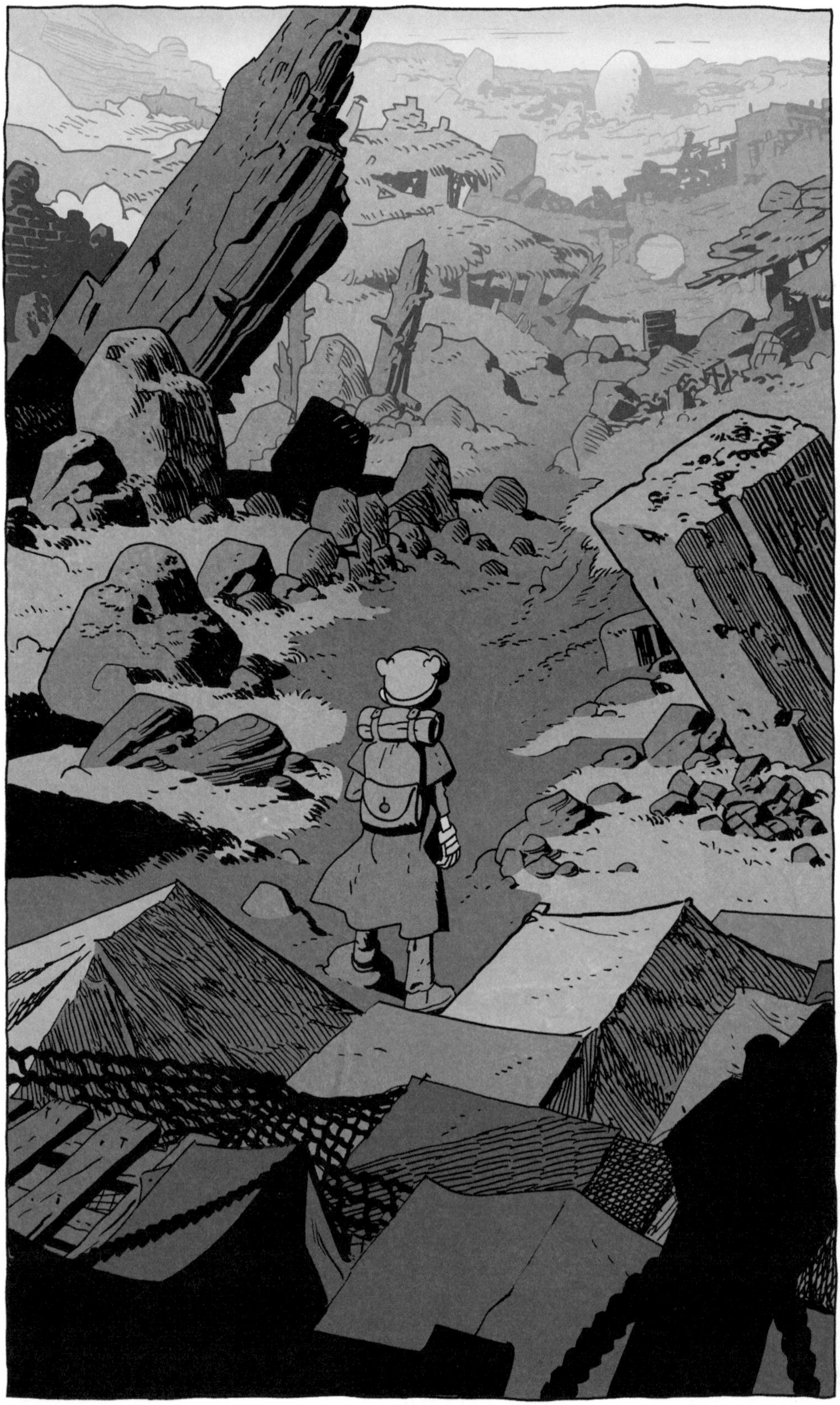

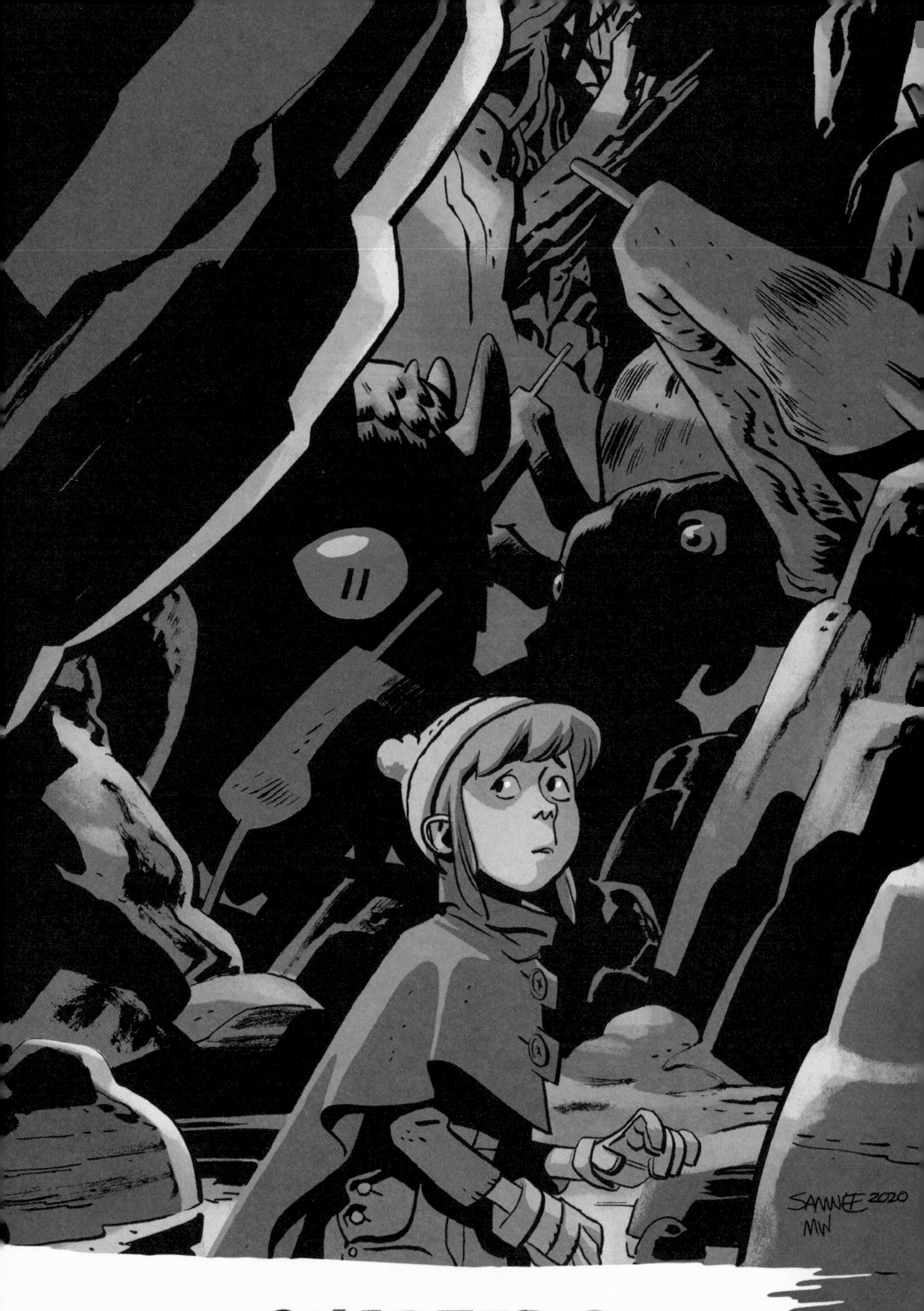
SAMNEE 2020
MW

CHAPTER 2

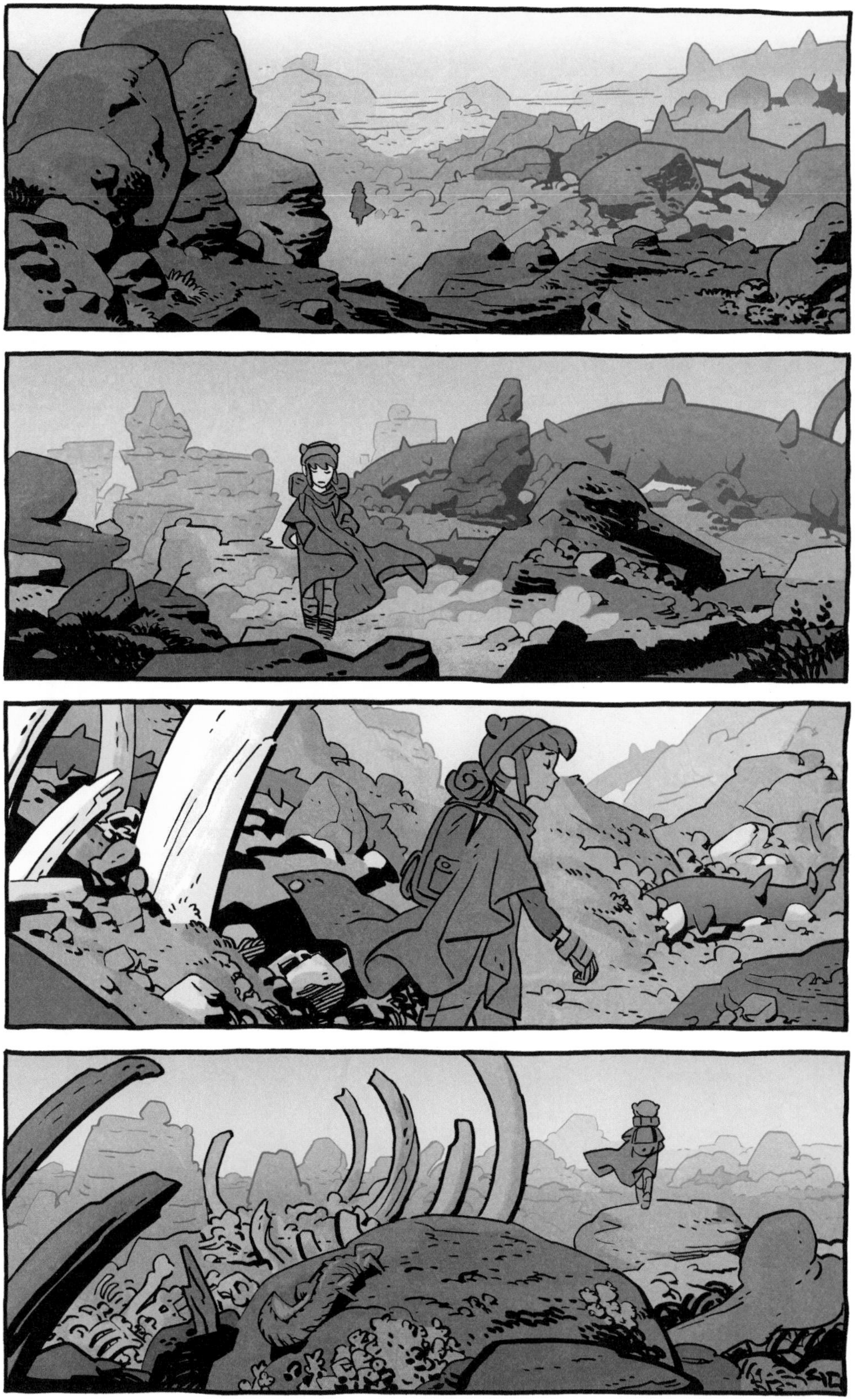

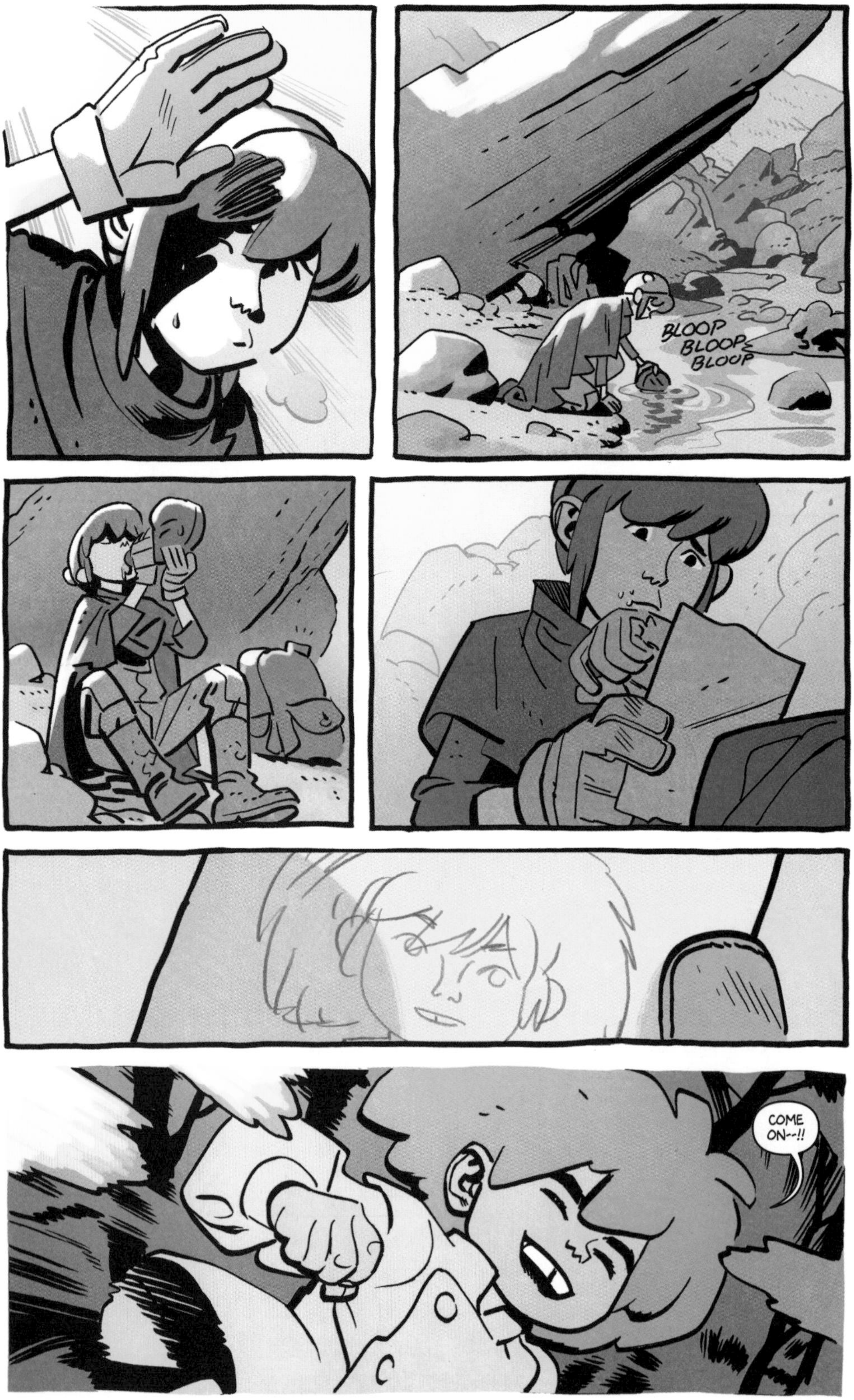
BLOOP
BLOOP
BLOOP
COME ON--!!

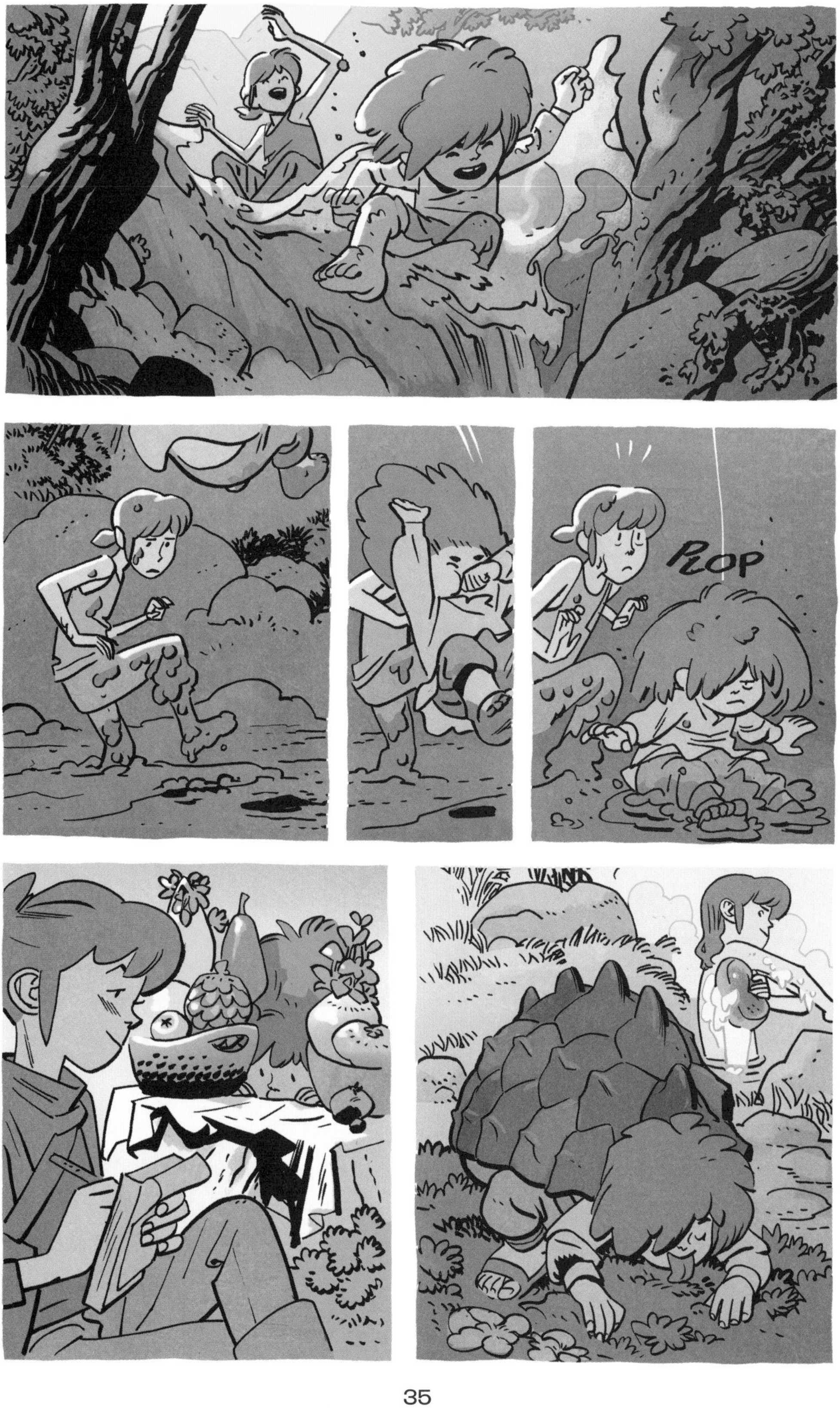
PLOP

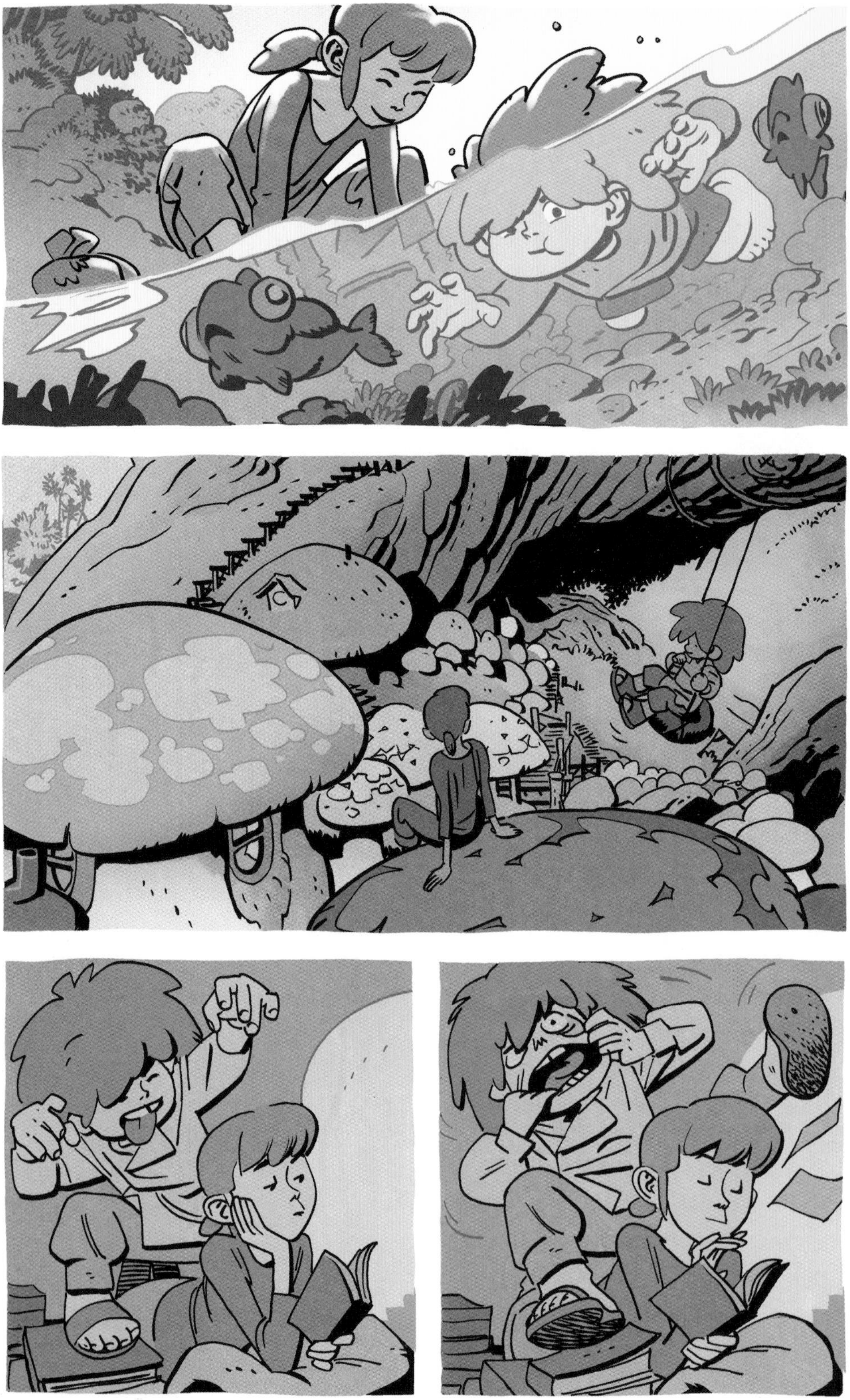

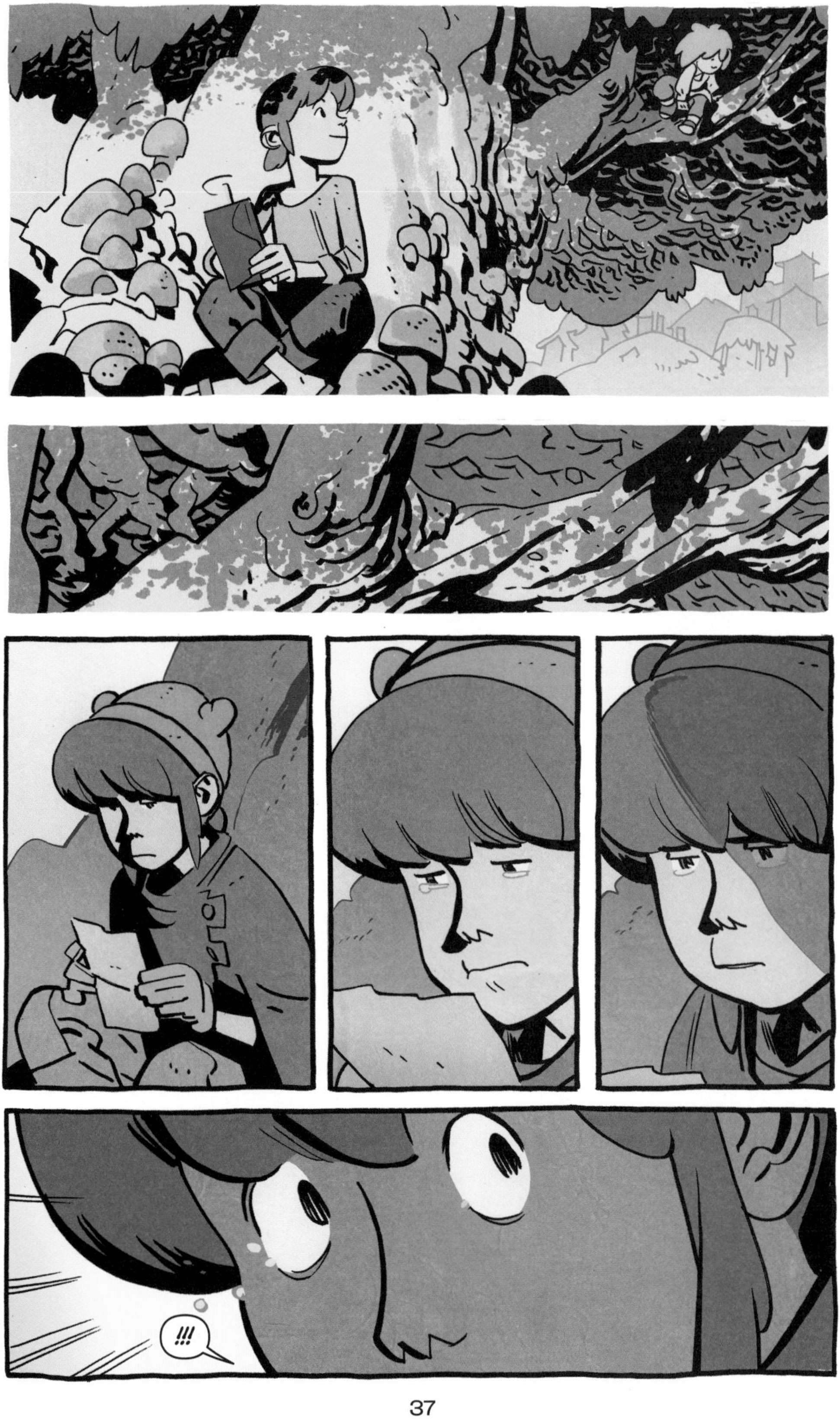
!!!

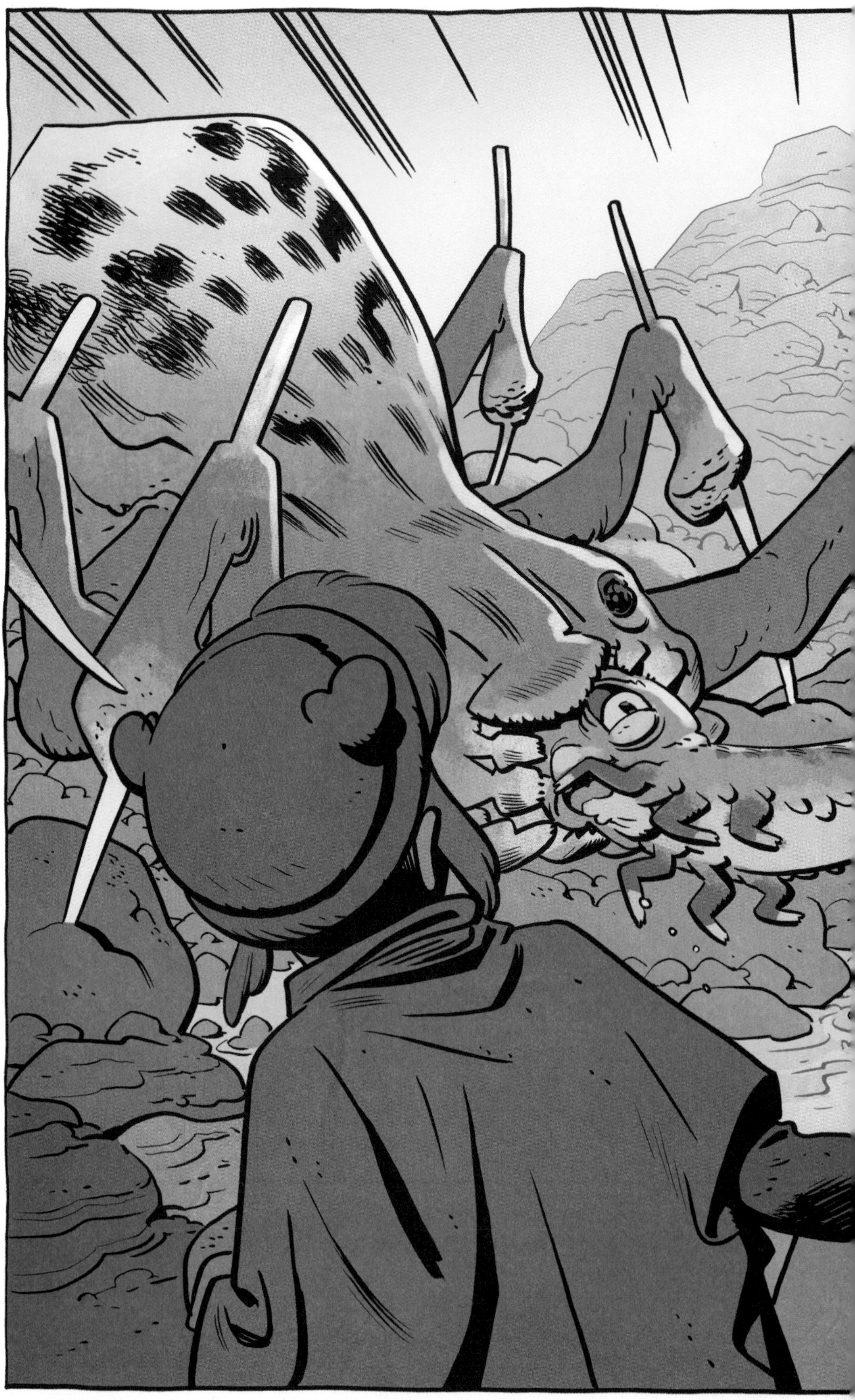

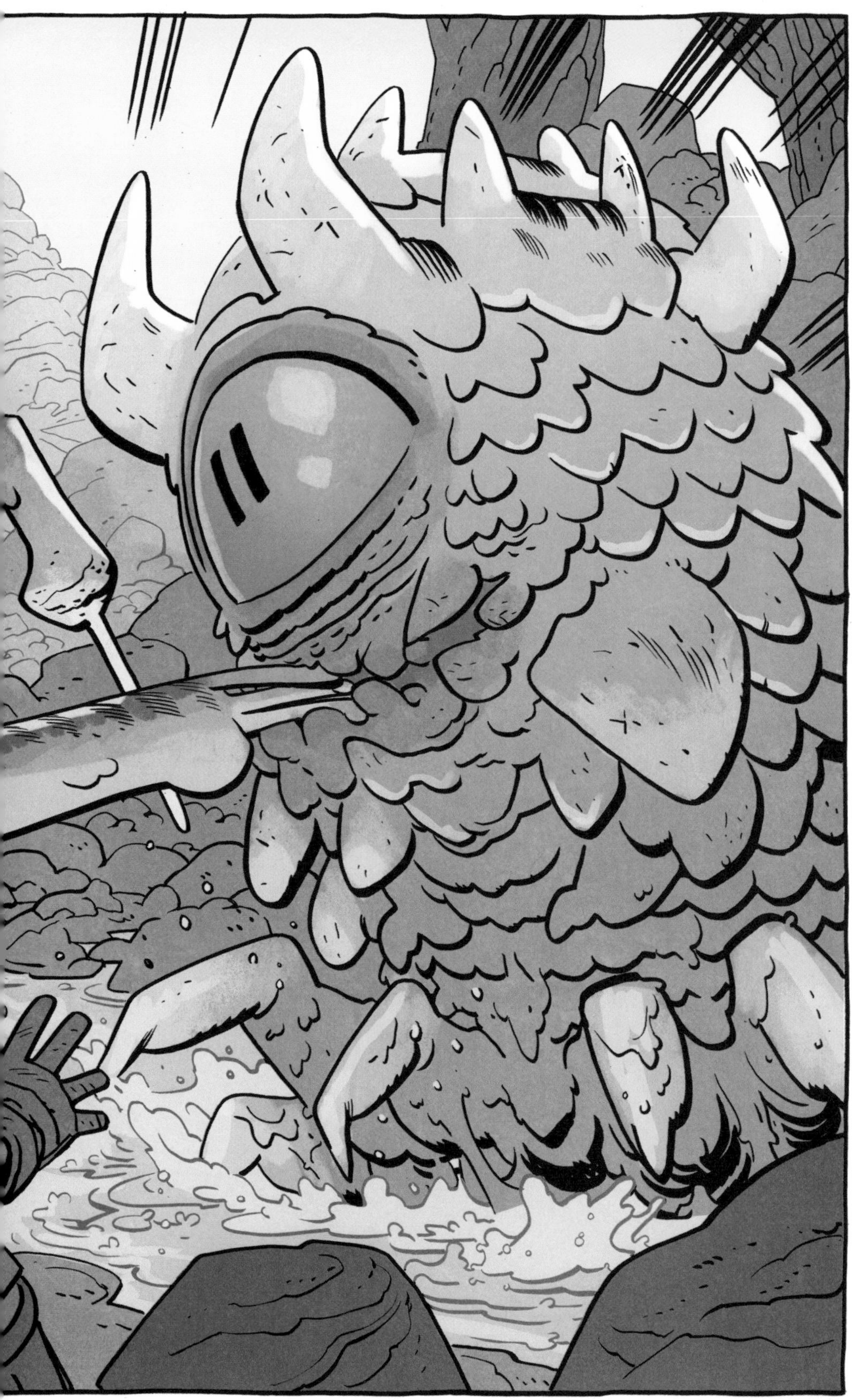

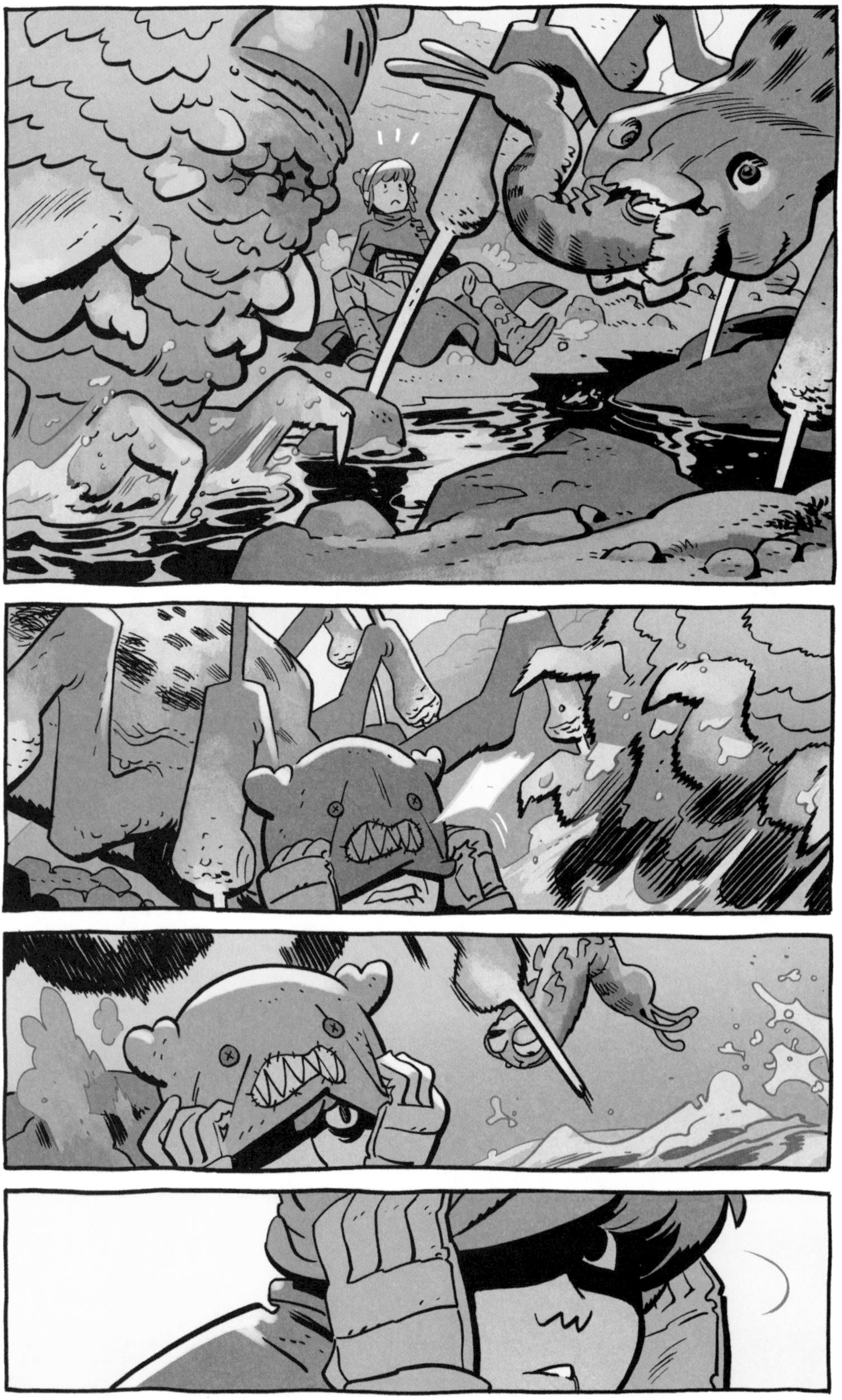

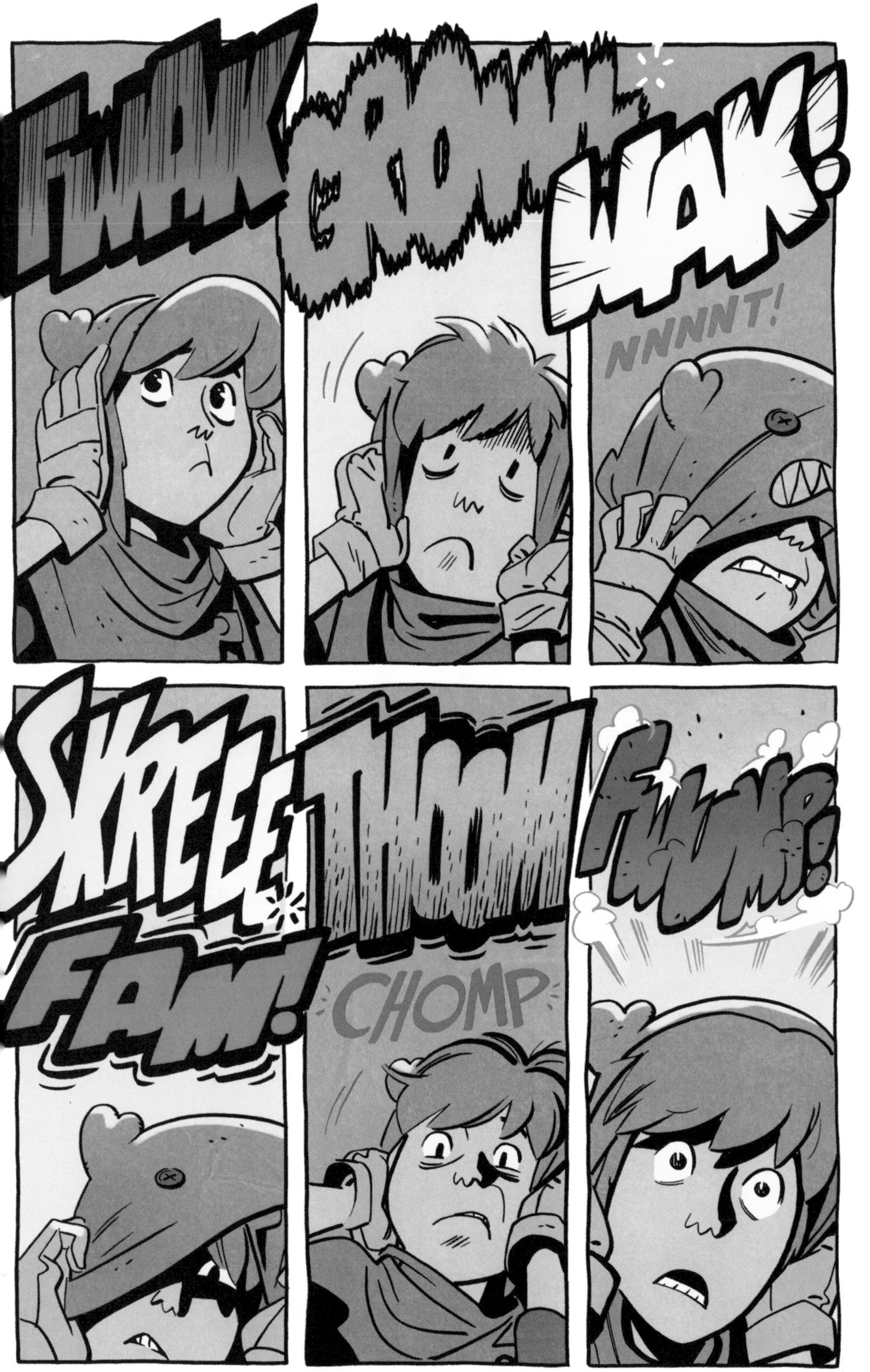
WAK!
NNNNT!
SKREEE
THOOM
FWUMP!
CHOMP

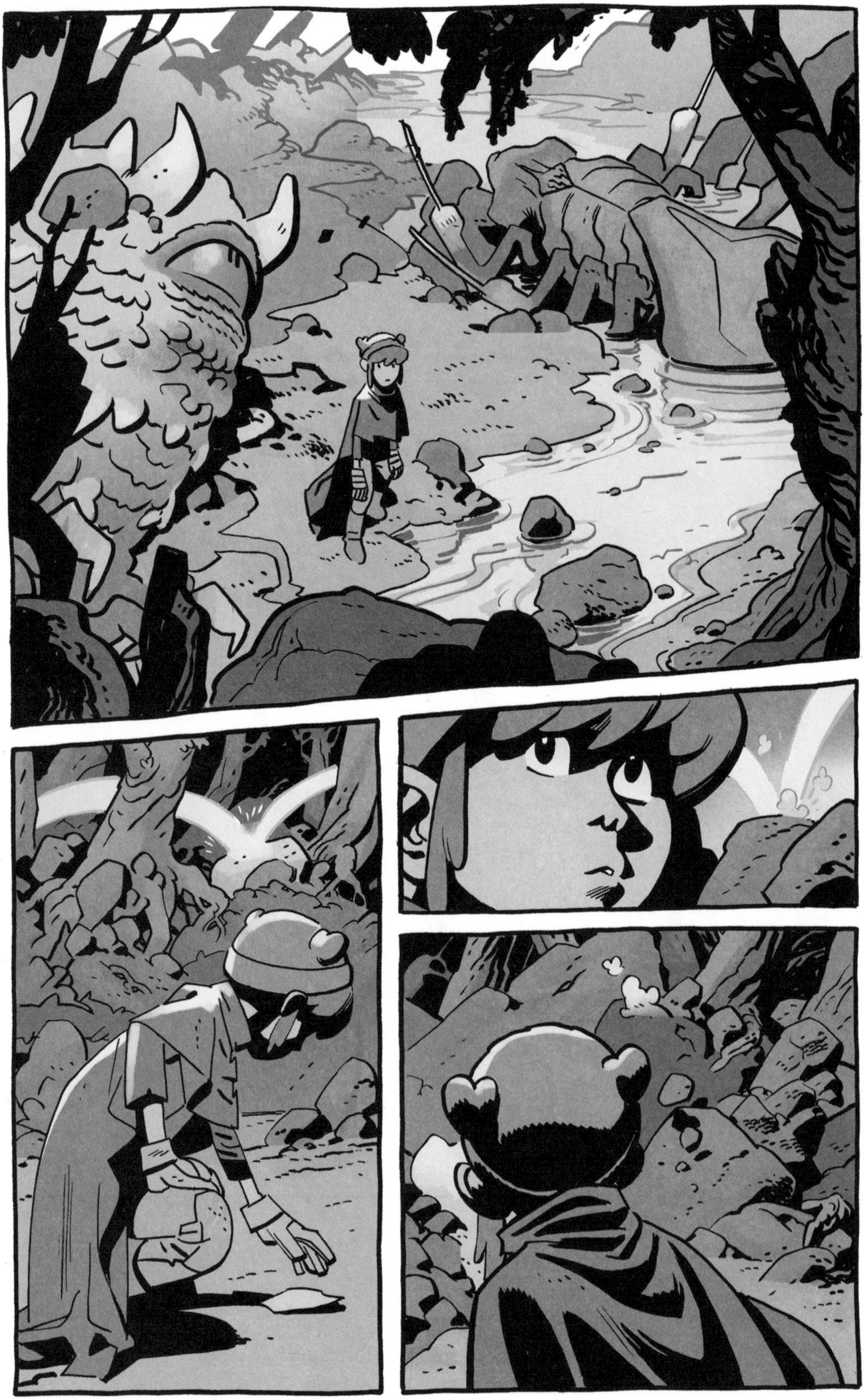

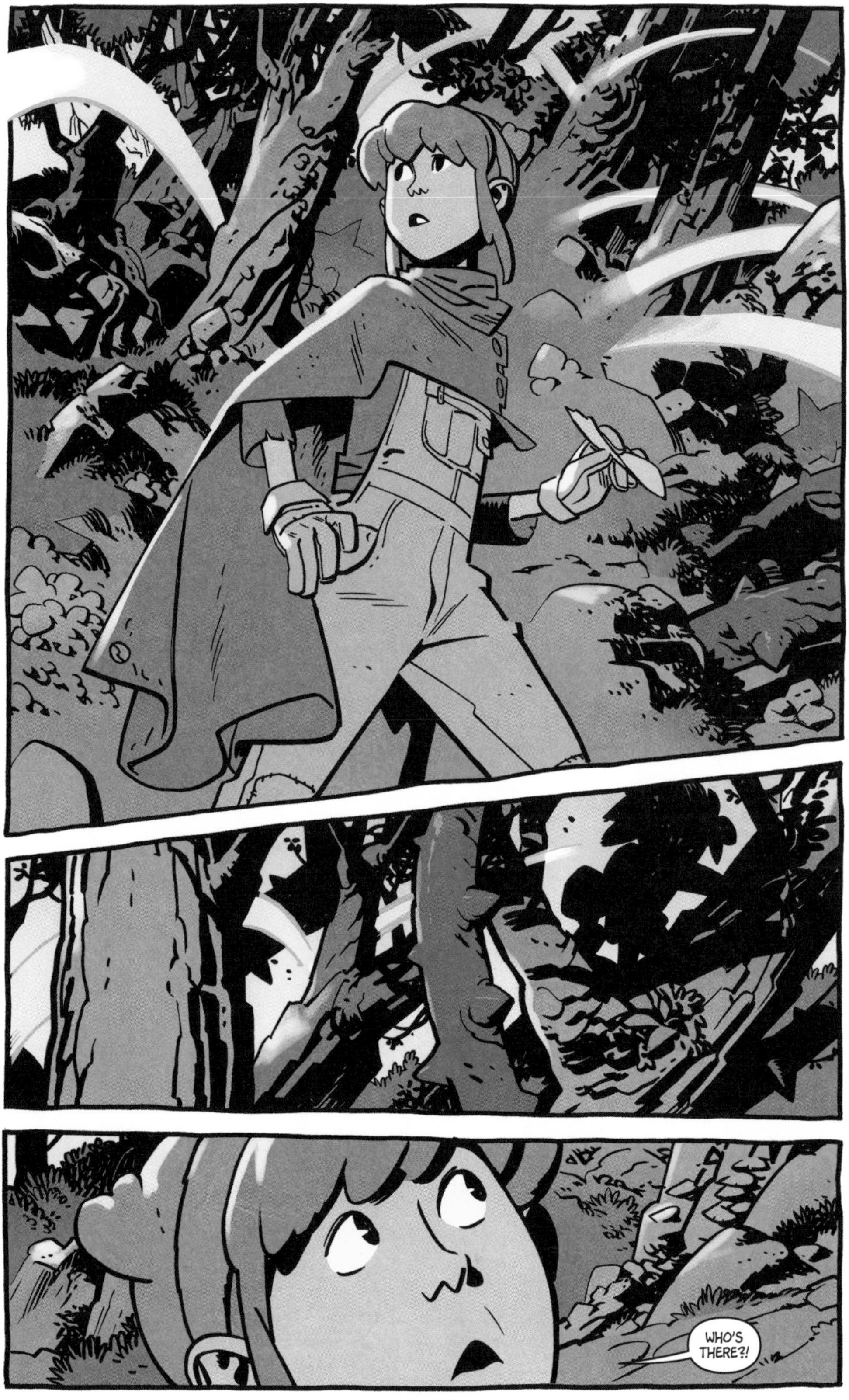
WHO'S
THERE?!

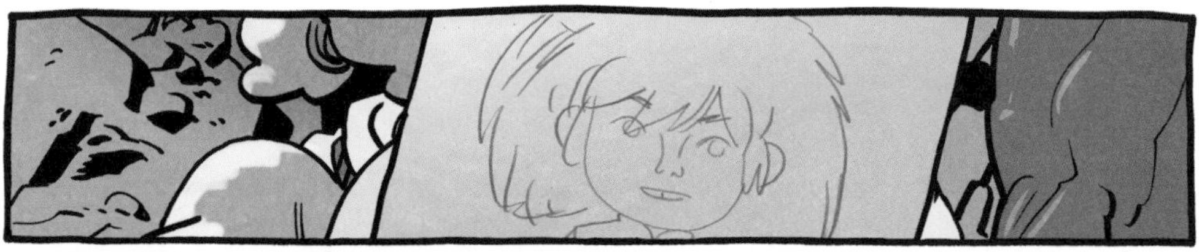

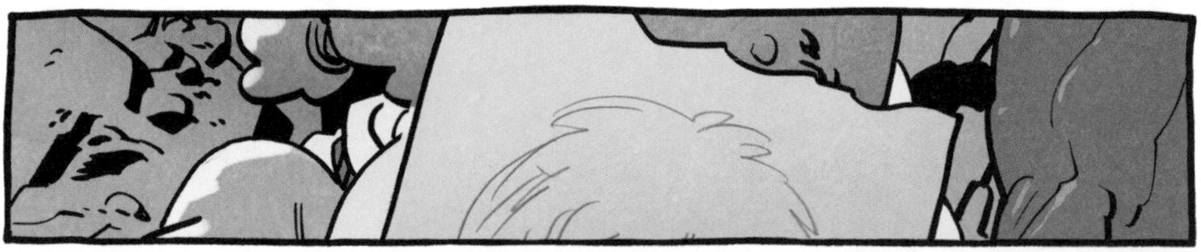

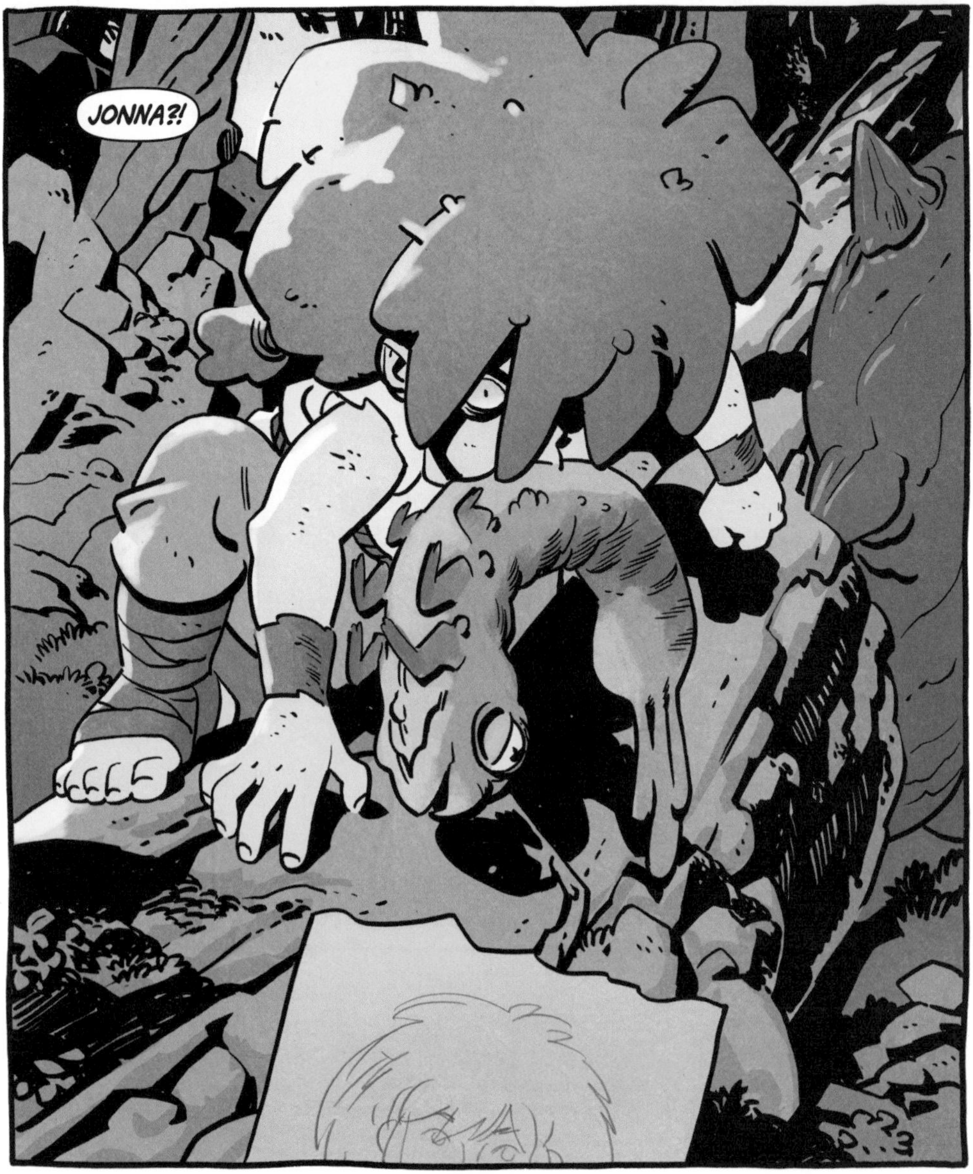
JONNA?!

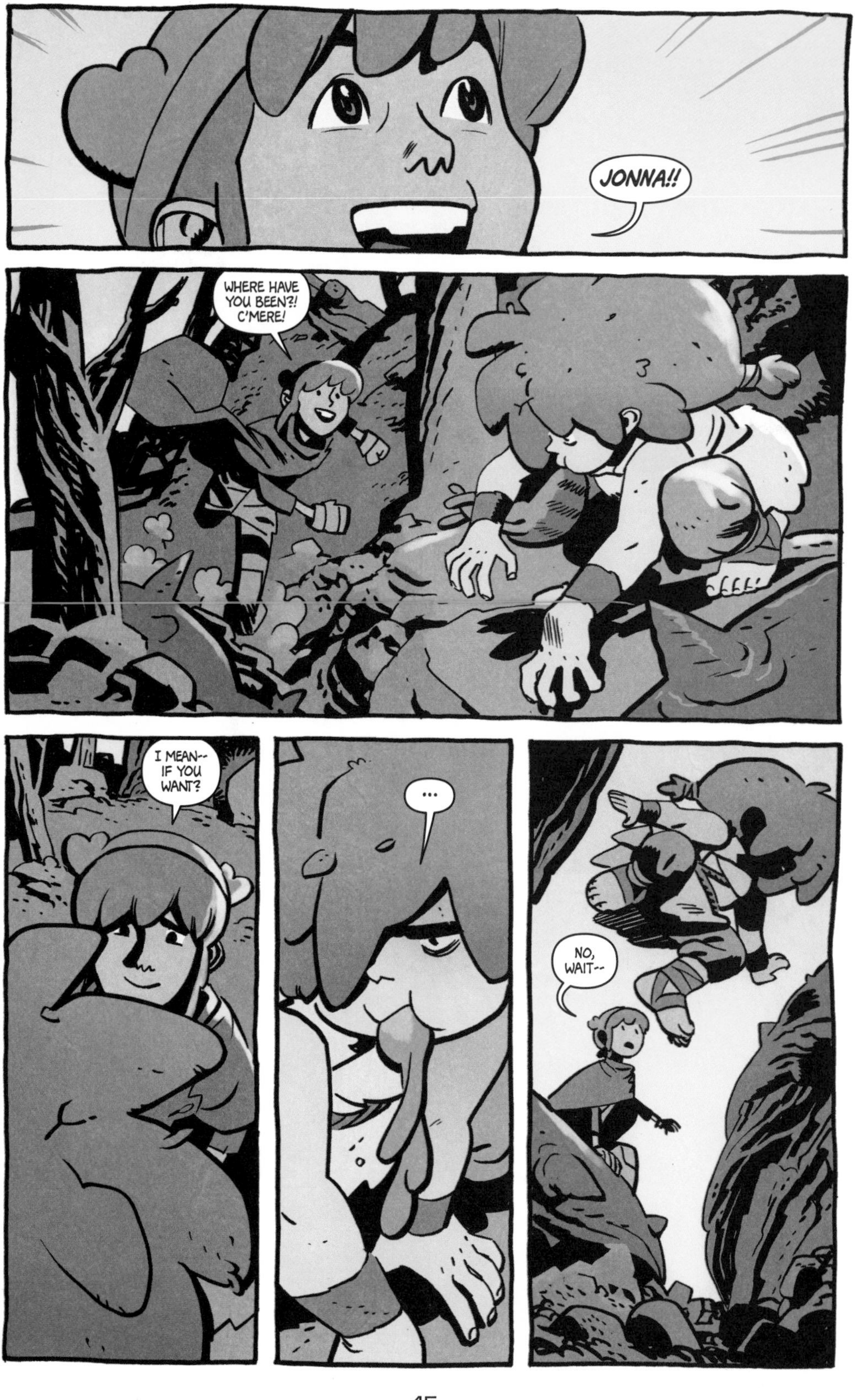
JONNA!!
WHERE HAVE YOU BEEN?! C'MERE!
I MEAN-- IF YOU WANT?
...
NO, WAIT--

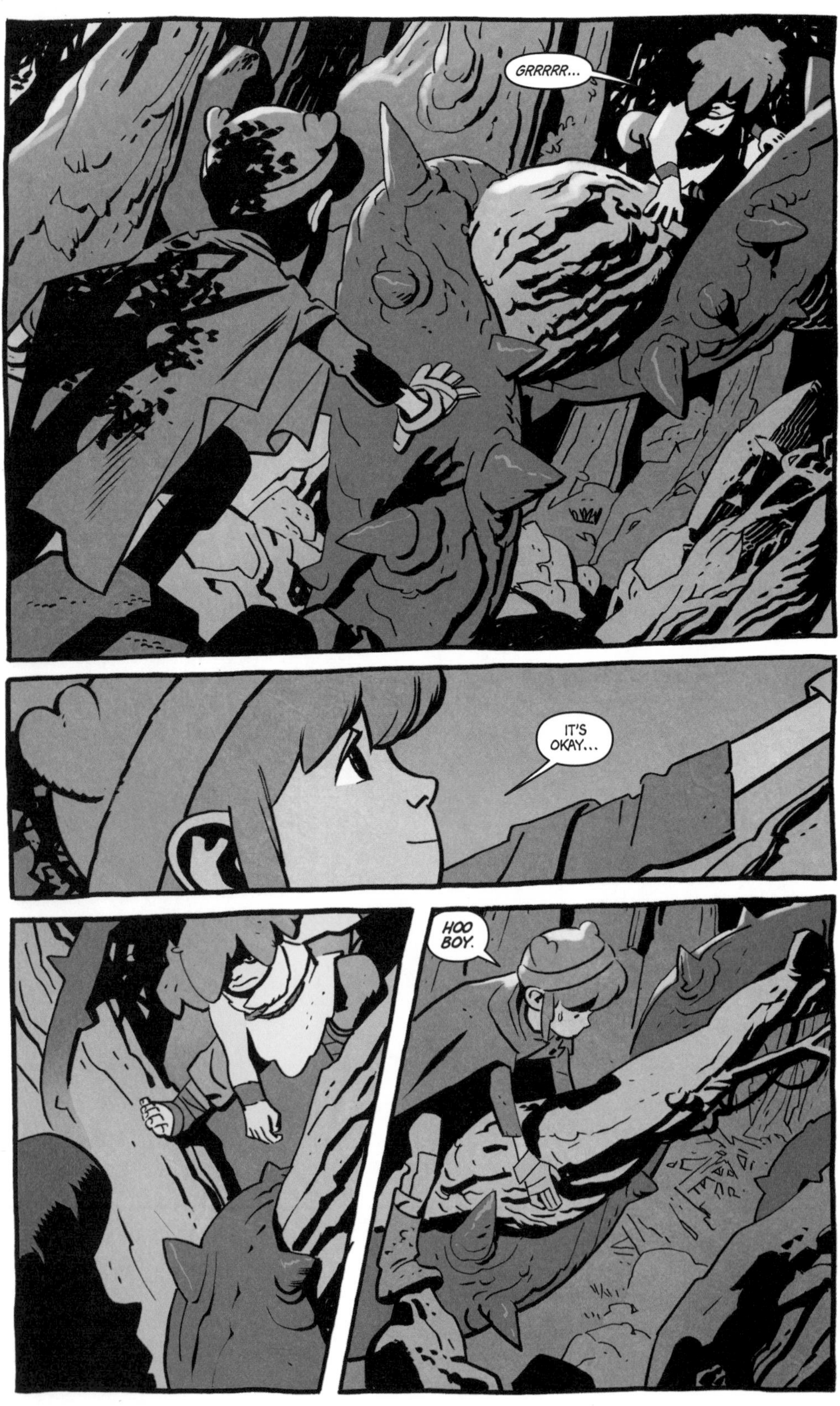
GRRRRR...
IT'S OKAY...
HOO BOY.

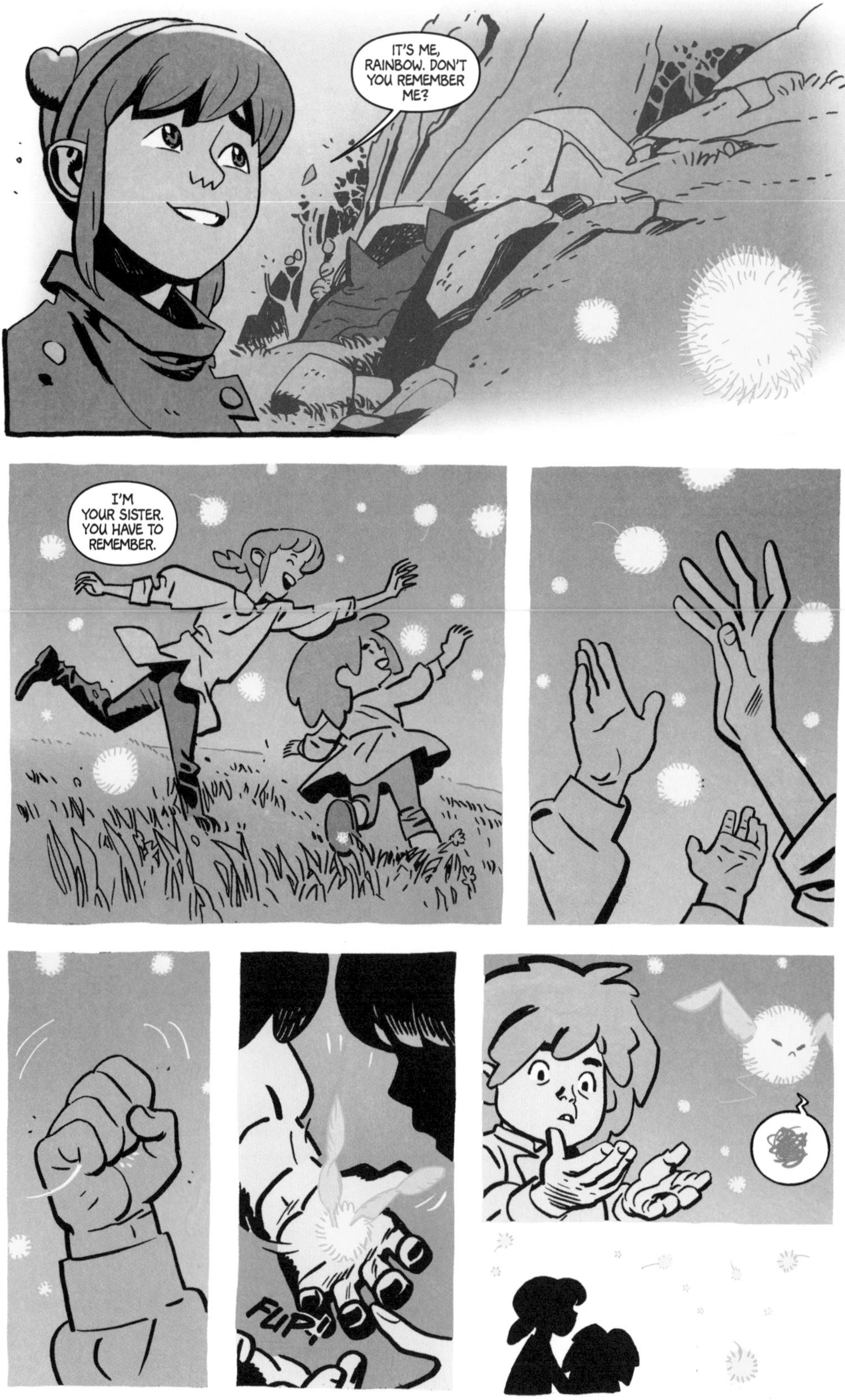
IT'S ME, RAINBOW. DON'T YOU REMEMBER ME?
I'M YOUR SISTER. YOU HAVE TO REMEMBER.
FLIP!!

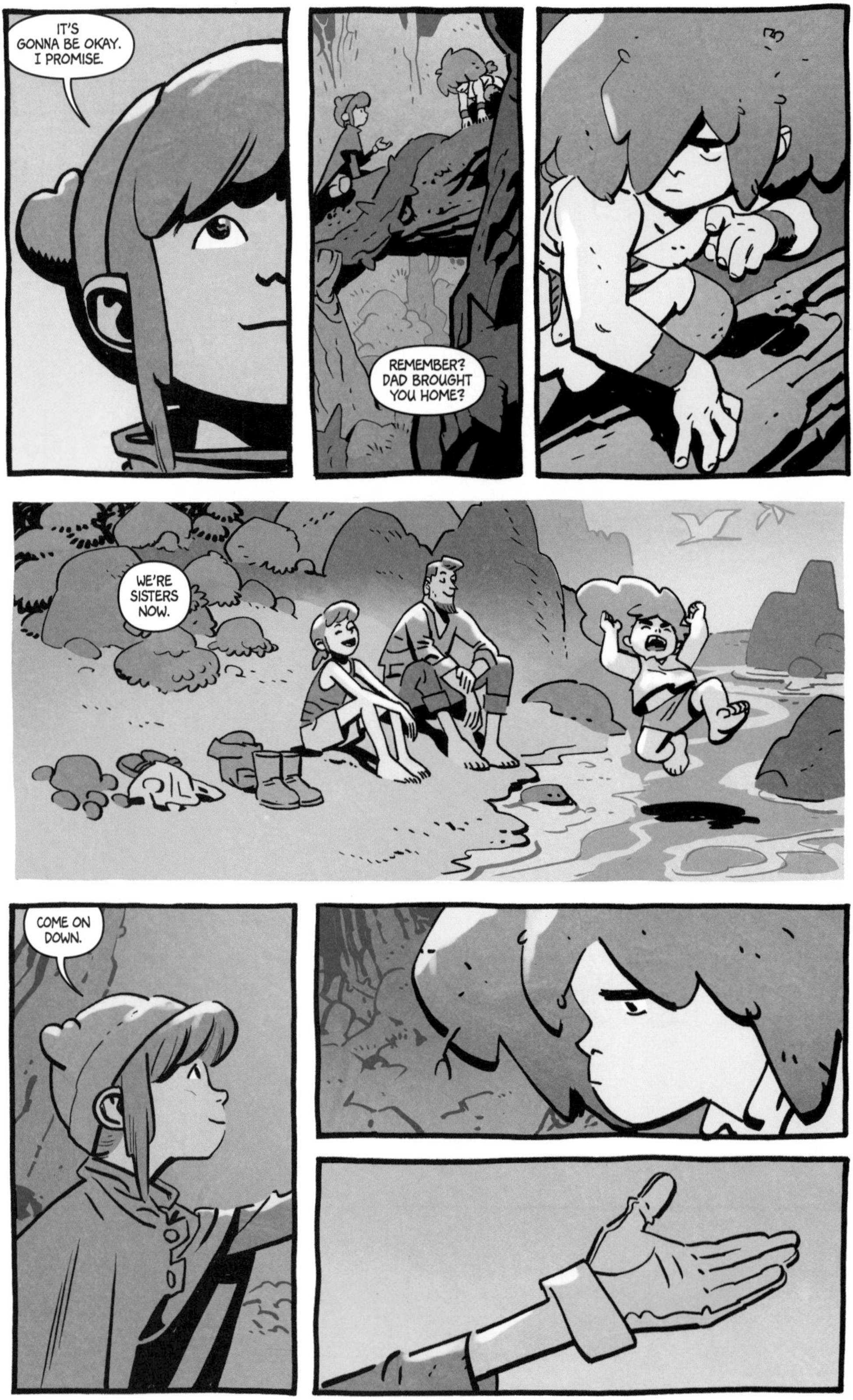
IT'S GONNA BE OKAY. I PROMISE.
REMEMBER? DAD BROUGHT YOU HOME?
WE'RE SISTERS NOW.
COME ON DOWN.

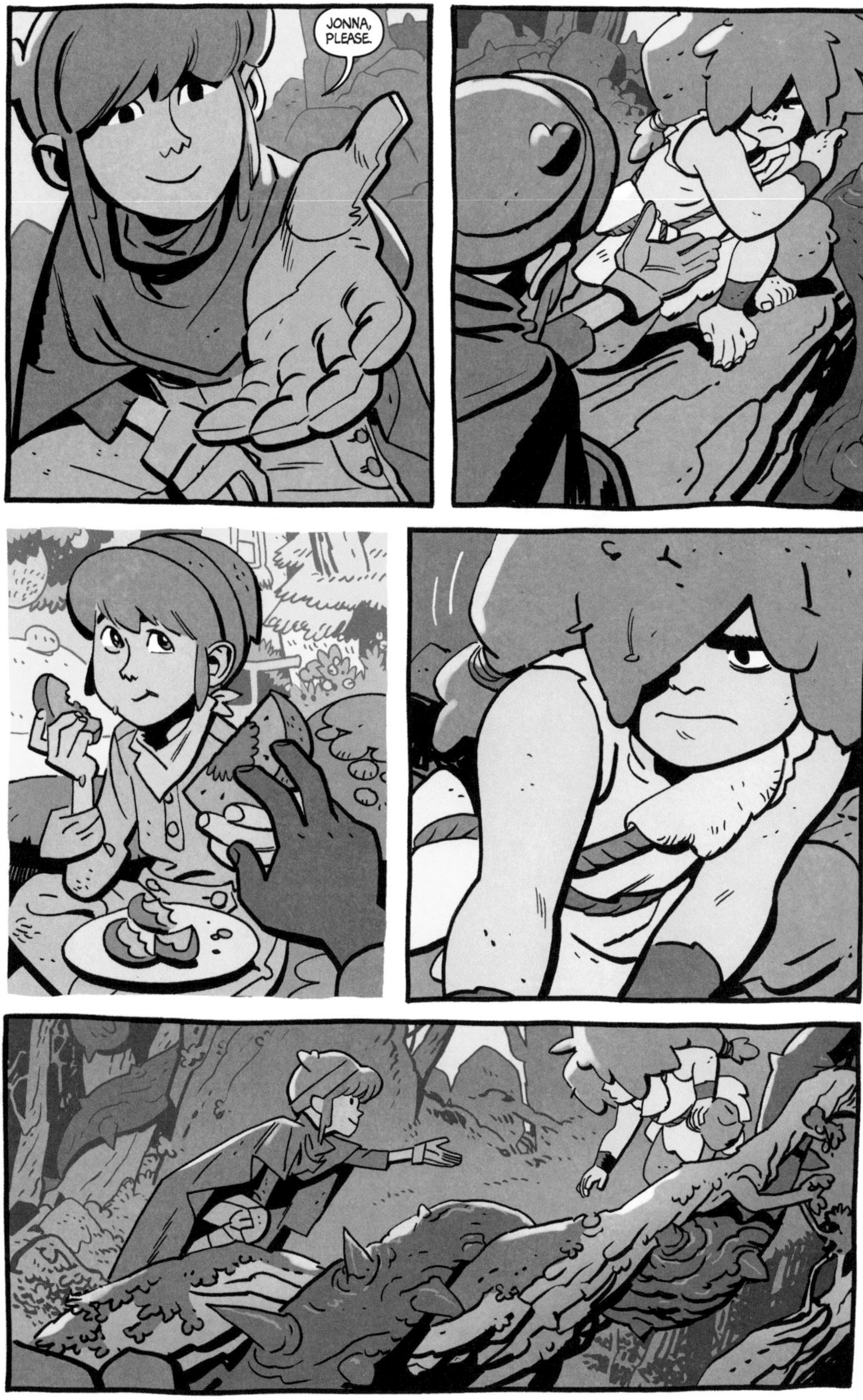
JONNA, PLEASE.

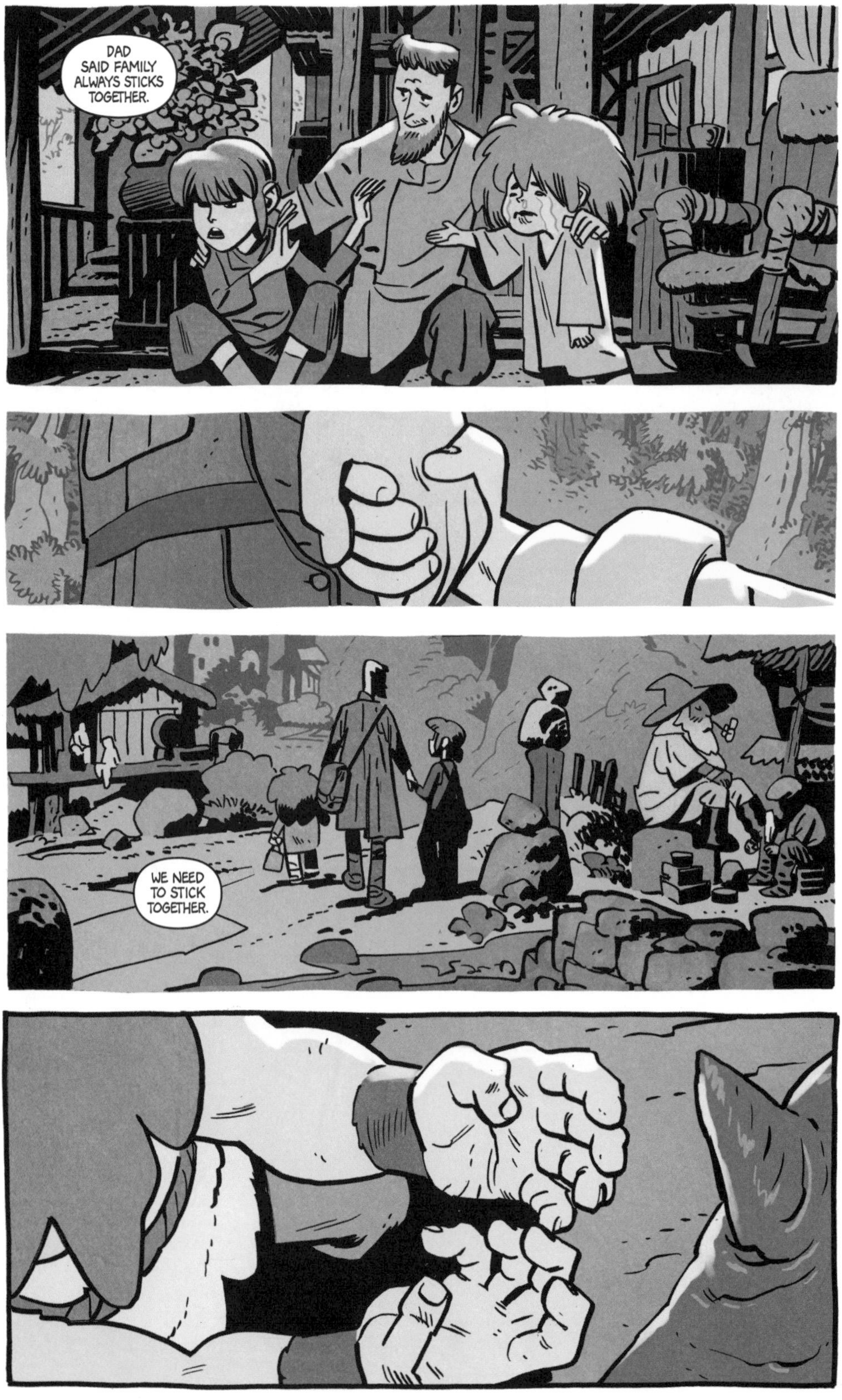
DAD SAID FAMILY ALWAYS STICKS TOGETHER.
WE NEED TO STICK TOGETHER.

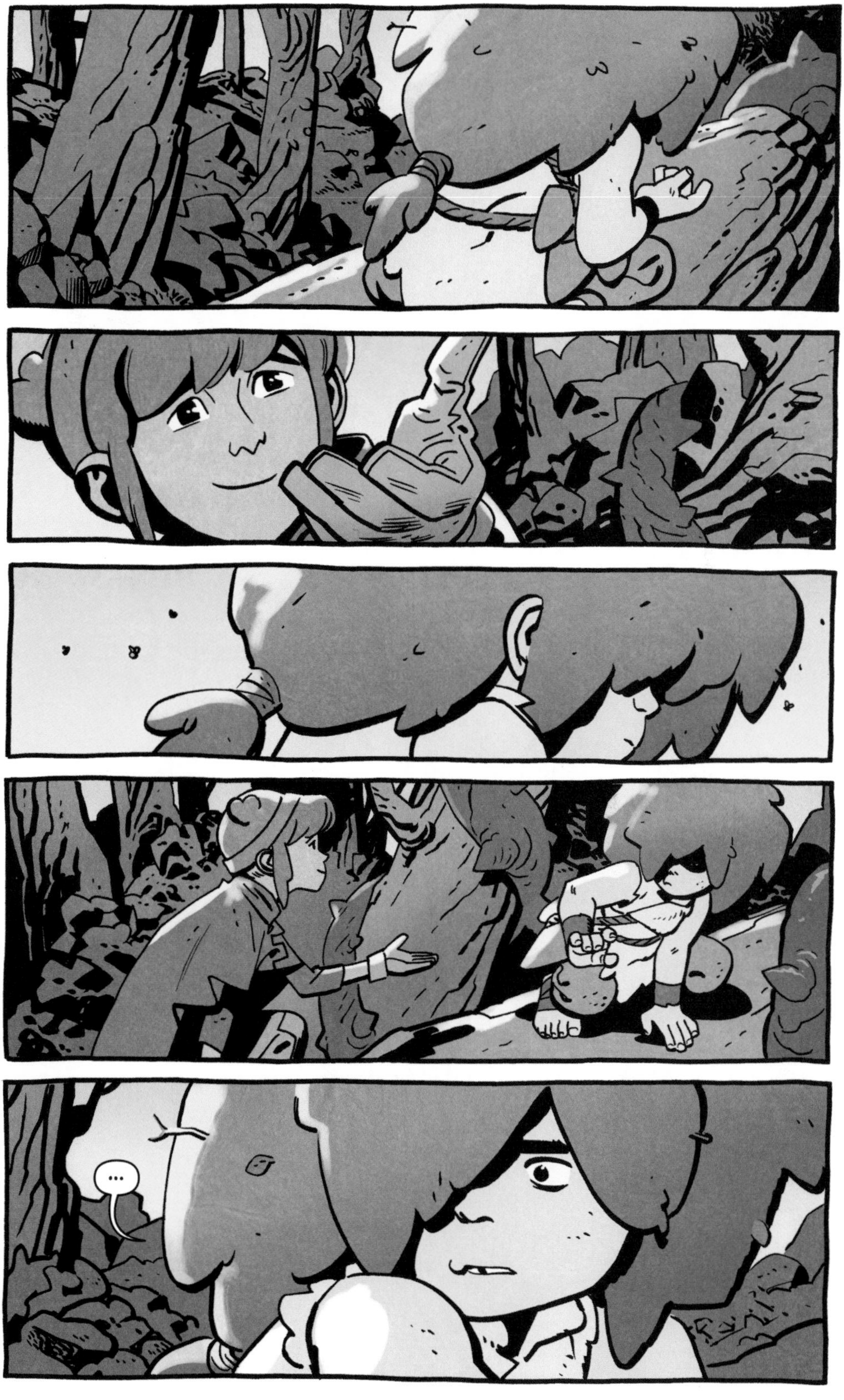
...

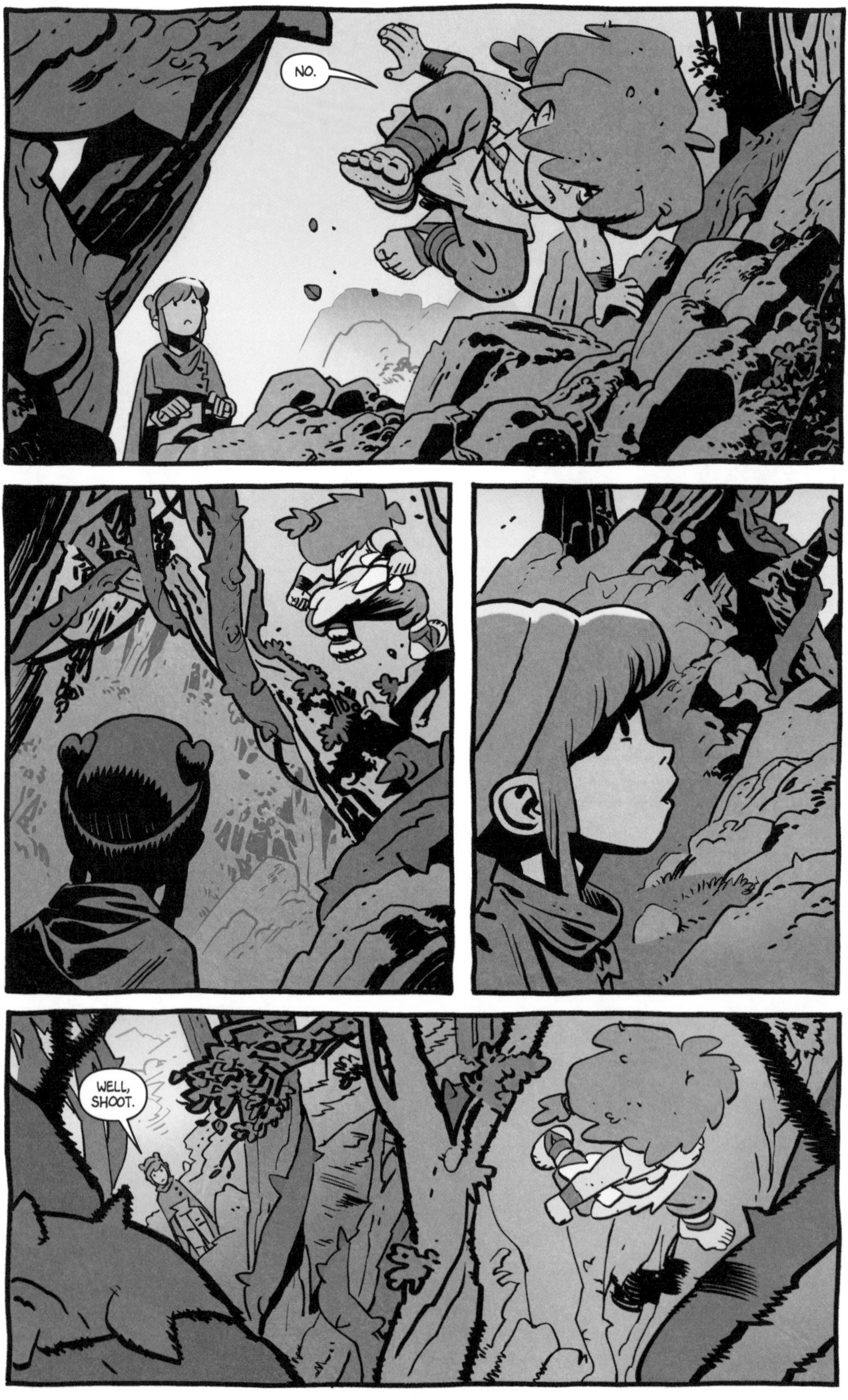
NO.
WELL, SHOOT.

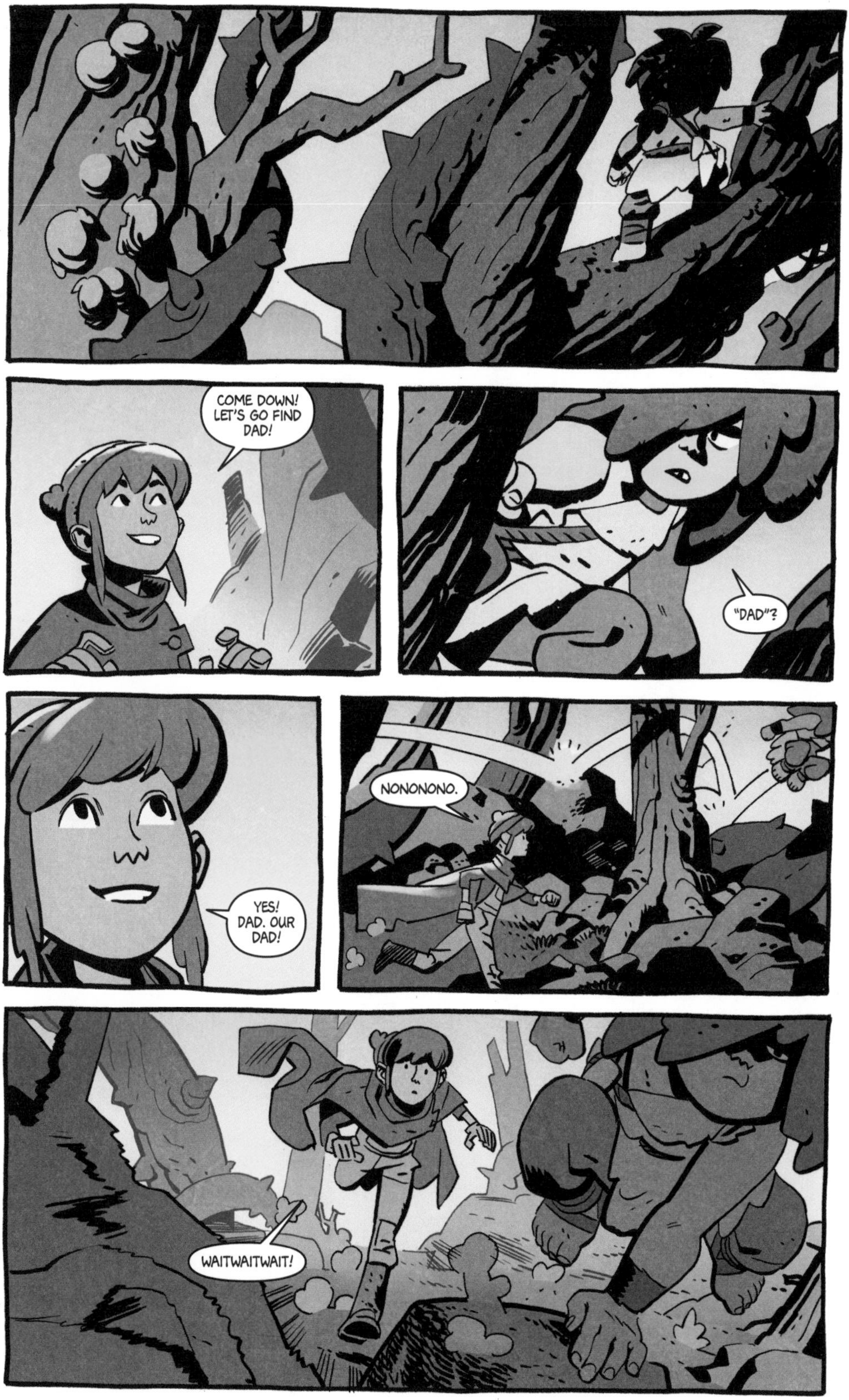
COME DOWN! LET'S GO FIND DAD!
"DAD"?
YES! DAD. OUR DAD!
NONONONO.
WAITWAITWAIT!

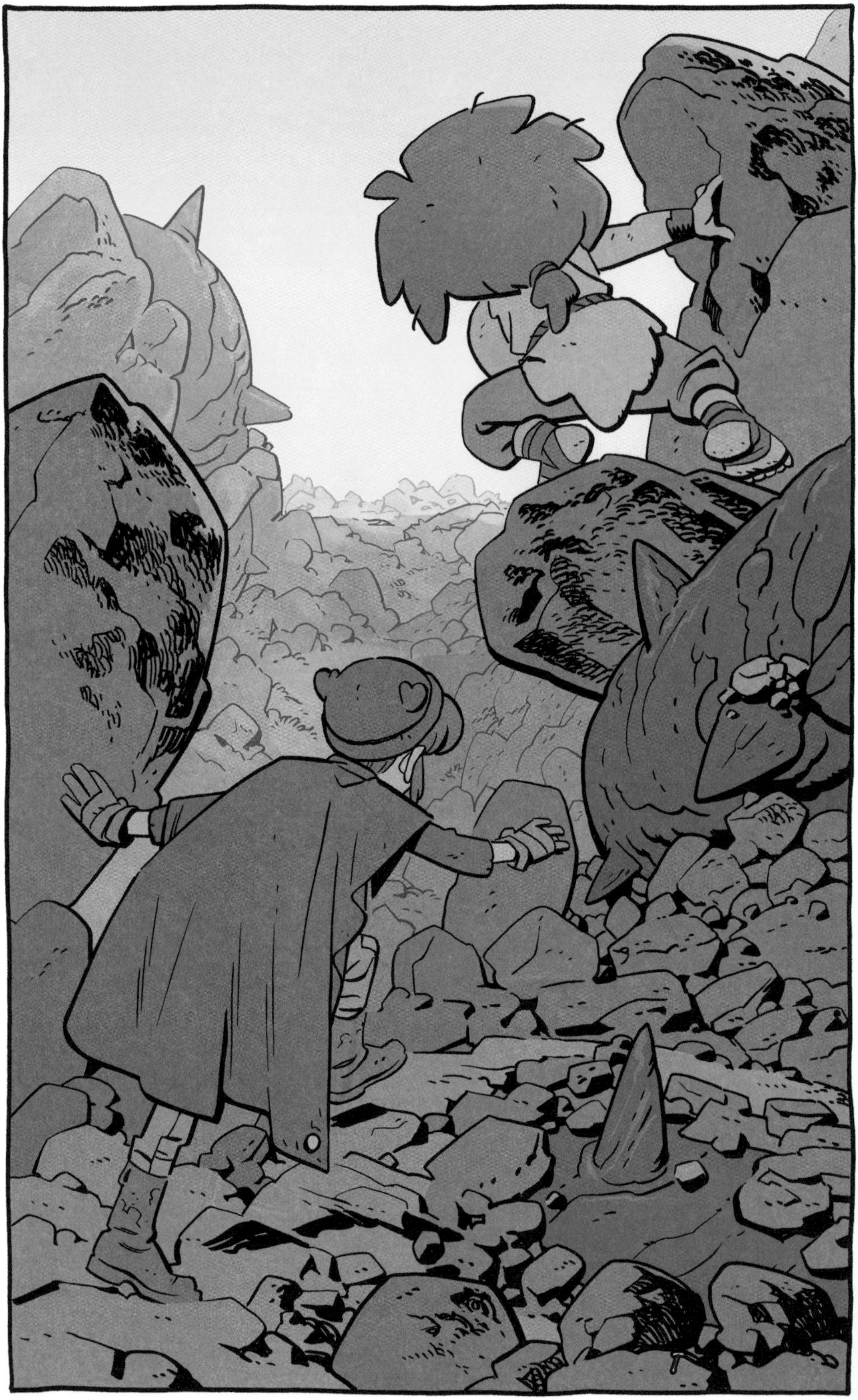

CHAPTER 3

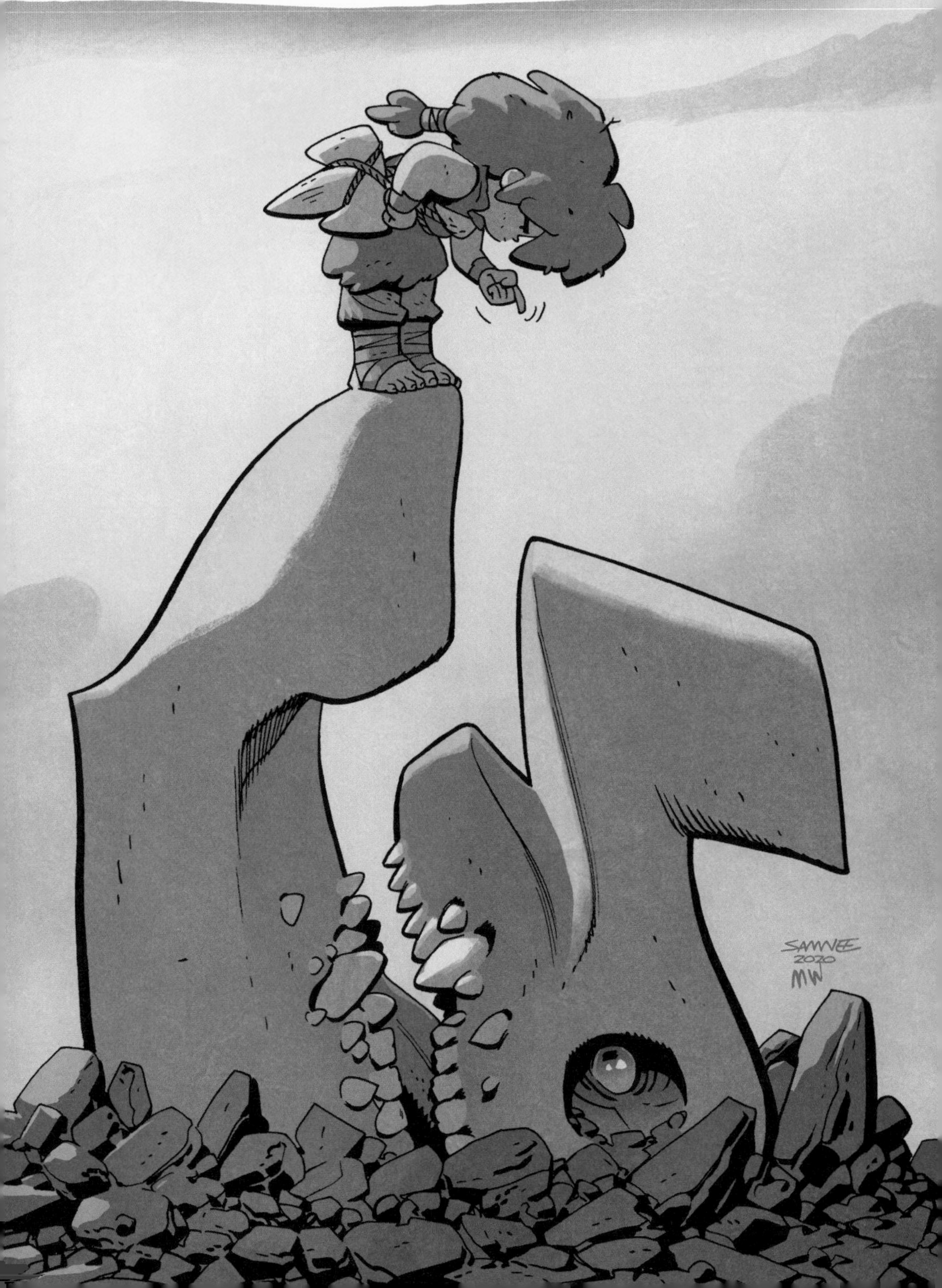
SAMNEE
2020
MW

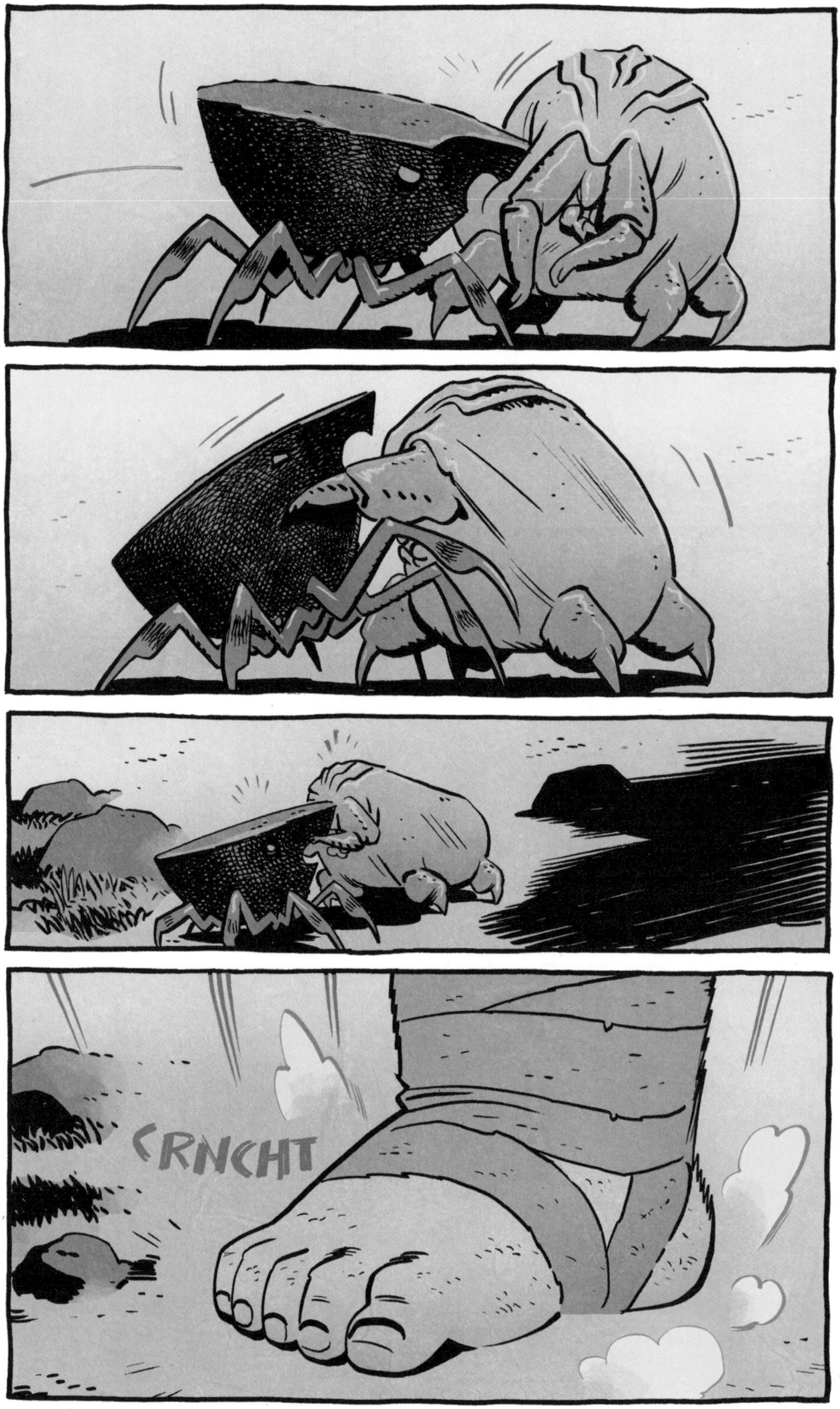
CRNCHT

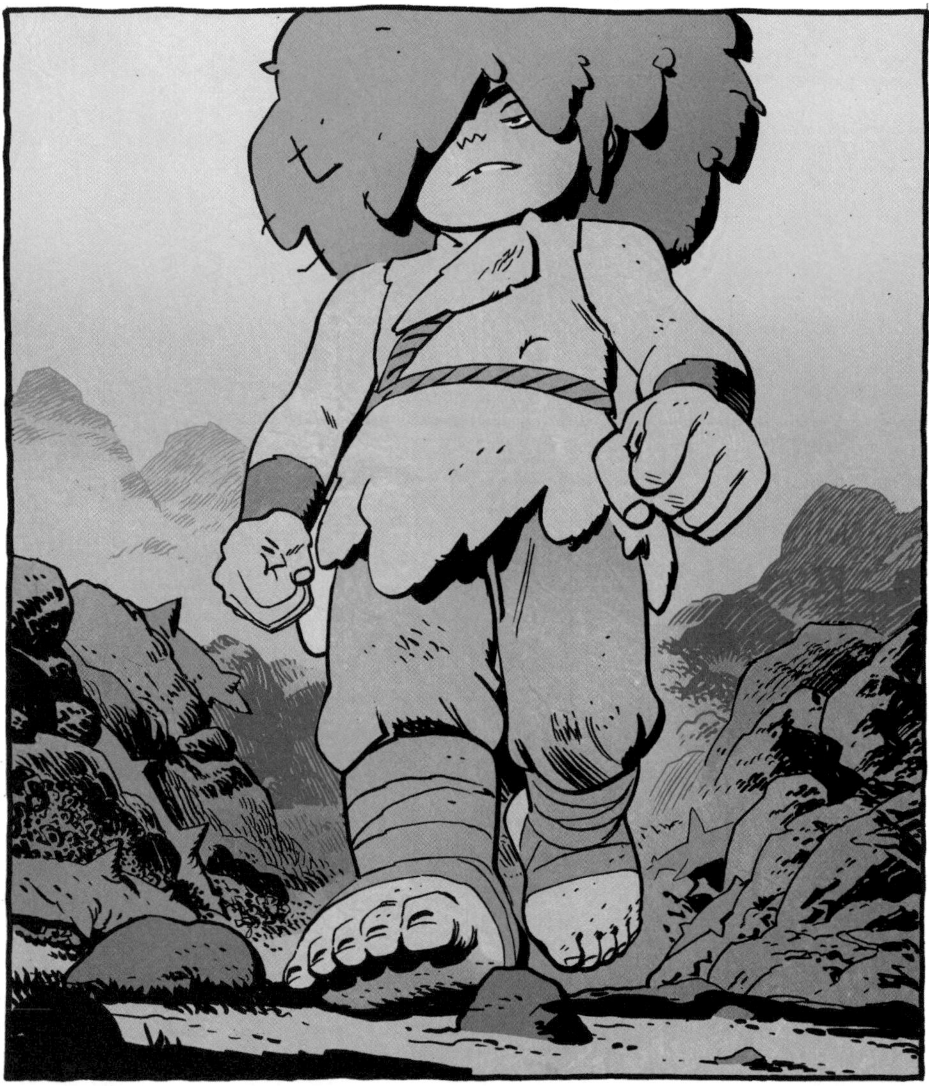

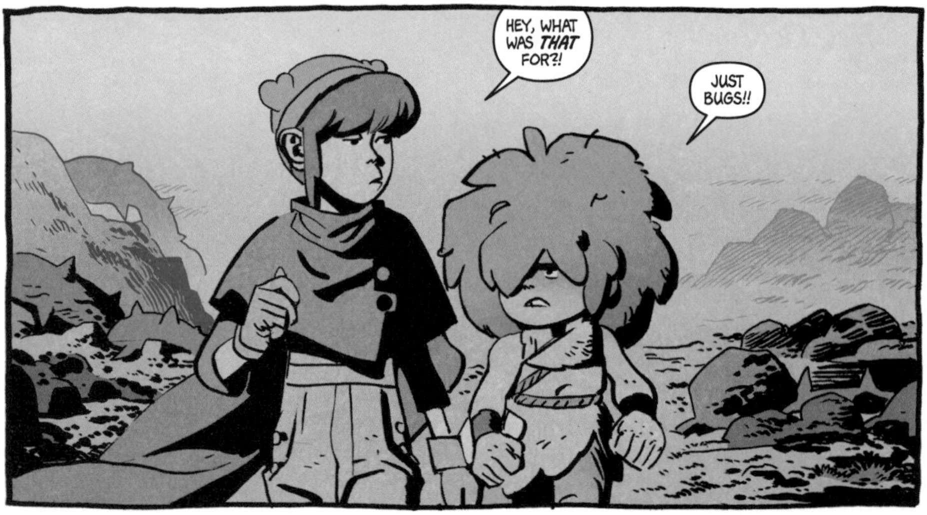
HEY, WHAT WAS *THAT* FOR?!
JUST BUGS!!

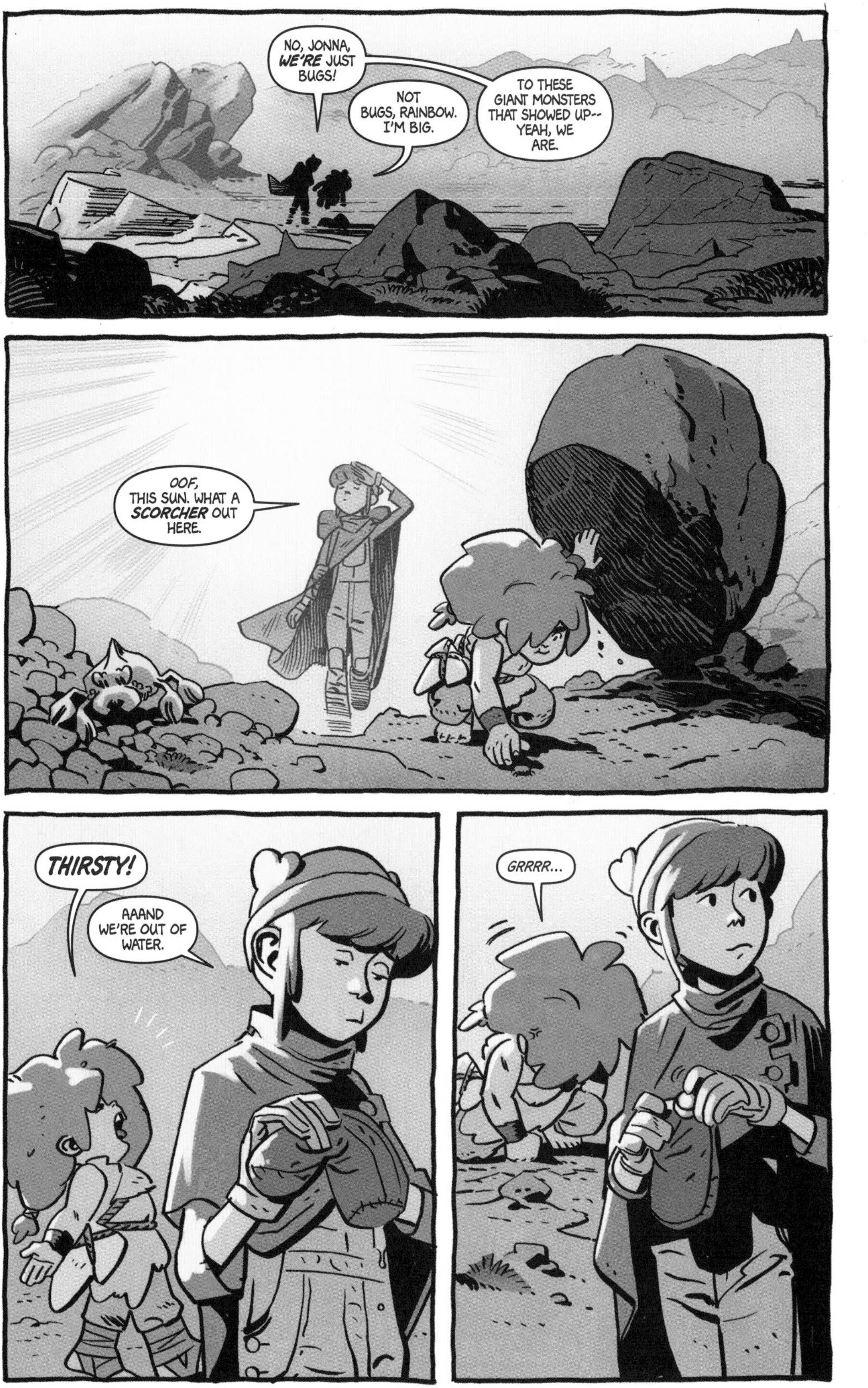
NO, JONNA, WE'RE JUST BUGS!
NOT BUGS, RAINBOW. I'M BIG.
TO THESE GIANT MONSTERS THAT SHOWED UP-- YEAH, WE ARE.
OOF, THIS SUN. WHAT A SCORCHER OUT HERE.
THIRSTY!
AAAND WE'RE OUT OF WATER.
GRRRR...

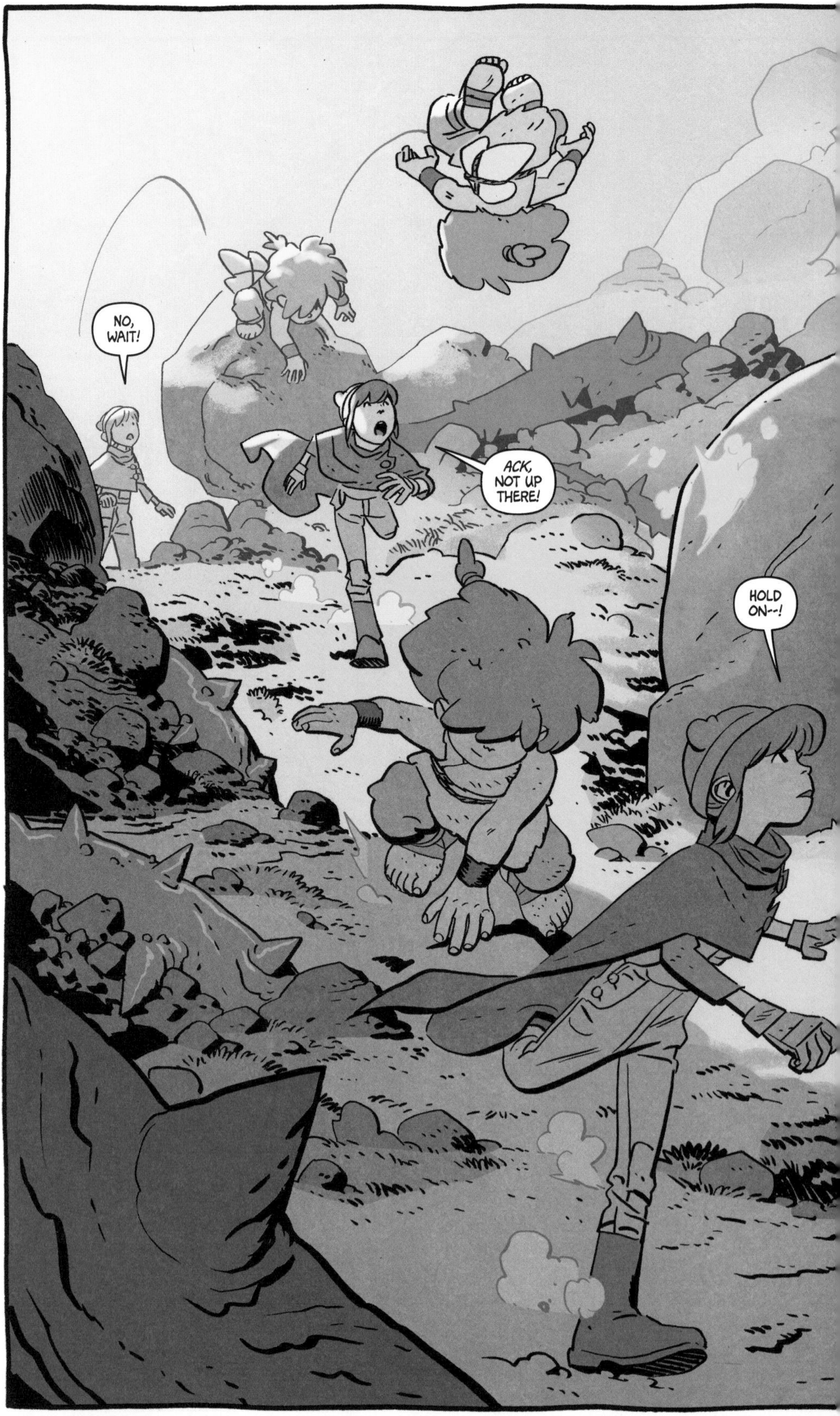
NO, WAIT!
ACK, NOT UP THERE!
HOLD ON--!

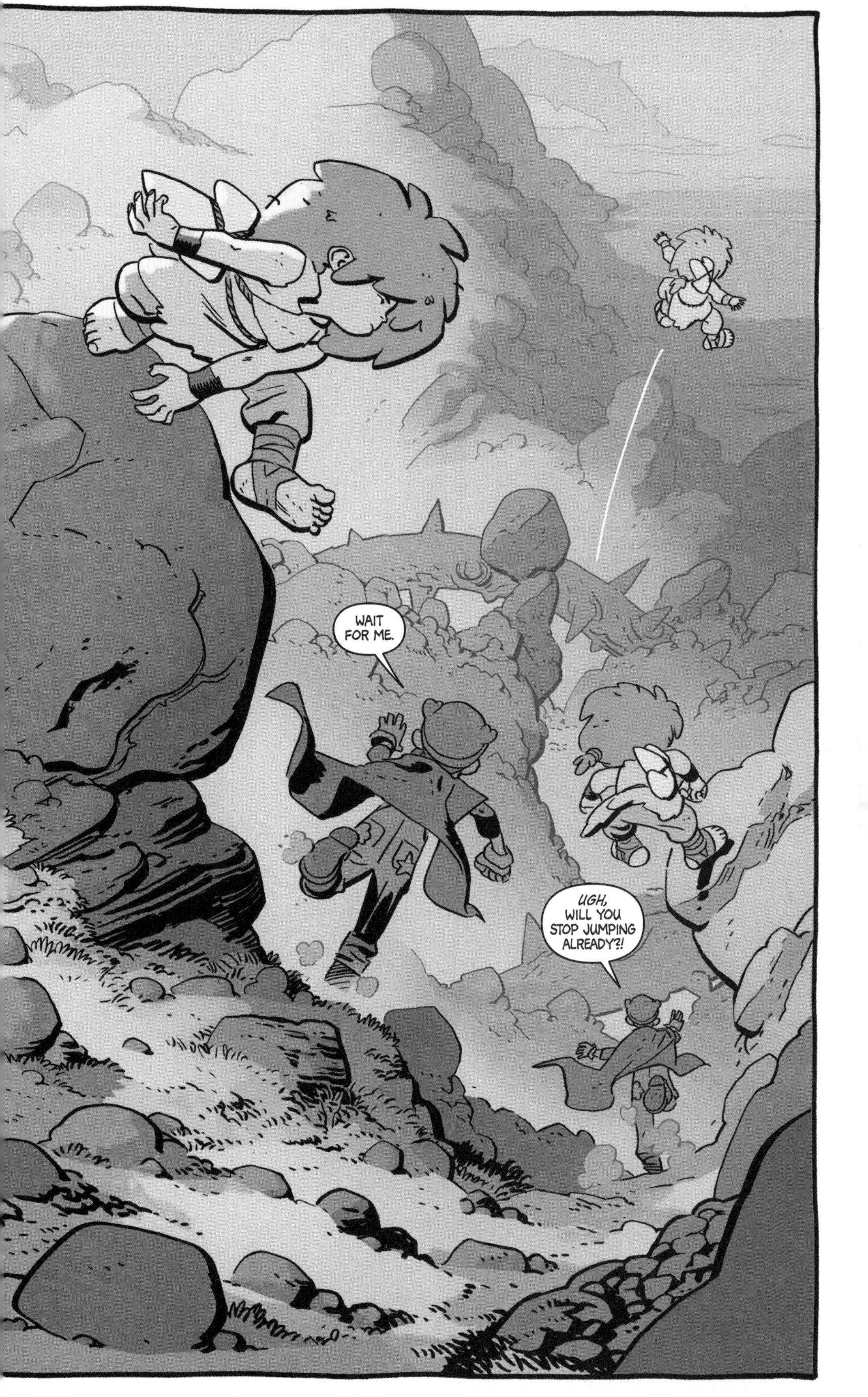
WAIT FOR ME.
UGH, WILL YOU STOP JUMPING ALREADY?!

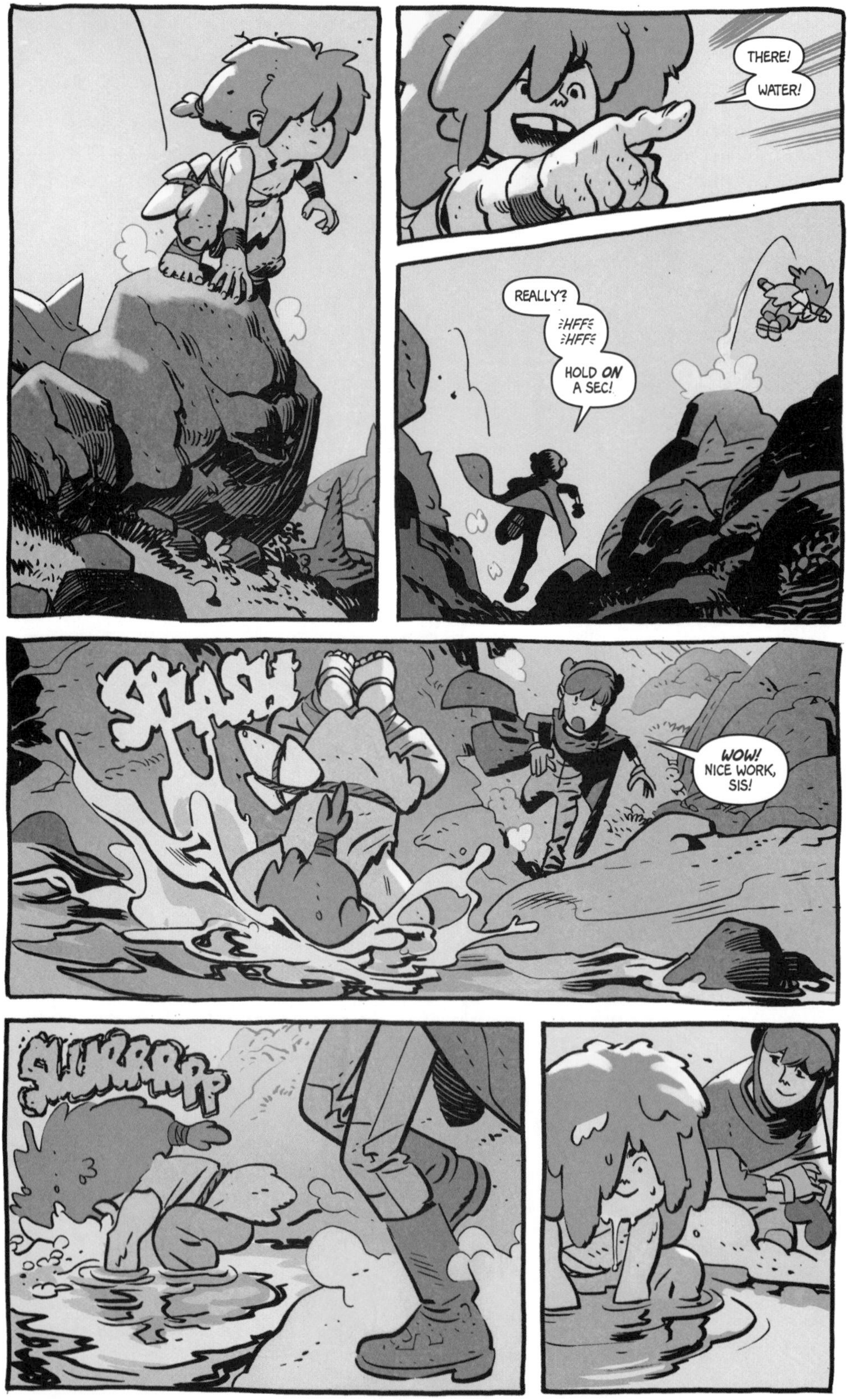
THERE!
WATER!
REALLY?
HFF HFF
HOLD ON A SEC!
SPLASH
WOW! NICE WORK, SIS!
SLURRRPP

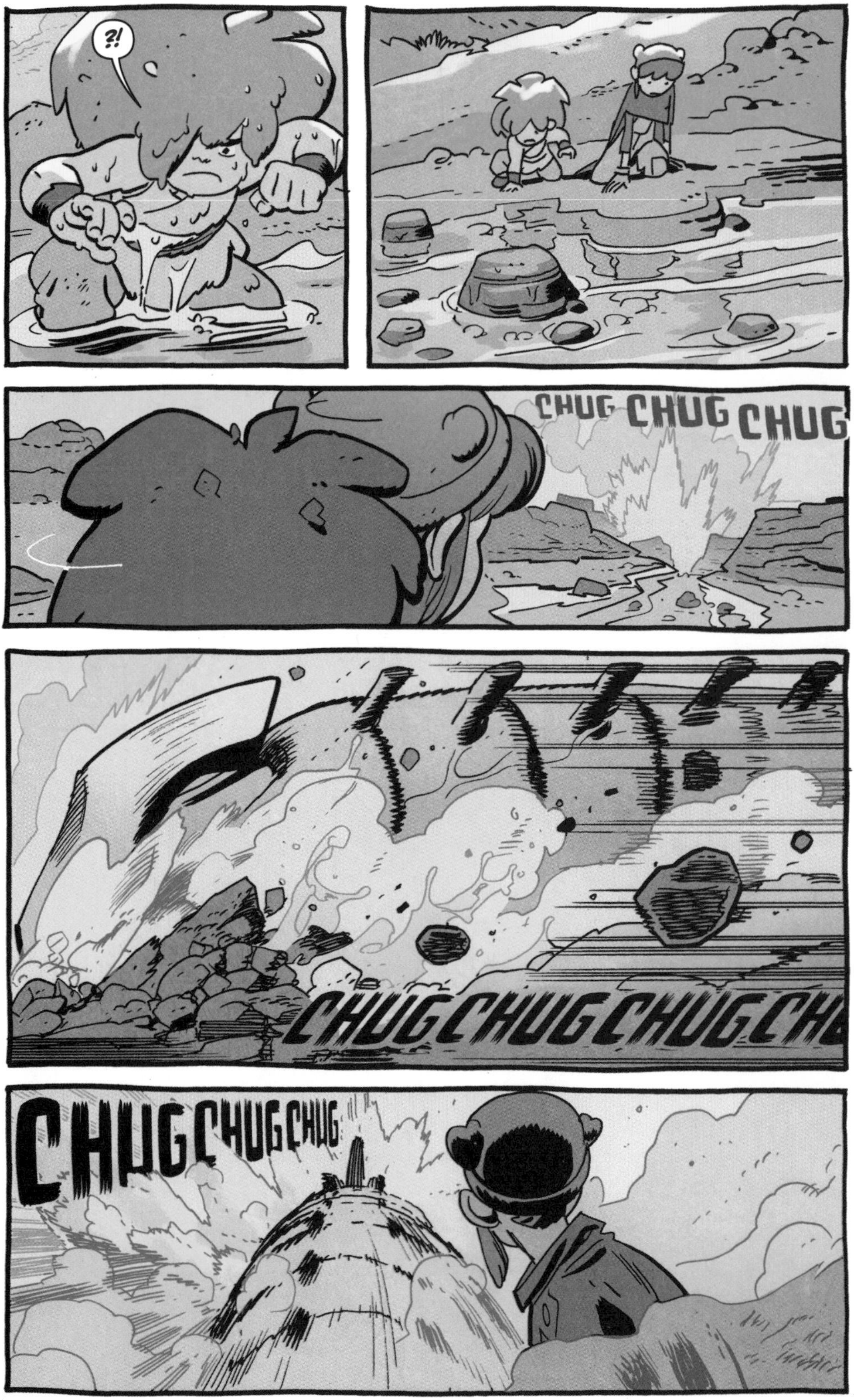
?!
CHUG CHUG CHUG
CHUG CHUG CHUG CH
CHUG CHUG CHUG

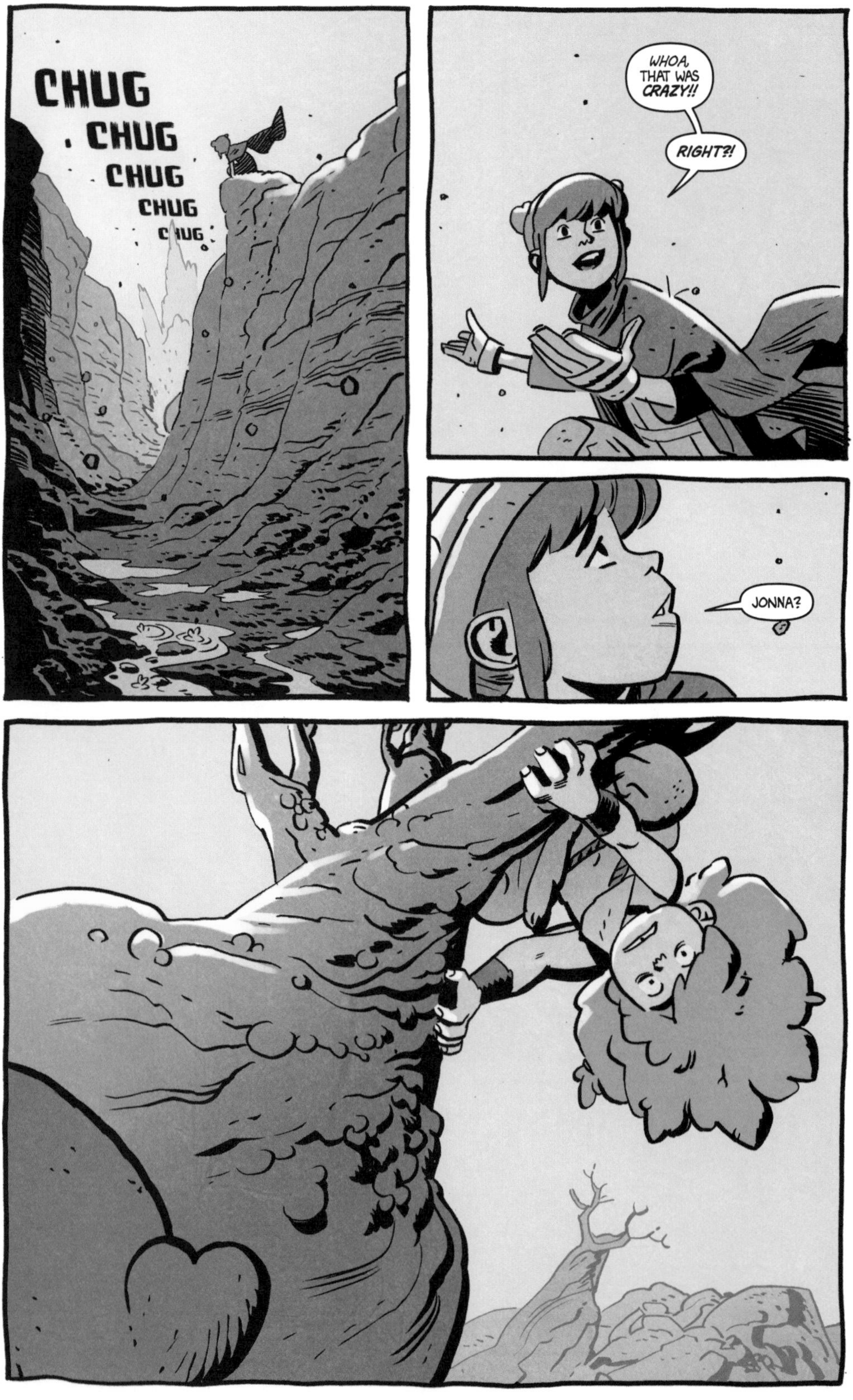
CHUG
CHUG
CHUG
CHUG
CHUG
WHOA, THAT WAS CRAZY!!
RIGHT?!
JONNA?

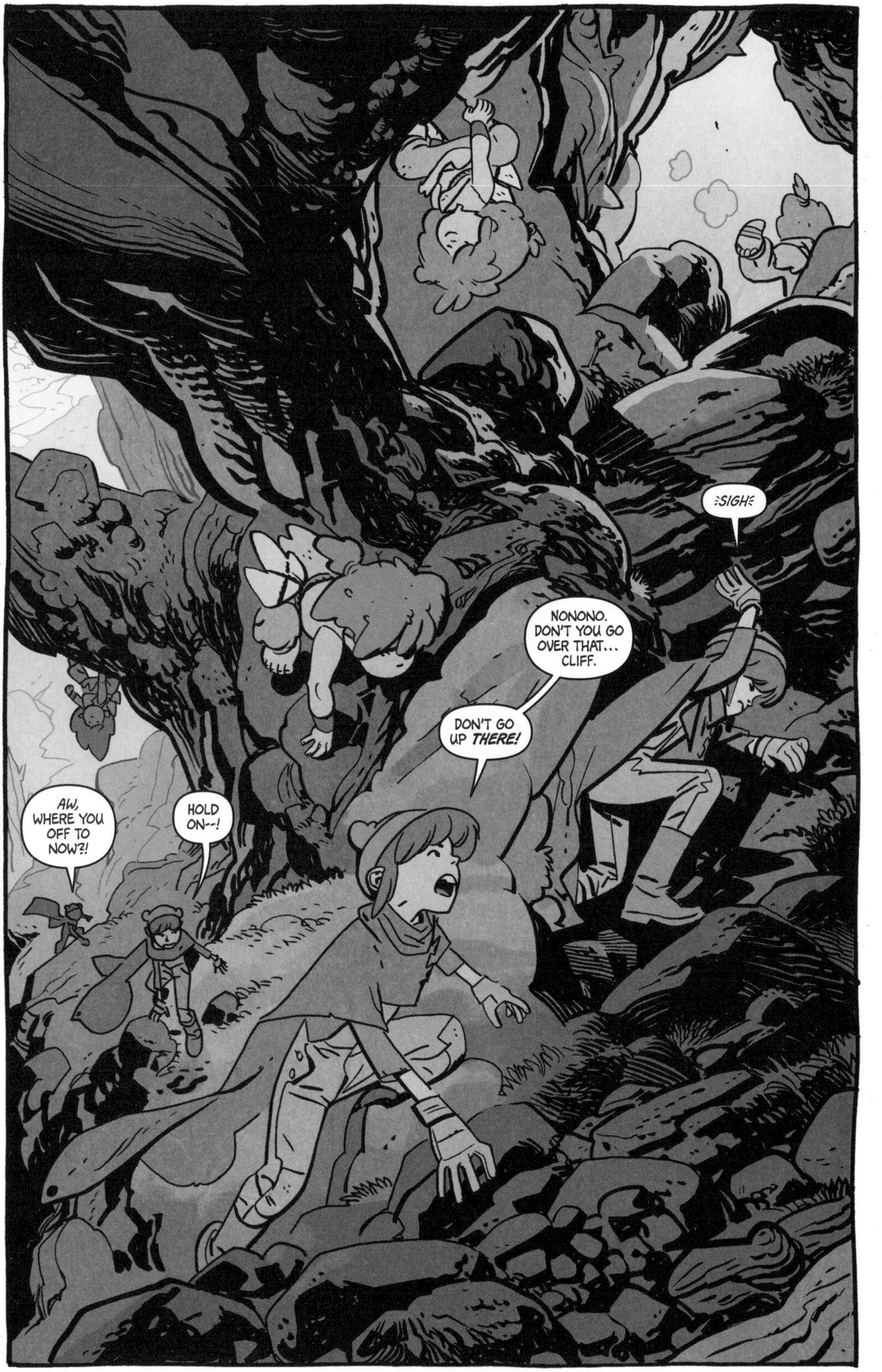

SIGH
NONONO. DON'T YOU GO OVER THAT... CLIFF.
DON'T GO UP *THERE!*
AW, WHERE YOU OFF TO NOW?!
HOLD ON--!

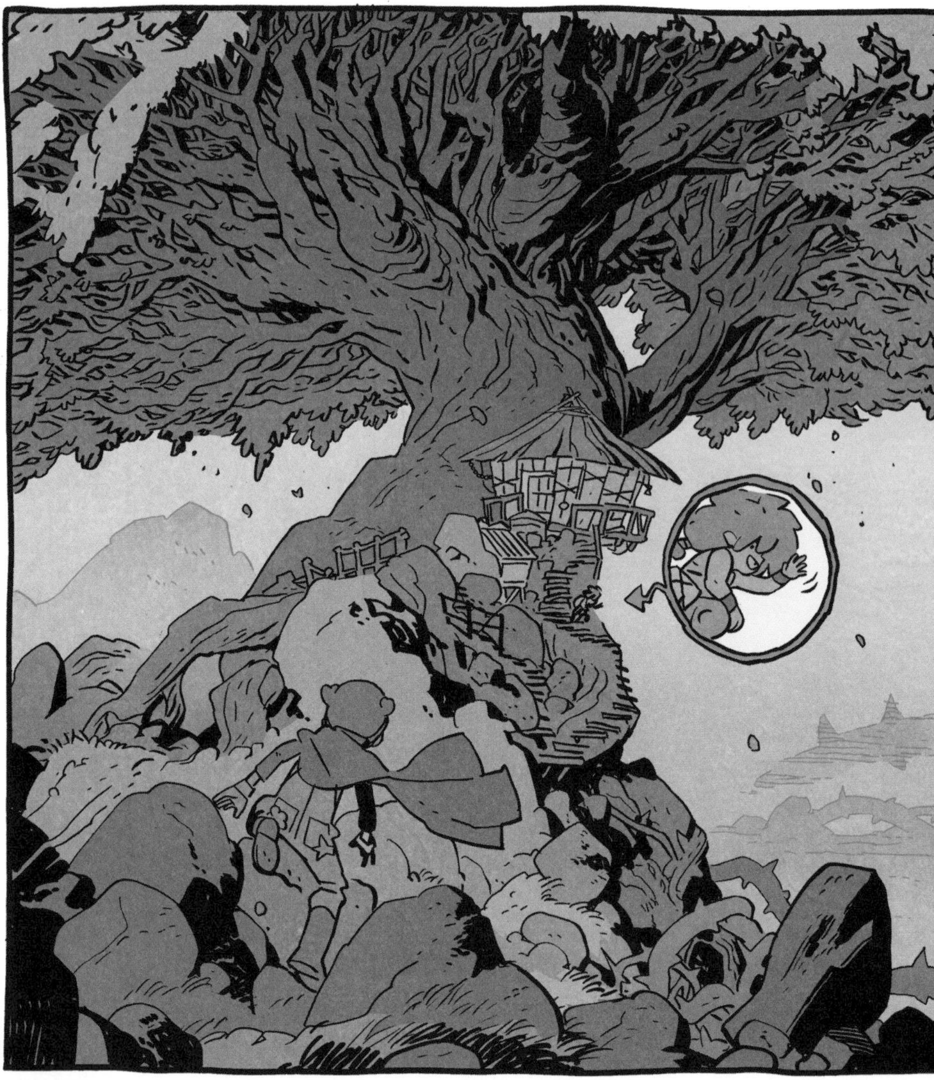

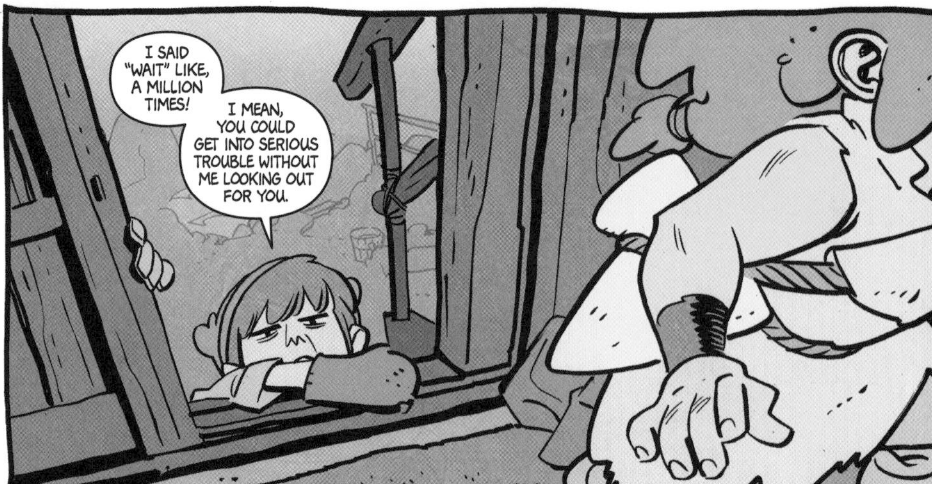
I SAID "WAIT" LIKE, A MILLION TIMES!
I MEAN, YOU COULD GET INTO SERIOUS TROUBLE WITHOUT ME LOOKING OUT FOR YOU.

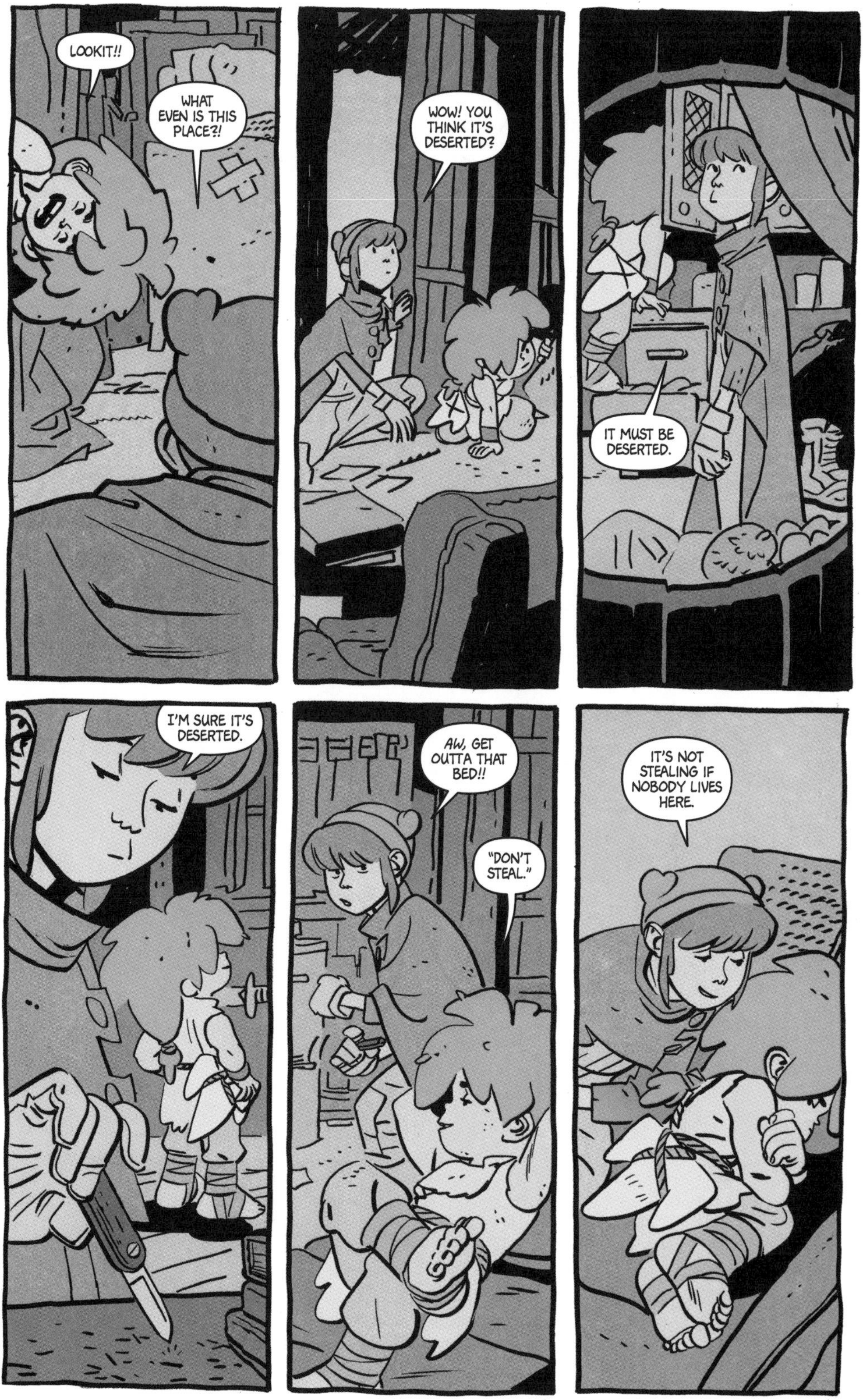
LOOKIT!!
WHAT EVEN IS THIS PLACE?!
WOW! YOU THINK IT'S DESERTED?
IT MUST BE DESERTED.
I'M SURE IT'S DESERTED.
AW, GET OUTTA THAT BED!!
"DON'T STEAL."
IT'S NOT STEALING IF NOBODY LIVES HERE.

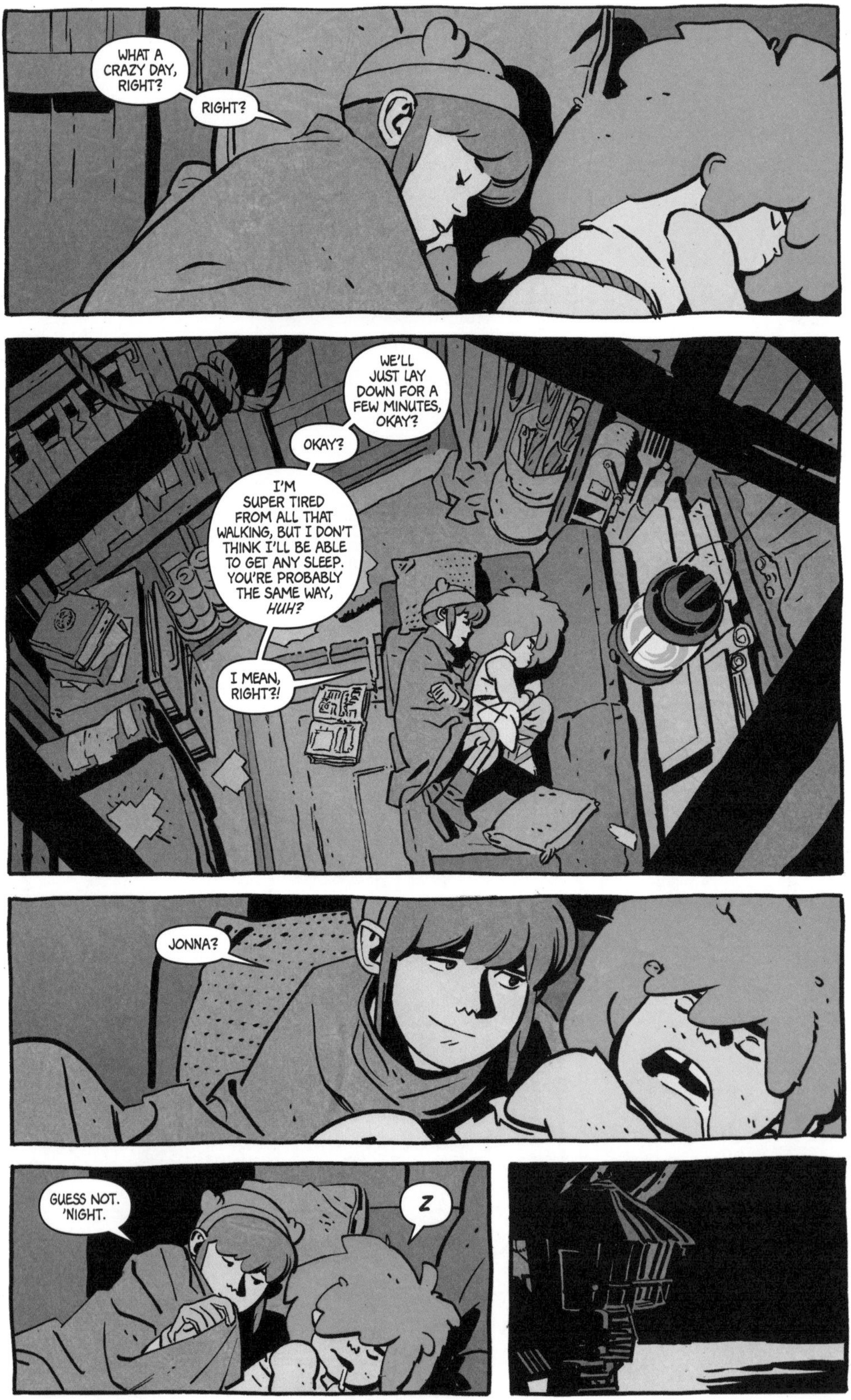
WHAT A CRAZY DAY, RIGHT?
RIGHT?
WE'LL JUST LAY DOWN FOR A FEW MINUTES, OKAY?
OKAY?
I'M SUPER TIRED FROM ALL THAT WALKING, BUT I DON'T THINK I'LL BE ABLE TO GET ANY SLEEP. YOU'RE PROBABLY THE SAME WAY, *HUH?*
I MEAN, RIGHT?!
JONNA?
GUESS NOT. 'NIGHT.
Z

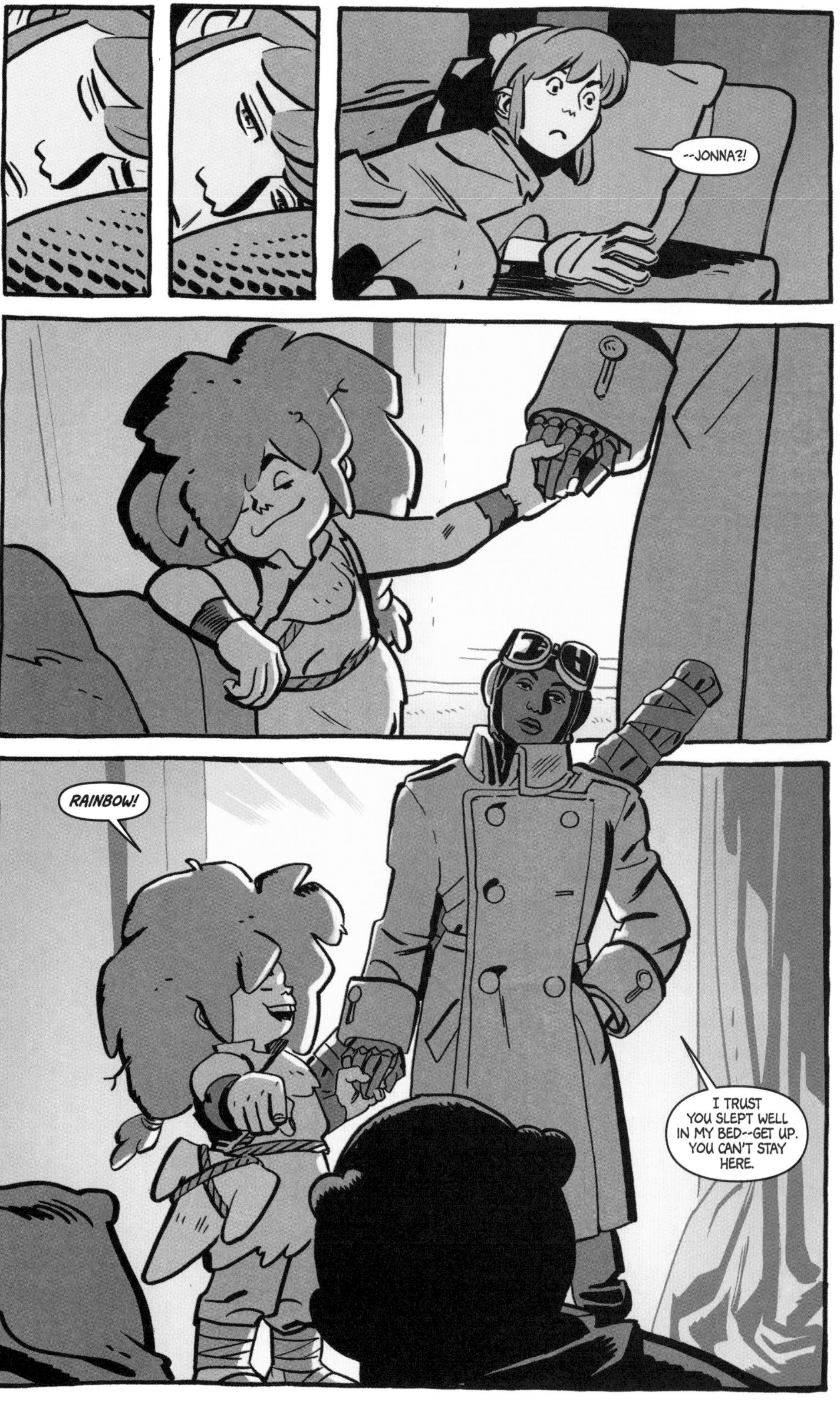
--JONNA?!
RAINBOW!
I TRUST YOU SLEPT WELL IN MY BED--GET UP. YOU CAN'T STAY HERE.

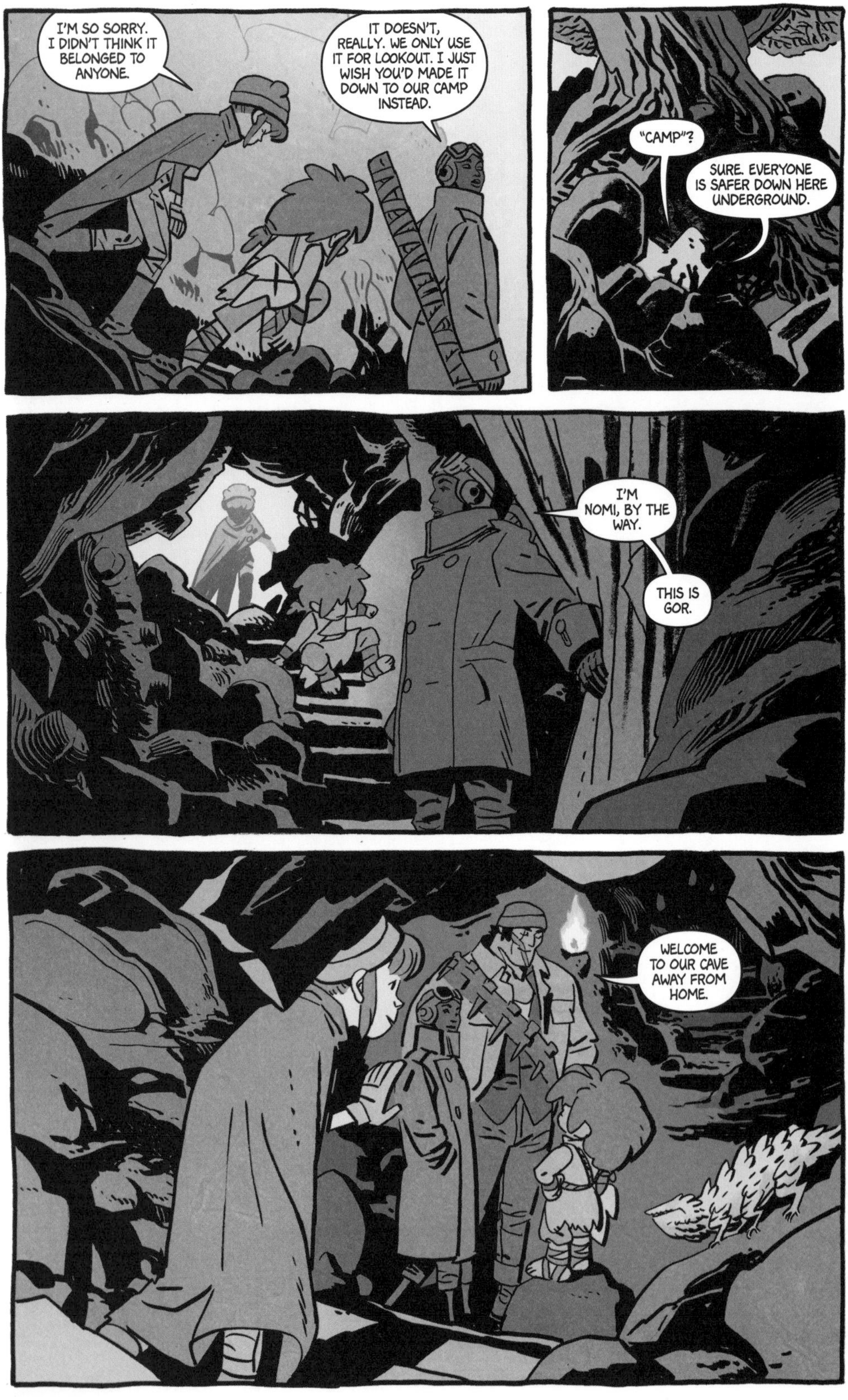
I'M SO SORRY. I DIDN'T THINK IT BELONGED TO ANYONE.
IT DOESN'T, REALLY. WE ONLY USE IT FOR LOOKOUT. I JUST WISH YOU'D MADE IT DOWN TO OUR CAMP INSTEAD.
"CAMP"?
SURE. EVERYONE IS SAFER DOWN HERE UNDERGROUND.
I'M NOMI, BY THE WAY.
THIS IS GOR.
WELCOME TO OUR CAVE AWAY FROM HOME.

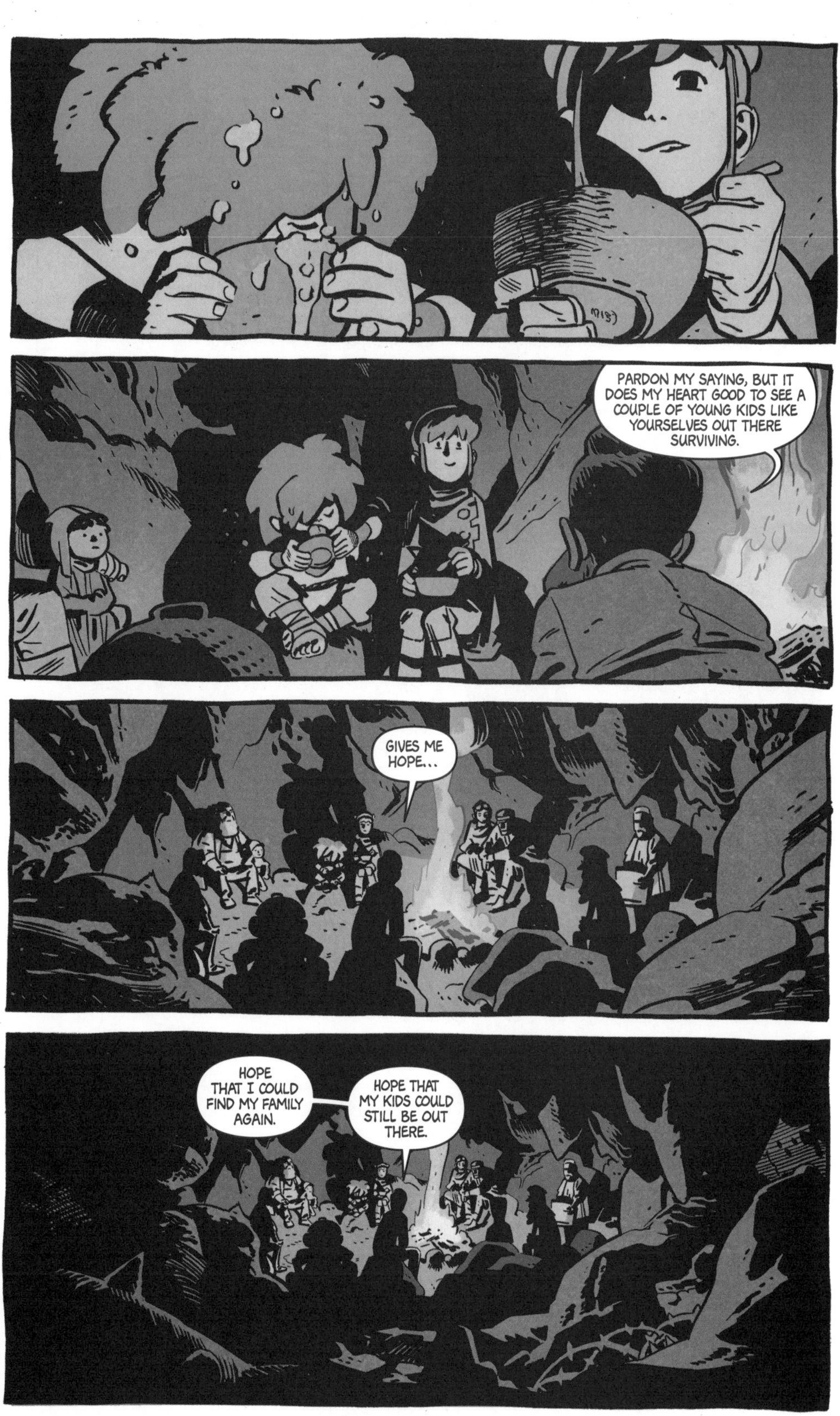
PARDON MY SAYING, BUT IT DOES MY HEART GOOD TO SEE A COUPLE OF YOUNG KIDS LIKE YOURSELVES OUT THERE SURVIVING.
GIVES ME HOPE...
HOPE THAT I COULD FIND MY FAMILY AGAIN.
HOPE THAT MY KIDS COULD STILL BE OUT THERE.

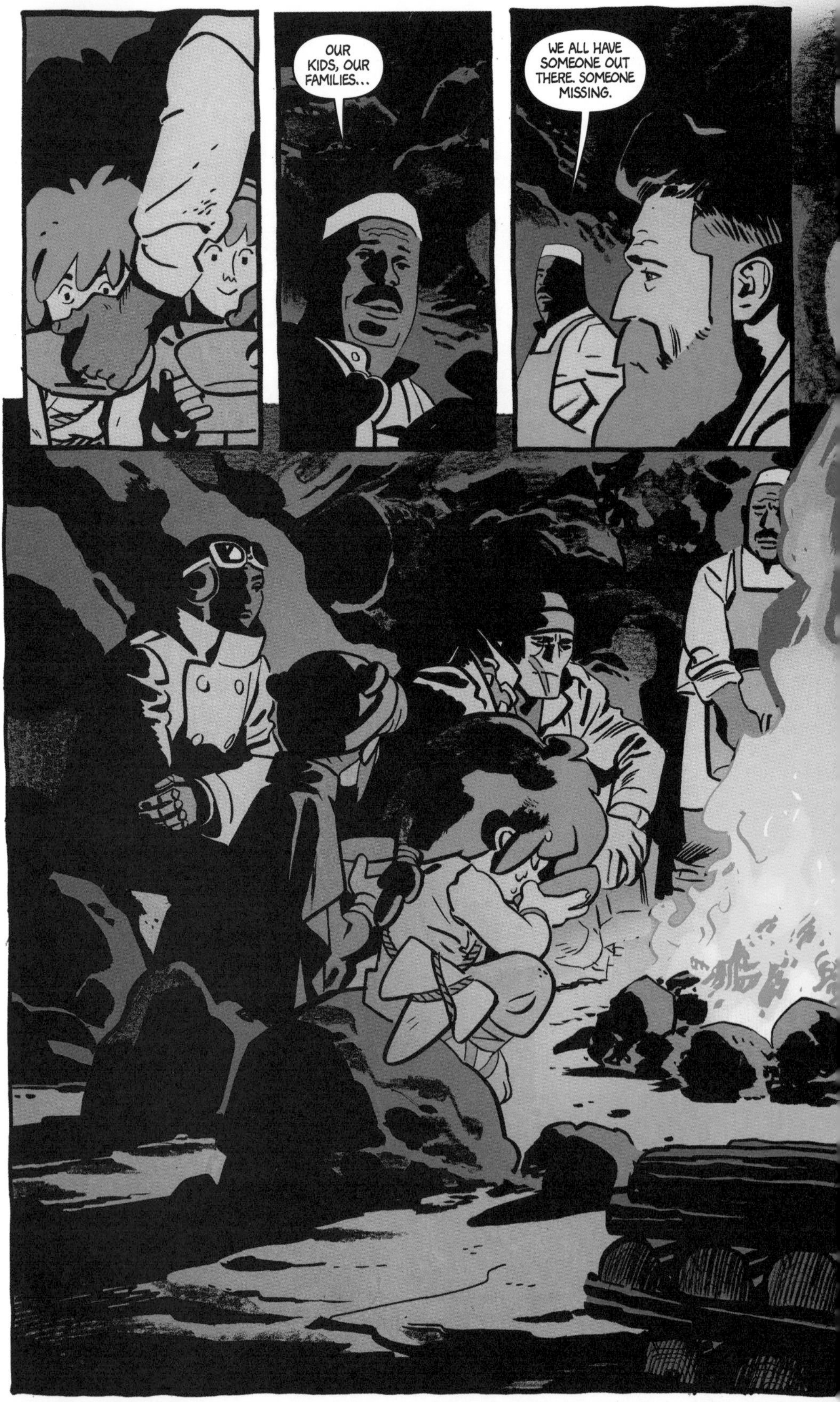
OUR KIDS, OUR FAMILIES...
WE ALL HAVE SOMEONE OUT THERE. SOMEONE MISSING.

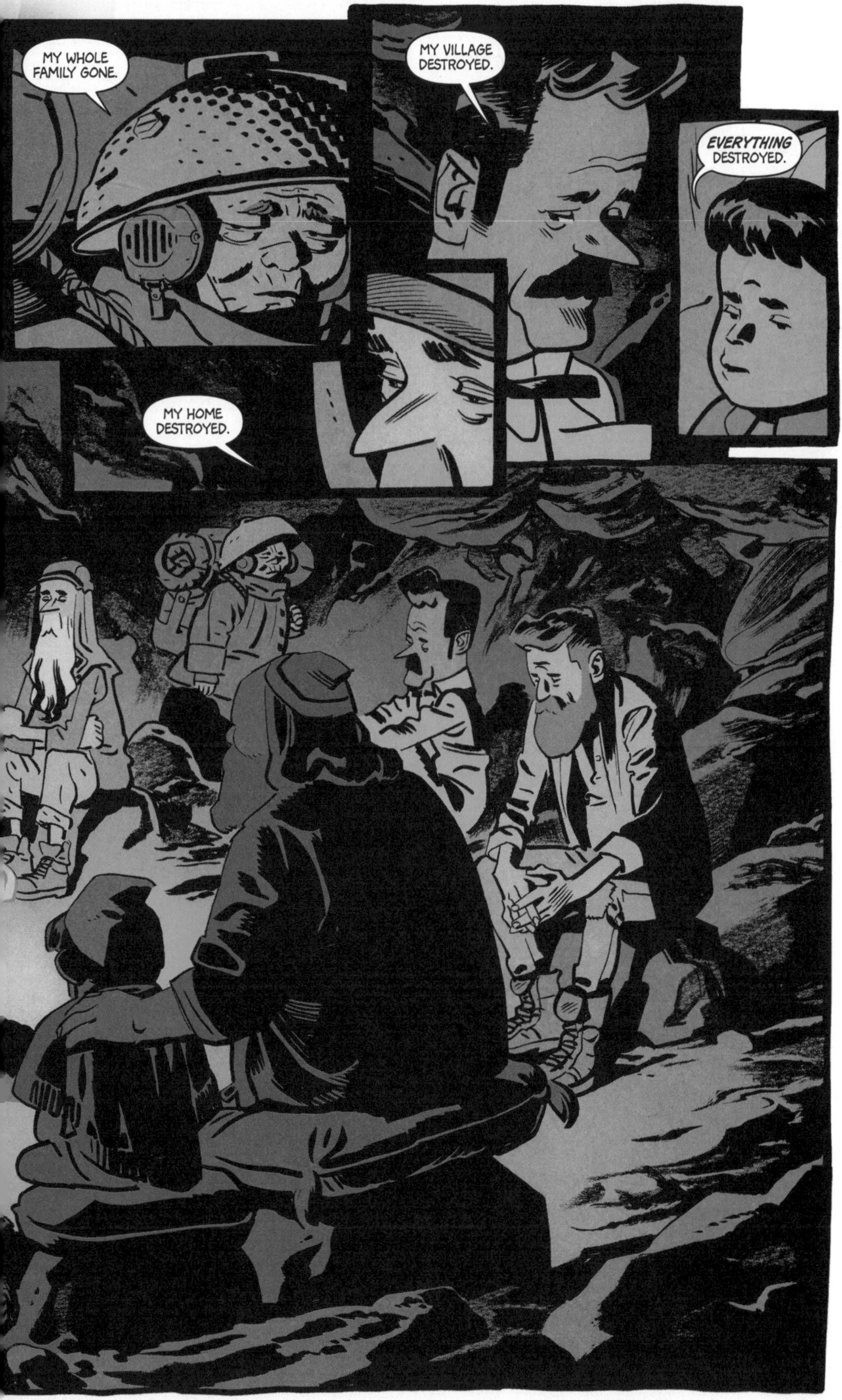
MY WHOLE FAMILY GONE.
MY VILLAGE DESTROYED.
EVERYTHING DESTROYED.
MY HOME DESTROYED.

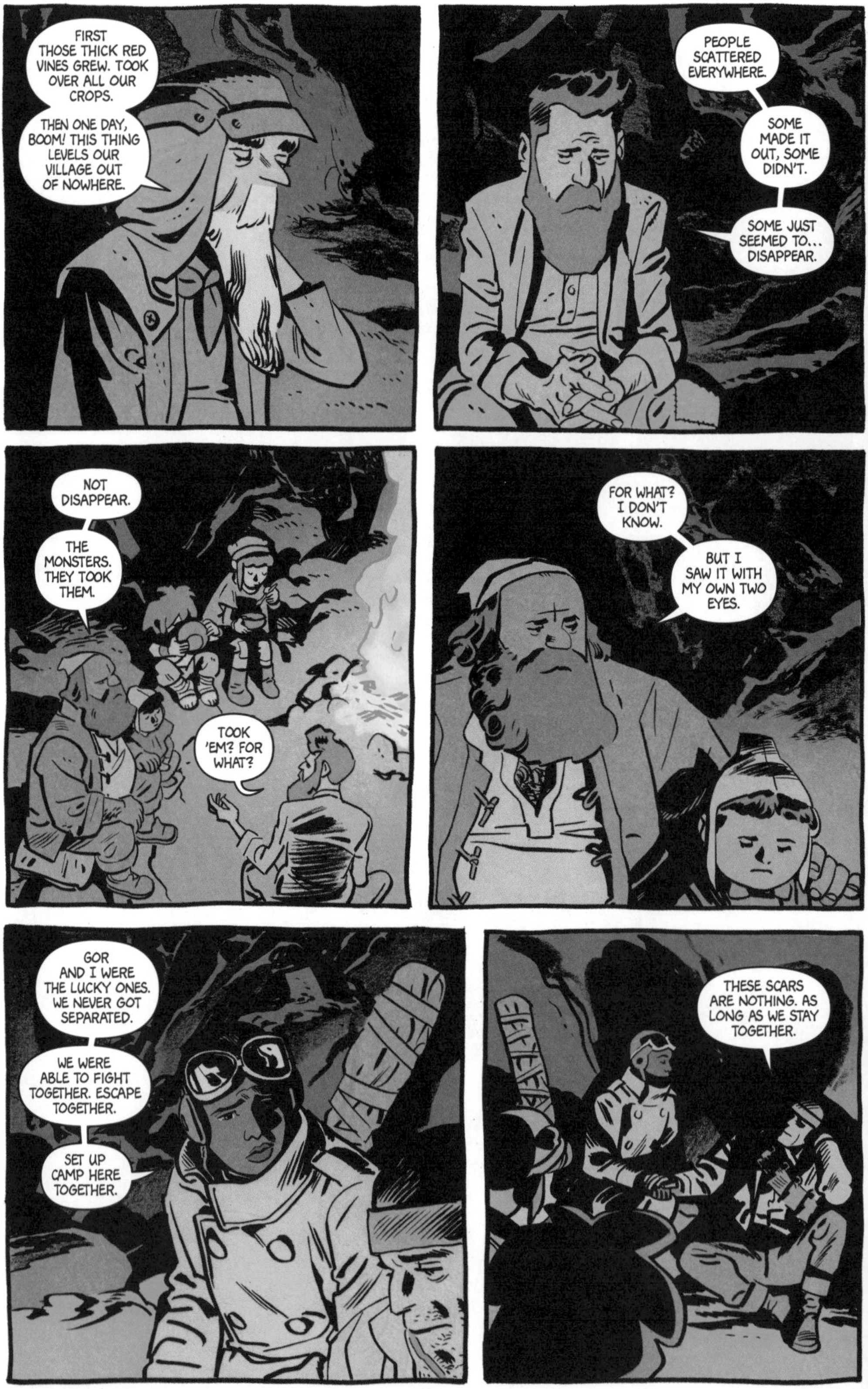
FIRST THOSE THICK RED VINES GREW. TOOK OVER ALL OUR CROPS.
THEN ONE DAY, BOOM! THIS THING LEVELS OUR VILLAGE OUT OF NOWHERE.
PEOPLE SCATTERED EVERYWHERE.
SOME MADE IT OUT, SOME DIDN'T.
SOME JUST SEEMED TO... DISAPPEAR.
NOT DISAPPEAR.
THE MONSTERS. THEY TOOK THEM.
TOOK 'EM? FOR WHAT?
FOR WHAT? I DON'T KNOW.
BUT I SAW IT WITH MY OWN TWO EYES.
GOR AND I WERE THE LUCKY ONES. WE NEVER GOT SEPARATED.
WE WERE ABLE TO FIGHT TOGETHER. ESCAPE TOGETHER.
SET UP CAMP HERE TOGETHER.
THESE SCARS ARE NOTHING. AS LONG AS WE STAY TOGETHER.

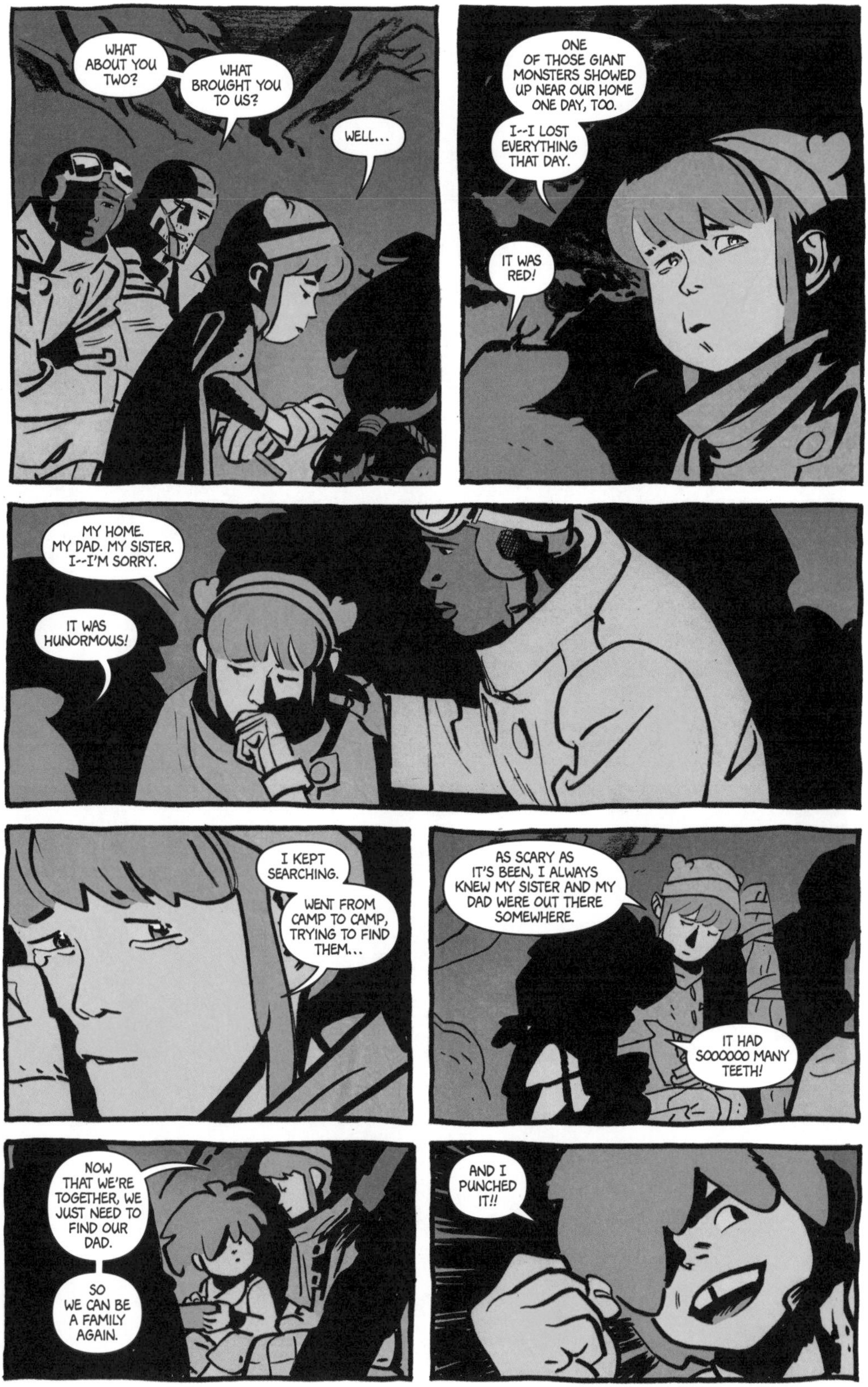
WHAT ABOUT YOU TWO?
WHAT BROUGHT YOU TO US?
WELL...
ONE OF THOSE GIANT MONSTERS SHOWED UP NEAR OUR HOME ONE DAY, TOO.
I--I LOST EVERYTHING THAT DAY.
IT WAS RED!
MY HOME. MY DAD. MY SISTER. I--I'M SORRY.
IT WAS HUNORMOUS!
I KEPT SEARCHING.
WENT FROM CAMP TO CAMP, TRYING TO FIND THEM...
AS SCARY AS IT'S BEEN, I ALWAYS KNEW MY SISTER AND MY DAD WERE OUT THERE SOMEWHERE.
IT HAD SOOOOOO MANY TEETH!
NOW THAT WE'RE TOGETHER, WE JUST NEED TO FIND OUR DAD.
SO WE CAN BE A FAMILY AGAIN.
AND I PUNCHED IT!!

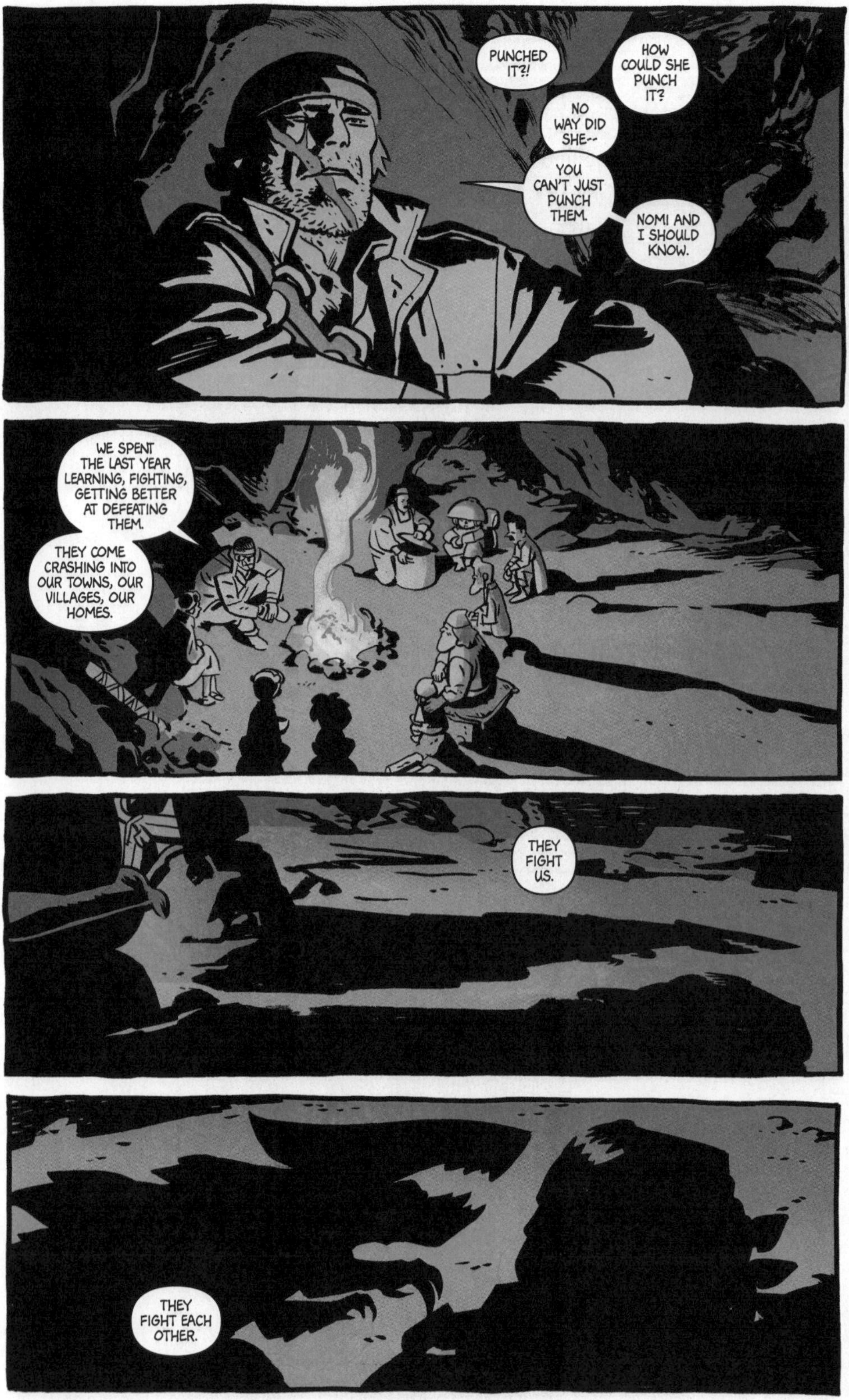
PUNCHED IT?!
HOW COULD SHE PUNCH IT?
NO WAY DID SHE--
YOU CAN'T JUST PUNCH THEM.
NOMI AND I SHOULD KNOW.
WE SPENT THE LAST YEAR LEARNING, FIGHTING, GETTING BETTER AT DEFEATING THEM.
THEY COME CRASHING INTO OUR TOWNS, OUR VILLAGES, OUR HOMES.
THEY FIGHT US.
THEY FIGHT EACH OTHER.

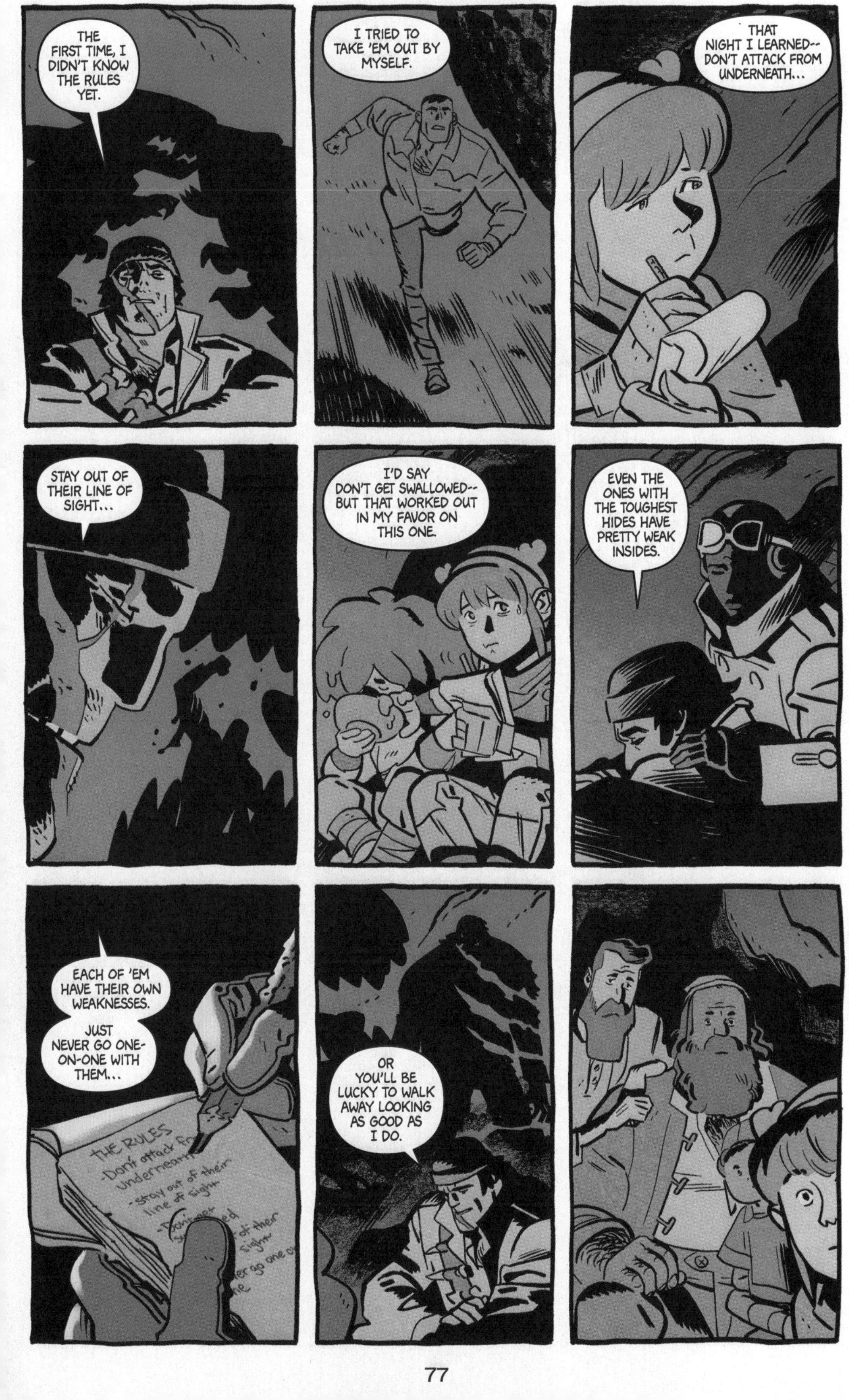
THE FIRST TIME, I DIDN'T KNOW THE RULES YET.
I TRIED TO TAKE 'EM OUT BY MYSELF.
THAT NIGHT I LEARNED-- DON'T ATTACK FROM UNDERNEATH...
STAY OUT OF THEIR LINE OF SIGHT...
I'D SAY DON'T GET SWALLOWED-- BUT THAT WORKED OUT IN MY FAVOR ON THIS ONE.
EVEN THE ONES WITH THE TOUGHEST HIDES HAVE PRETTY WEAK INSIDES.
EACH OF 'EM HAVE THEIR OWN WEAKNESSES.
JUST NEVER GO ONE-ON-ONE WITH THEM...
THE RULES
-stay out of their
line of sight
OR YOU'LL BE LUCKY TO WALK AWAY LOOKING AS GOOD AS I DO.

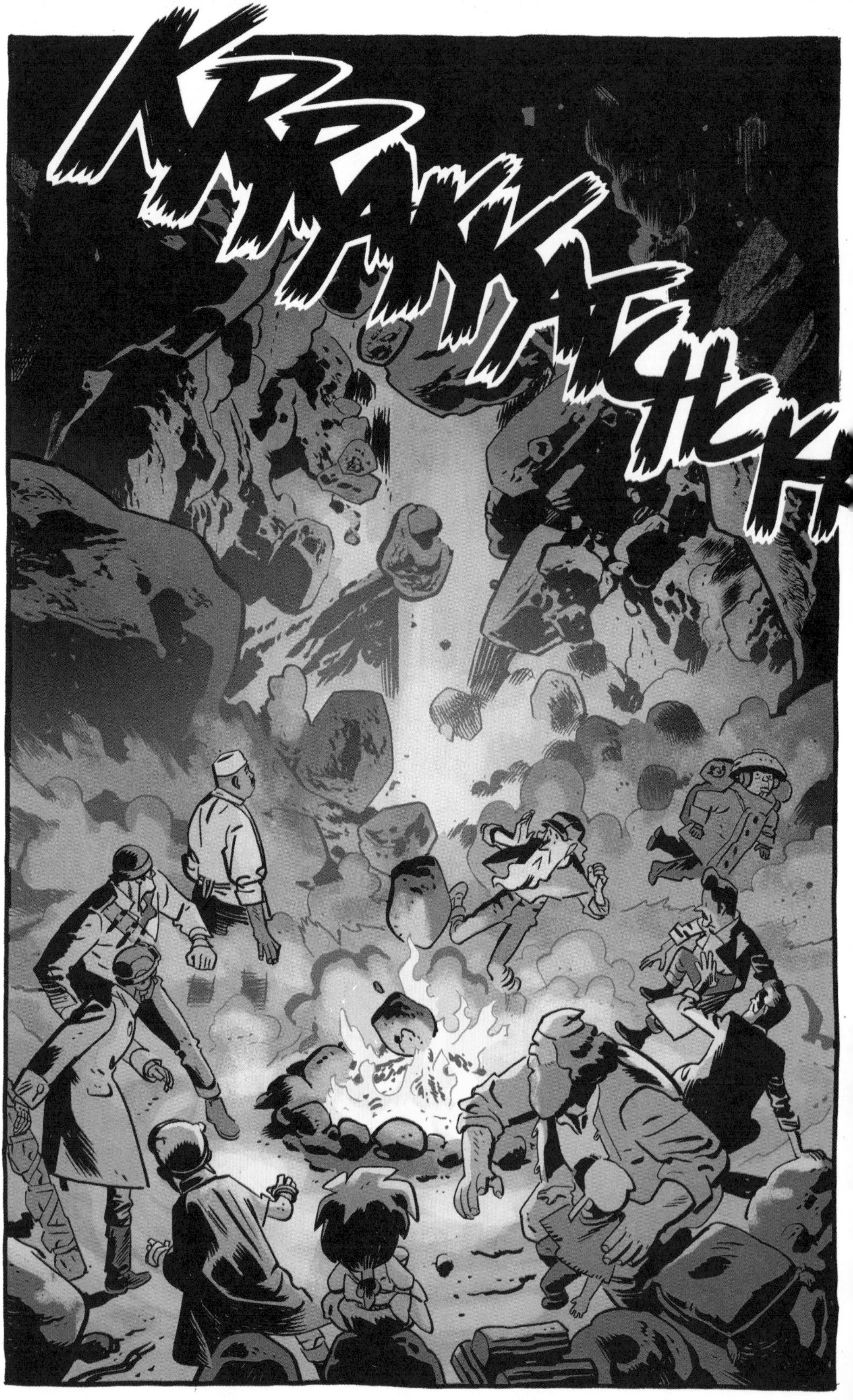

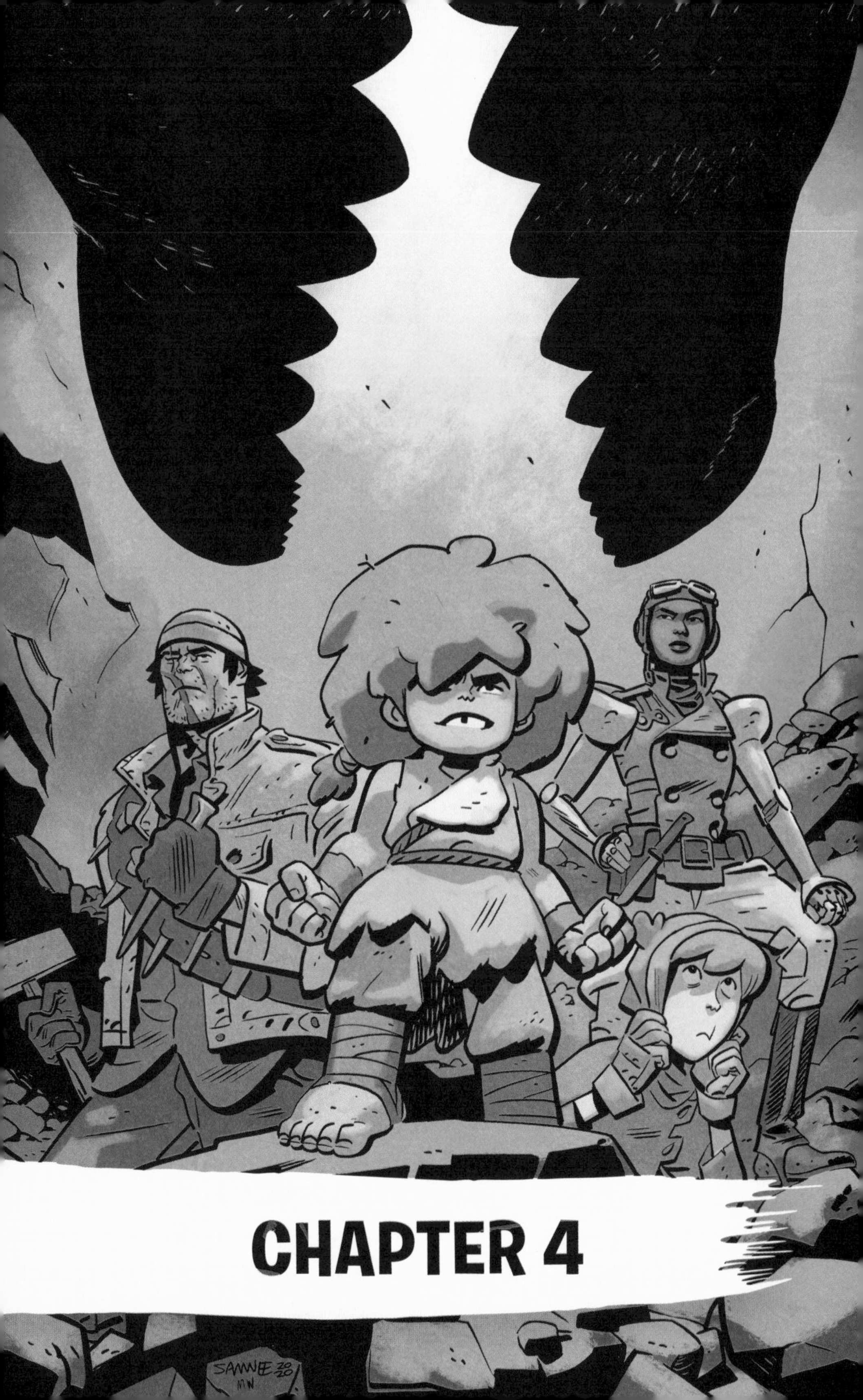
SAMNEE 2020
MW

CHAPTER 4

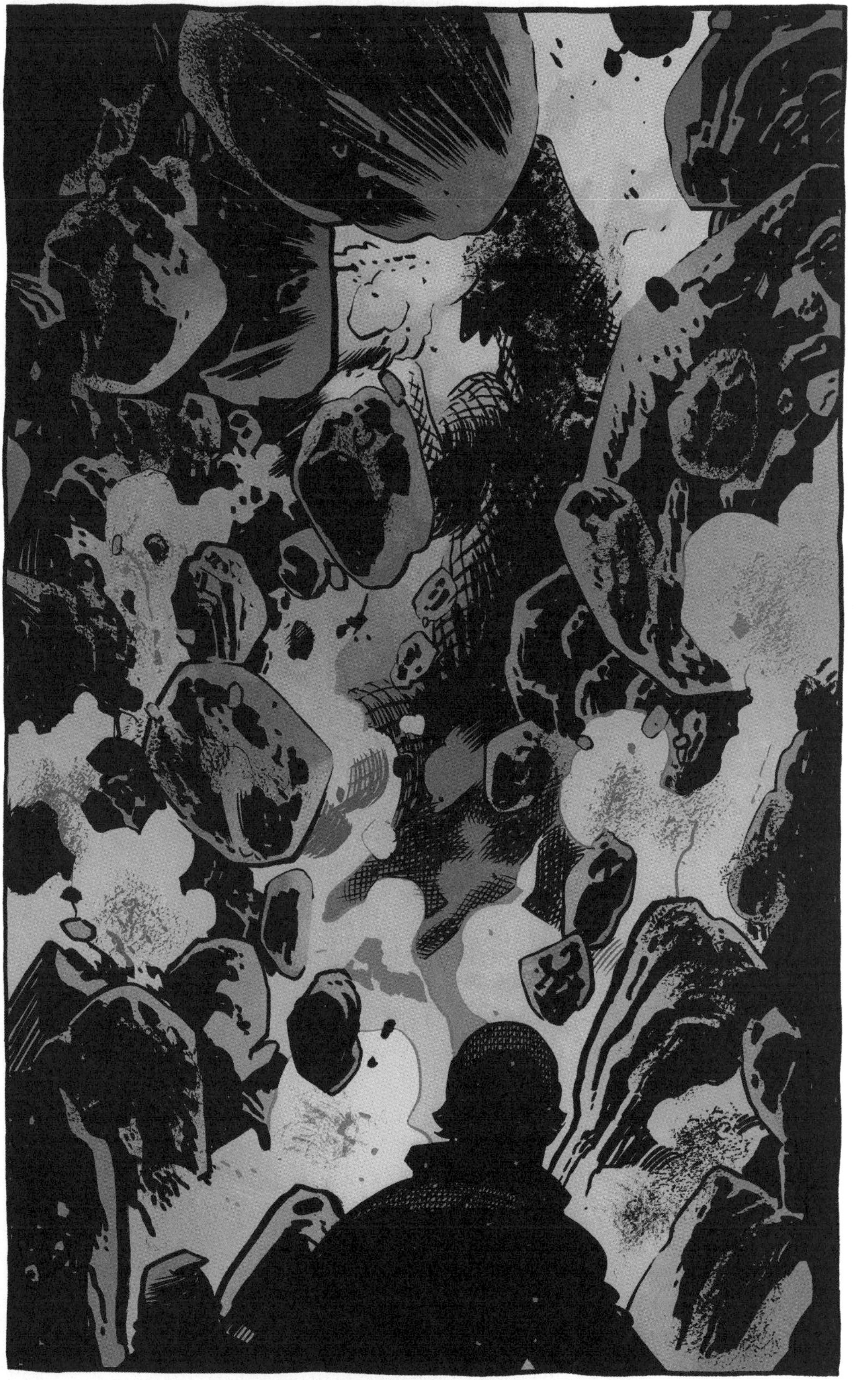

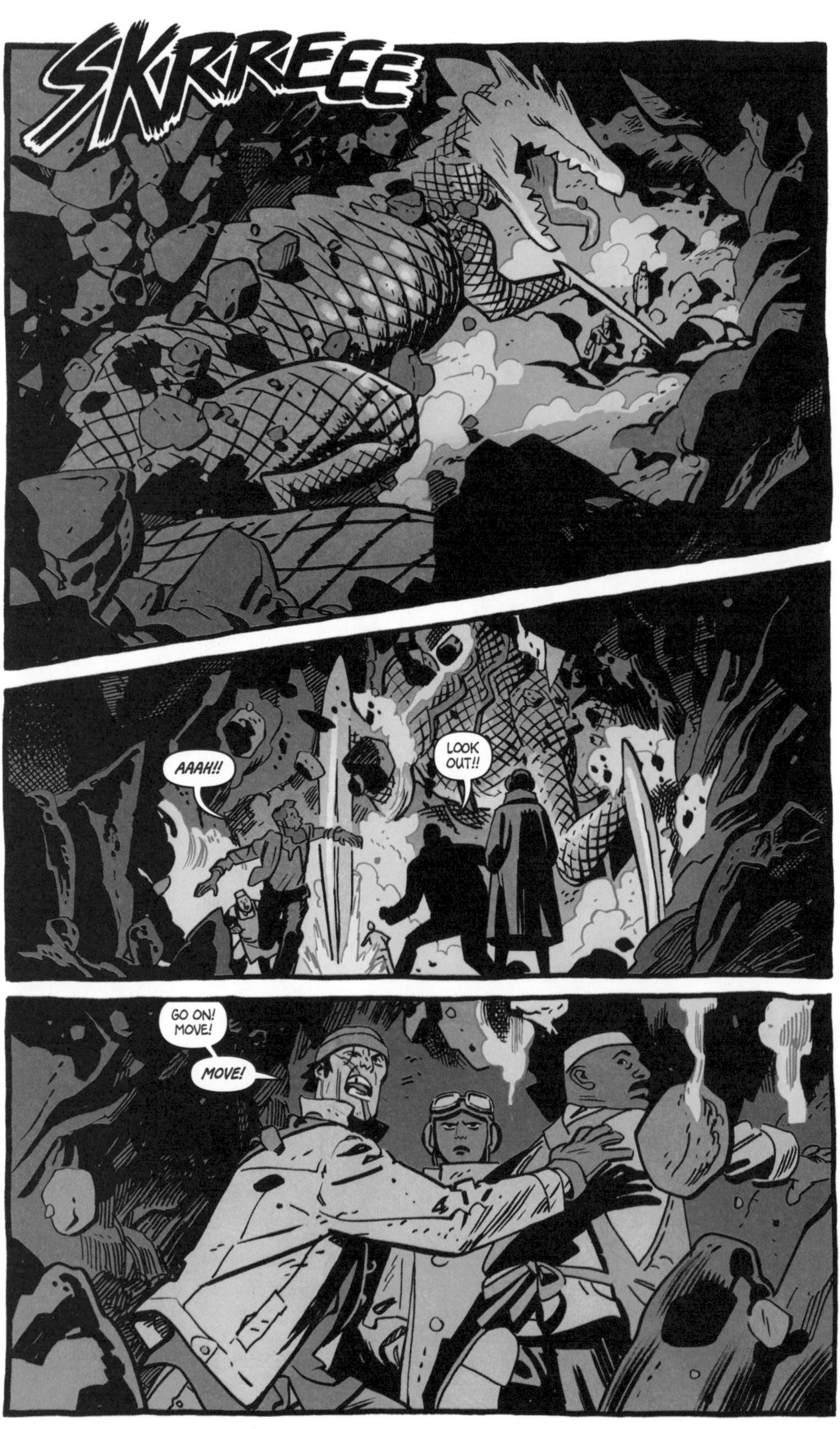
SKRREEE
AAAH!!
LOOK OUT!!
GO ON! MOVE!
MOVE!

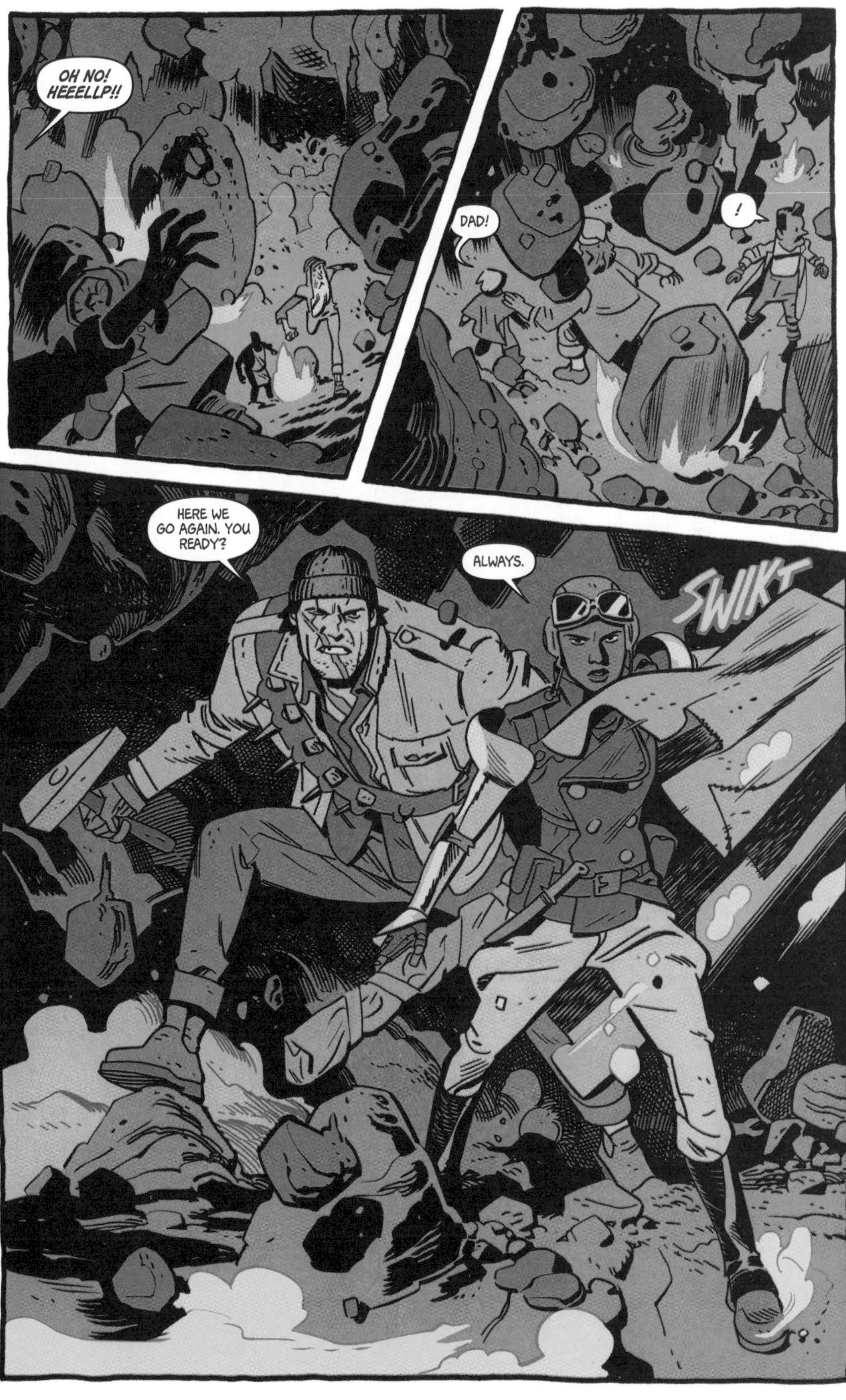
OH NO! HEEELLP!!
DAD!
!
HERE WE GO AGAIN. YOU READY?
ALWAYS.
SWIKT

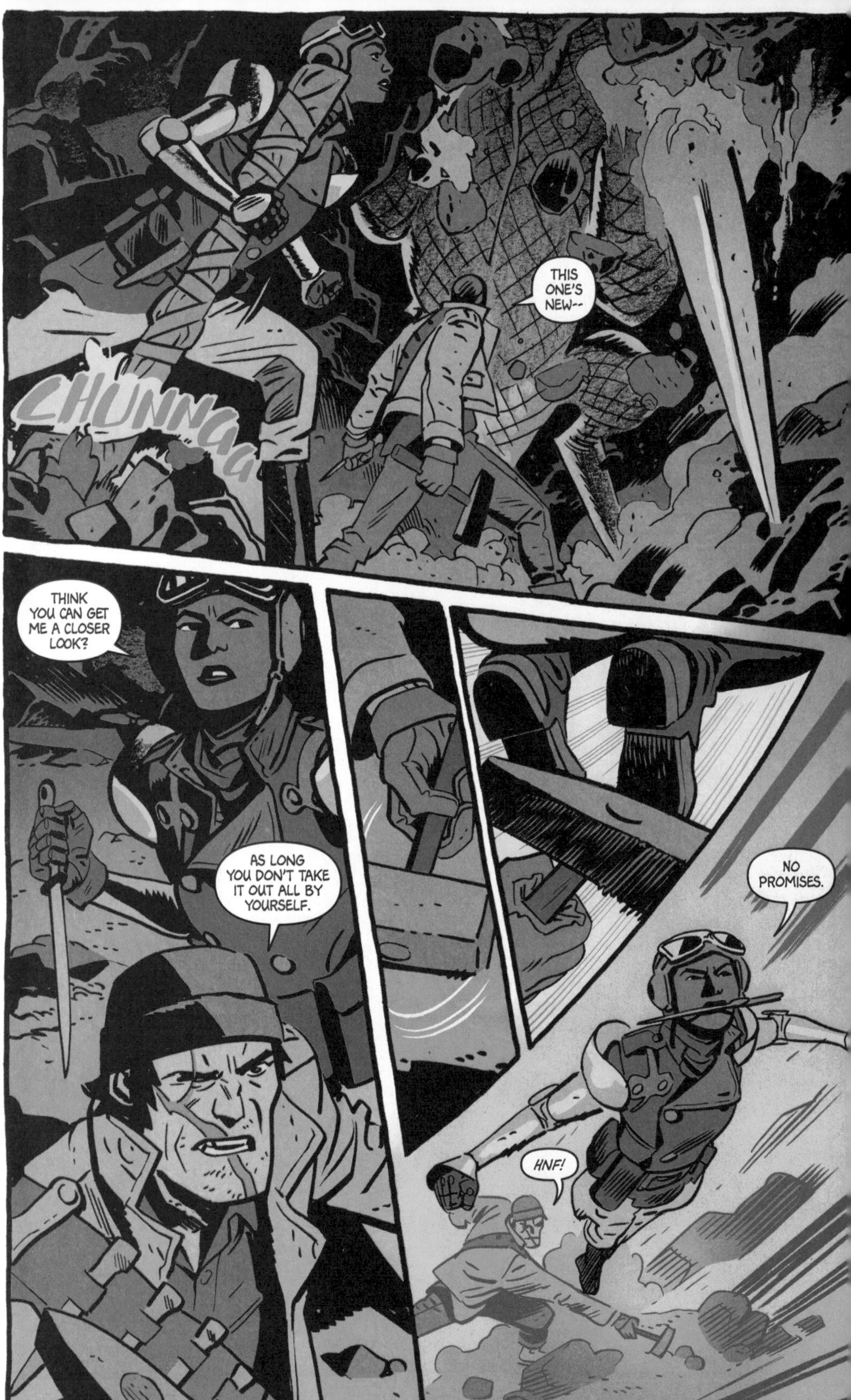
CHUNNGG
THIS ONE'S NEW--
THINK YOU CAN GET ME A CLOSER LOOK?
AS LONG YOU DON'T TAKE IT OUT ALL BY YOURSELF.
NO PROMISES.
HNF!

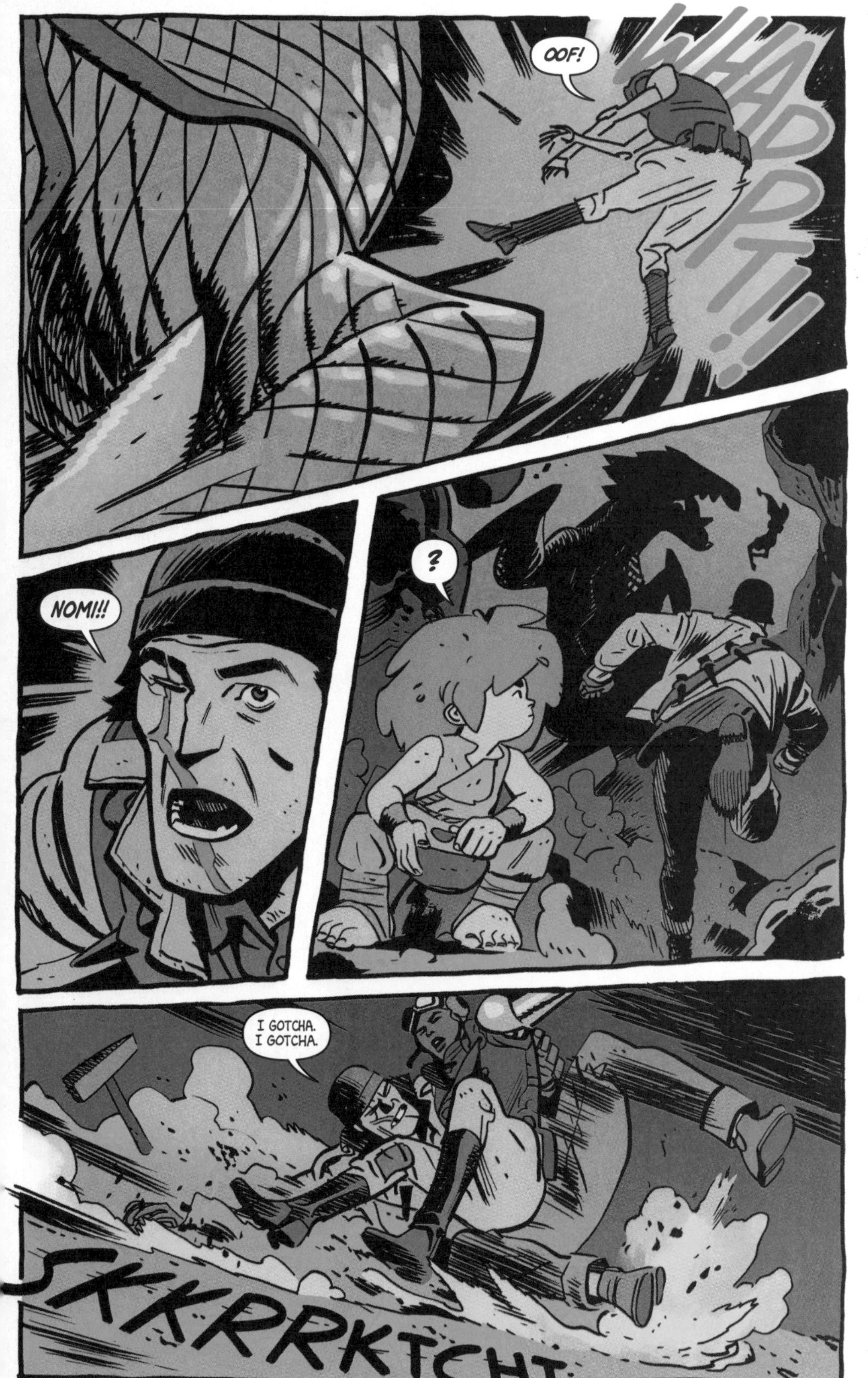
OOF!
WHAPPT!!!
NOMI!!!
?
I GOTCHA.
I GOTCHA.
SKKRRRKTCHT

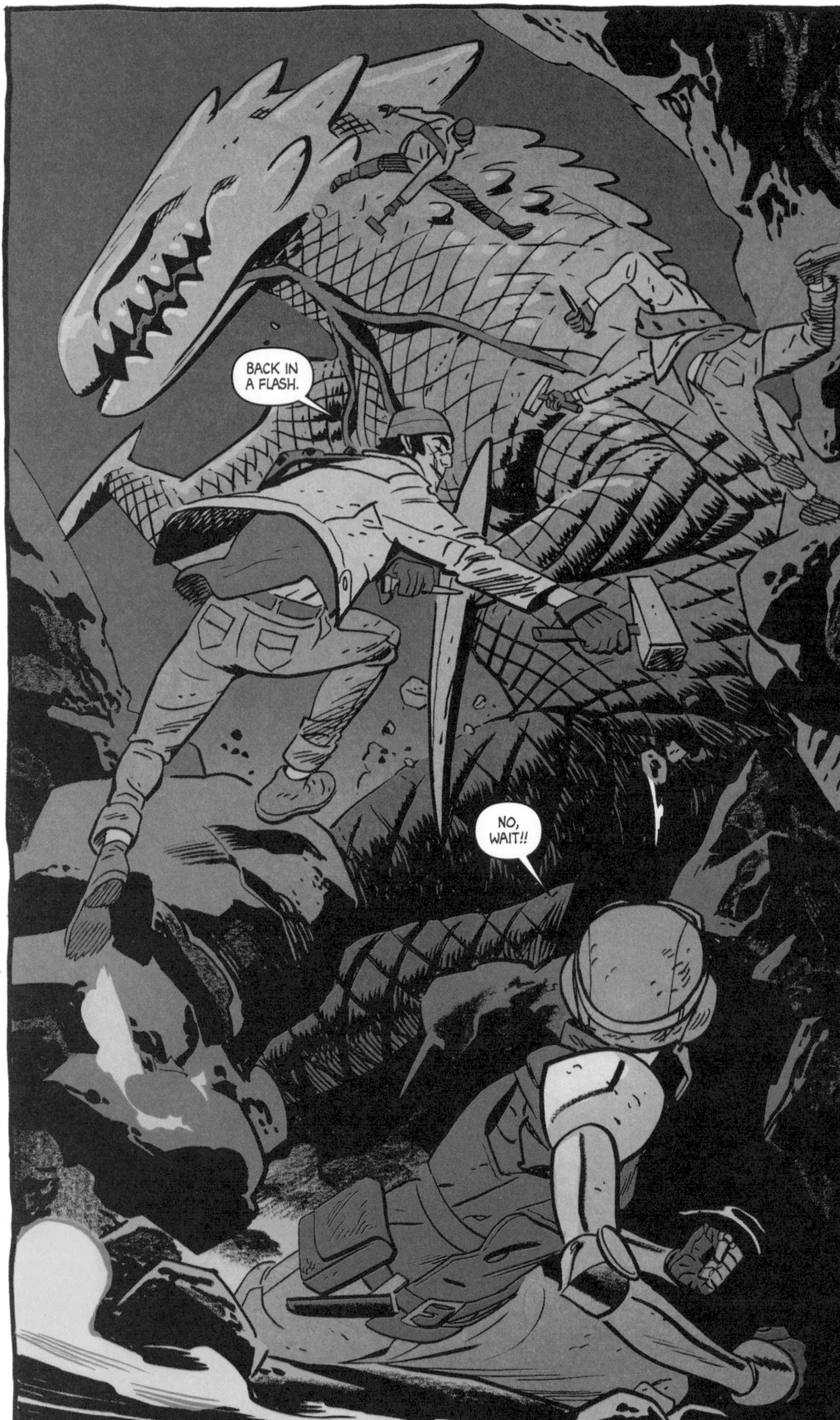
BACK IN A FLASH.
NO, WAIT!!

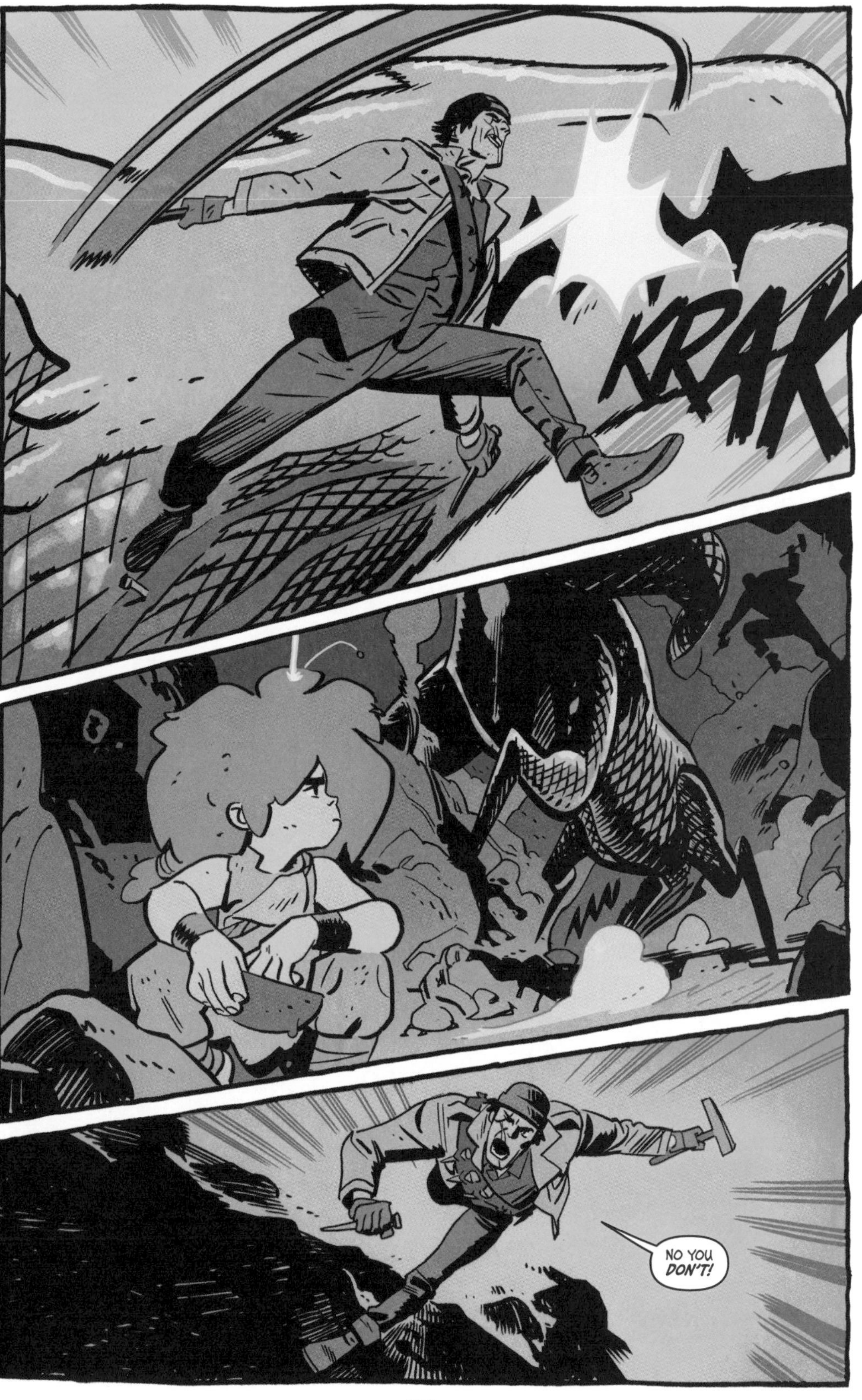
KRAK
NO YOU DON'T!

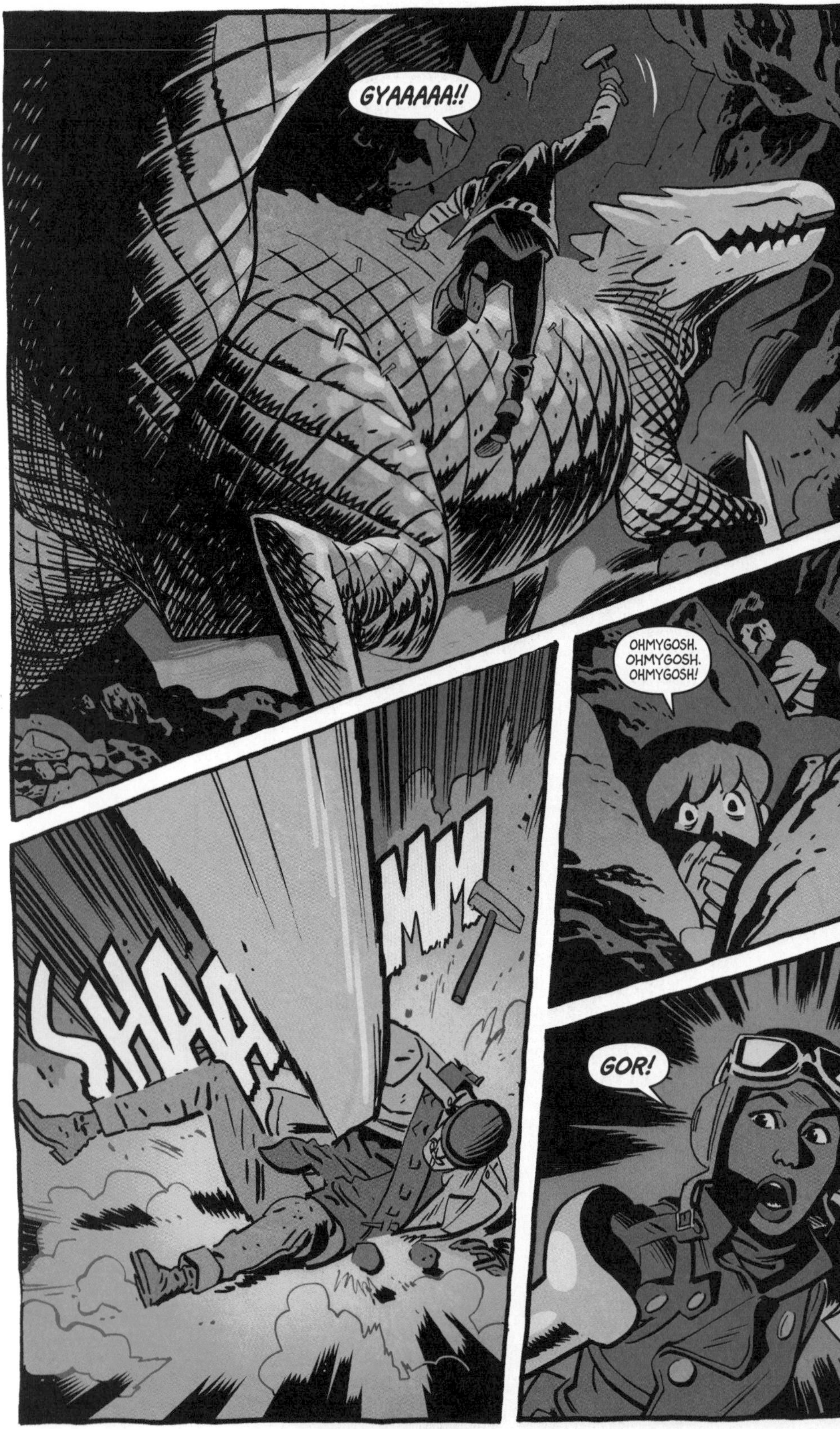
GYAAAAA!!
OHMYGOSH.
OHMYGOSH.
OHMYGOSH!
SHAA
MM
GOR!

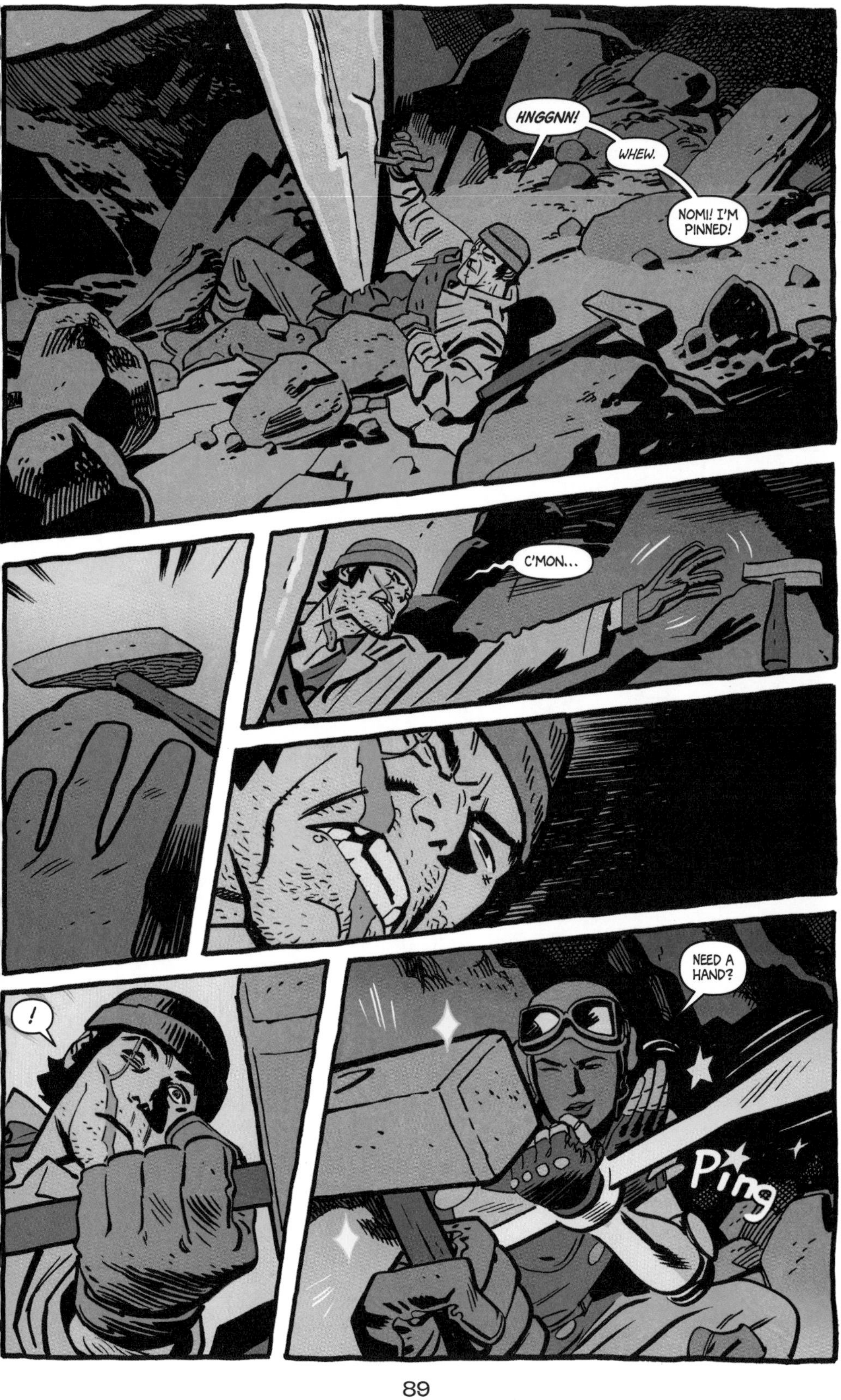
HNGGNN!
WHEW.
NOMI! I'M PINNED!
C'MON...
!
NEED A HAND?
Ping

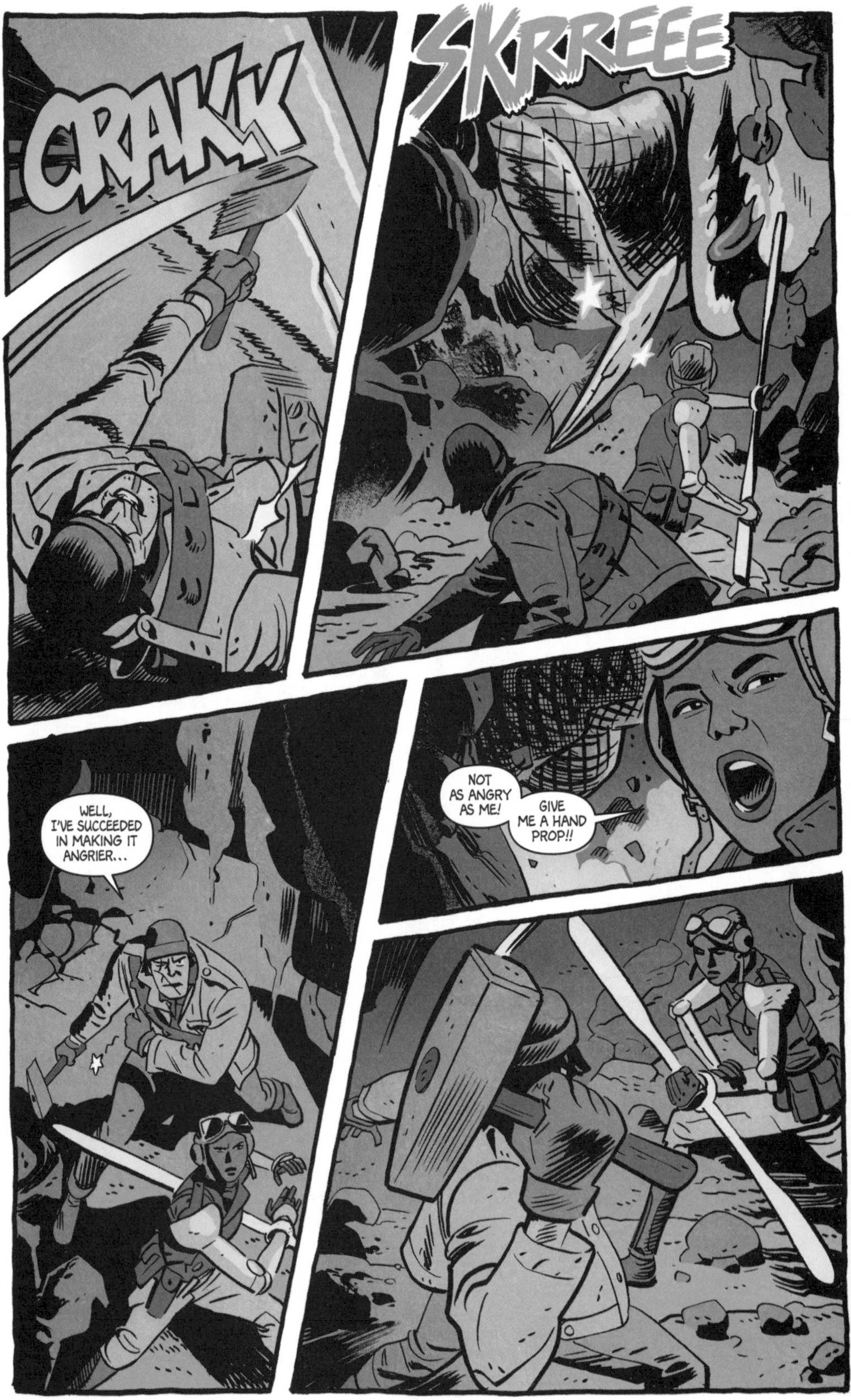
CRAKK
SKRREEE
WELL, I'VE SUCCEEDED IN MAKING IT ANGRIER...
NOT AS ANGRY AS ME!
GIVE ME A HAND PROP!!

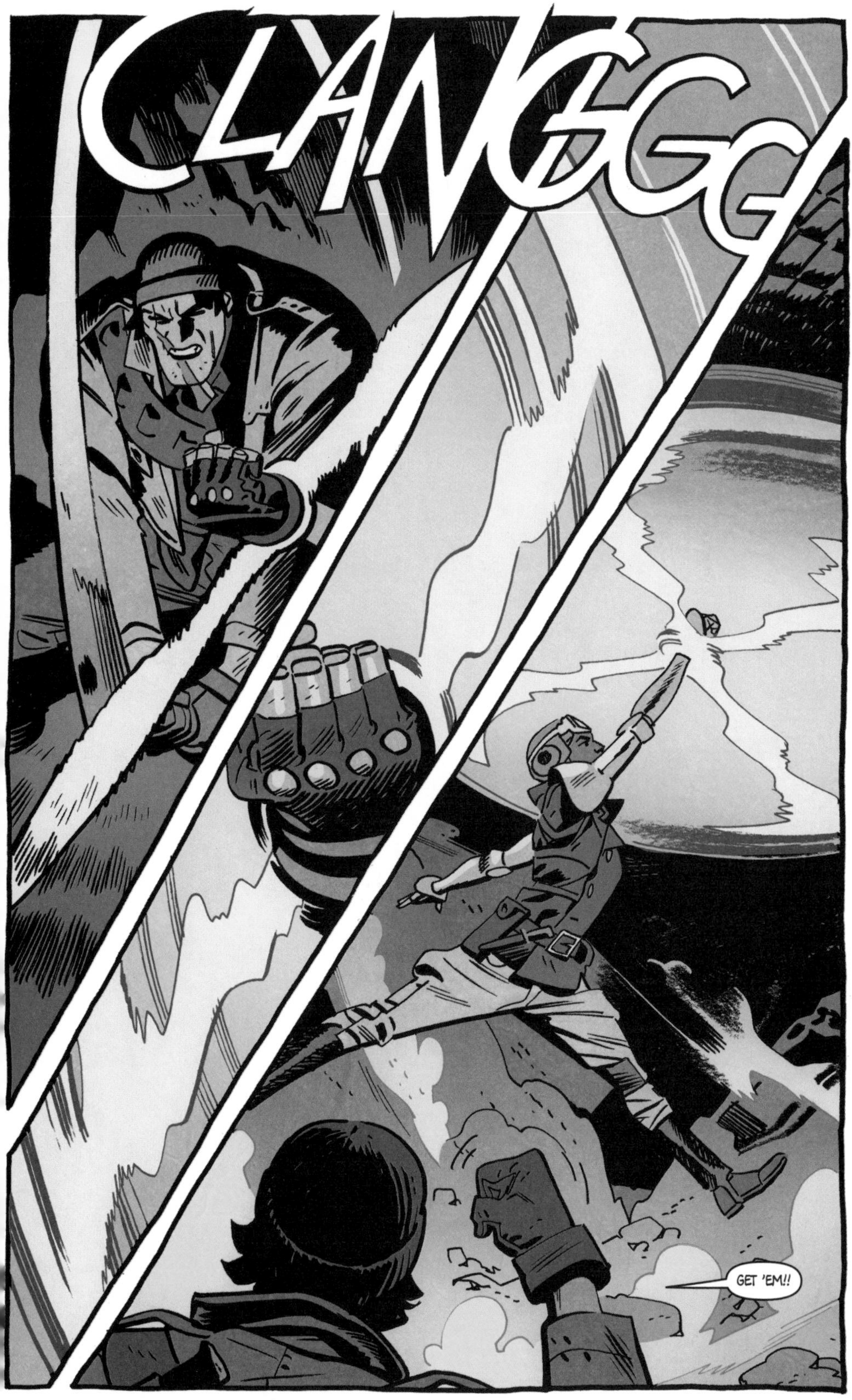
CLANGG
GET 'EM!!

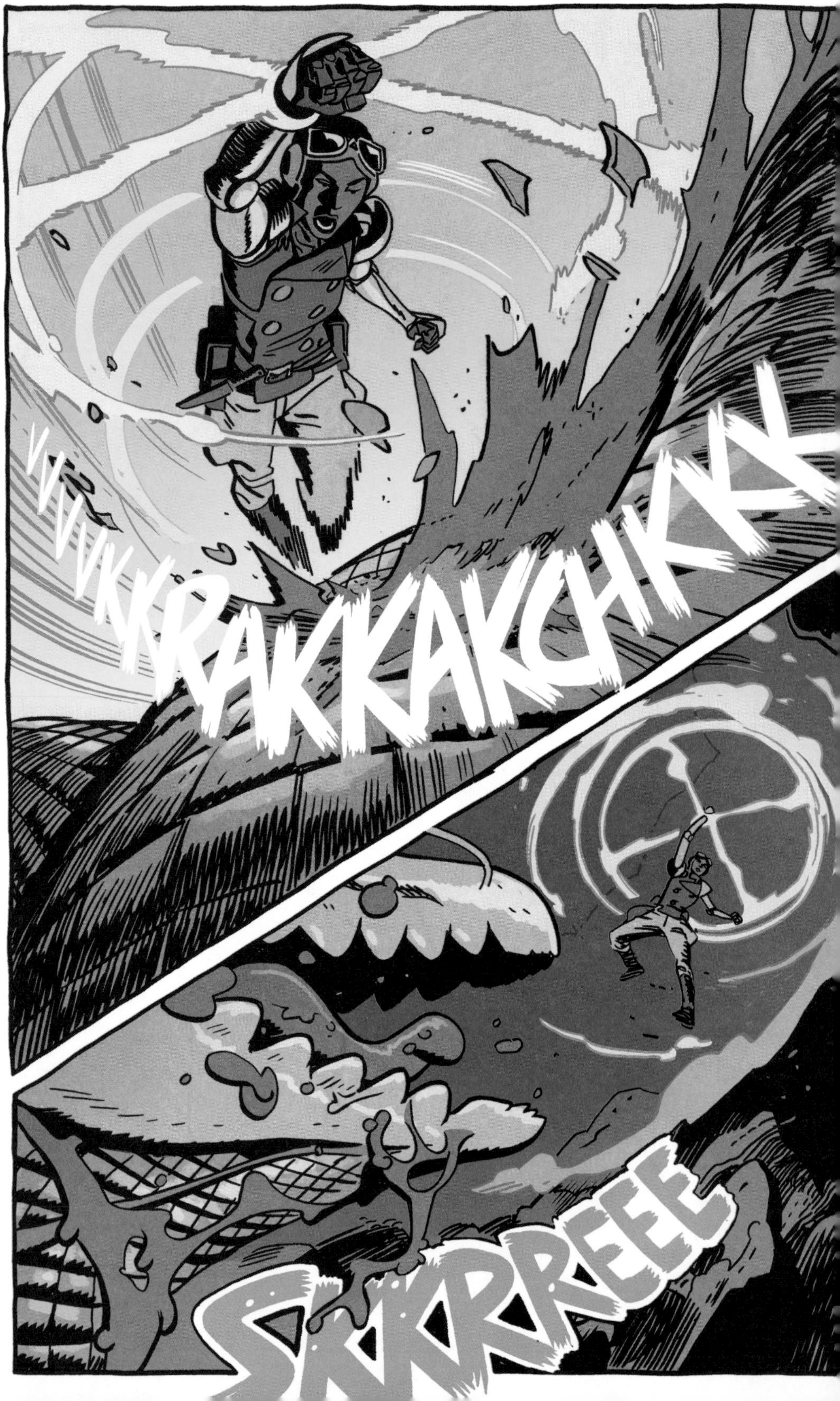
VVVVVKKRAKKAKCHKKK
SKRREEE

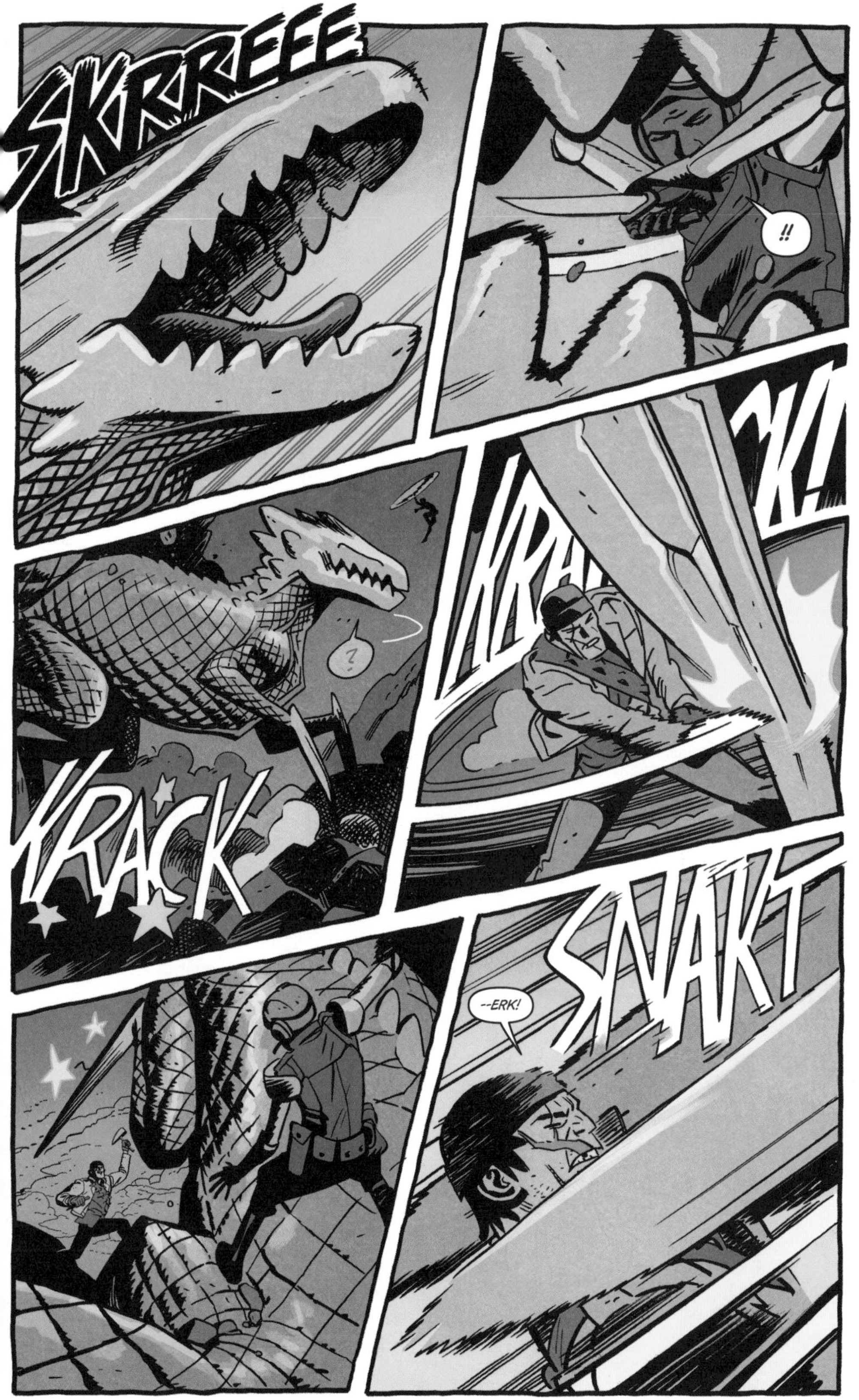
SKRREEE
!!
?
KRAK
KRACK
SNAKT
--ERK!

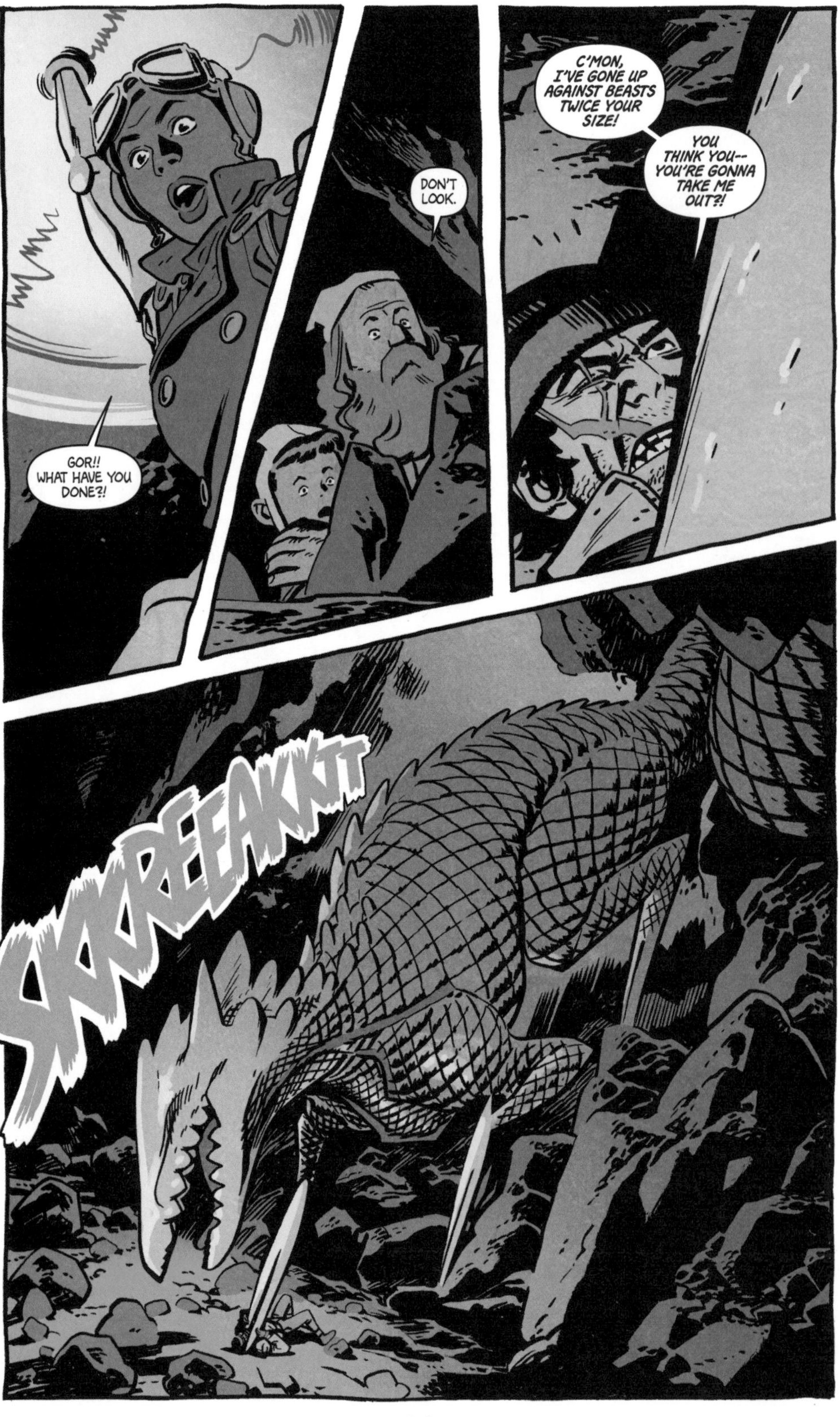
GOR!! WHAT HAVE YOU DONE?!
DON'T LOOK.
C'MON, I'VE GONE UP AGAINST BEASTS TWICE YOUR SIZE!
YOU THINK YOU-- YOU'RE GONNA TAKE ME OUT?!
SKKREEAKKTT

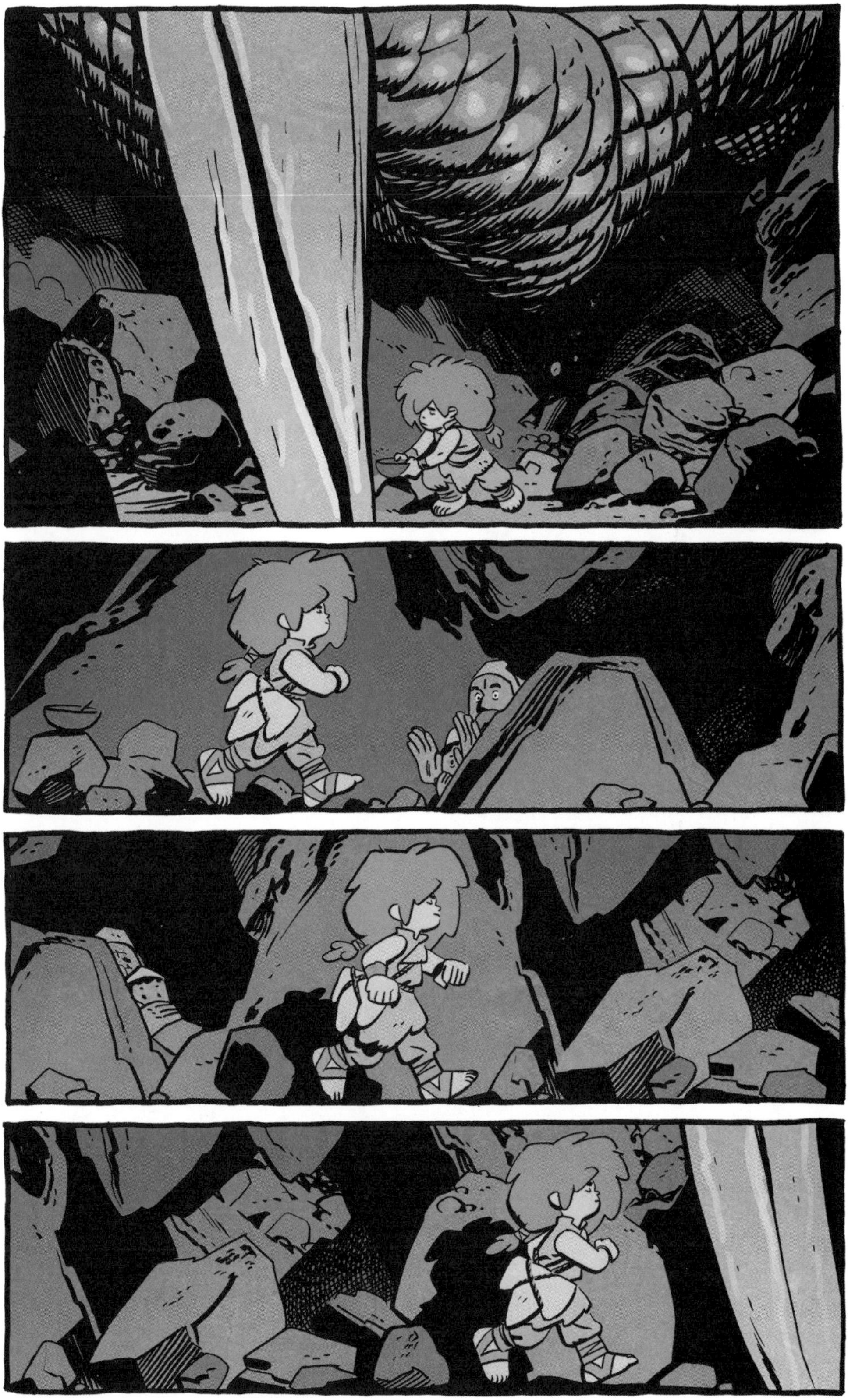

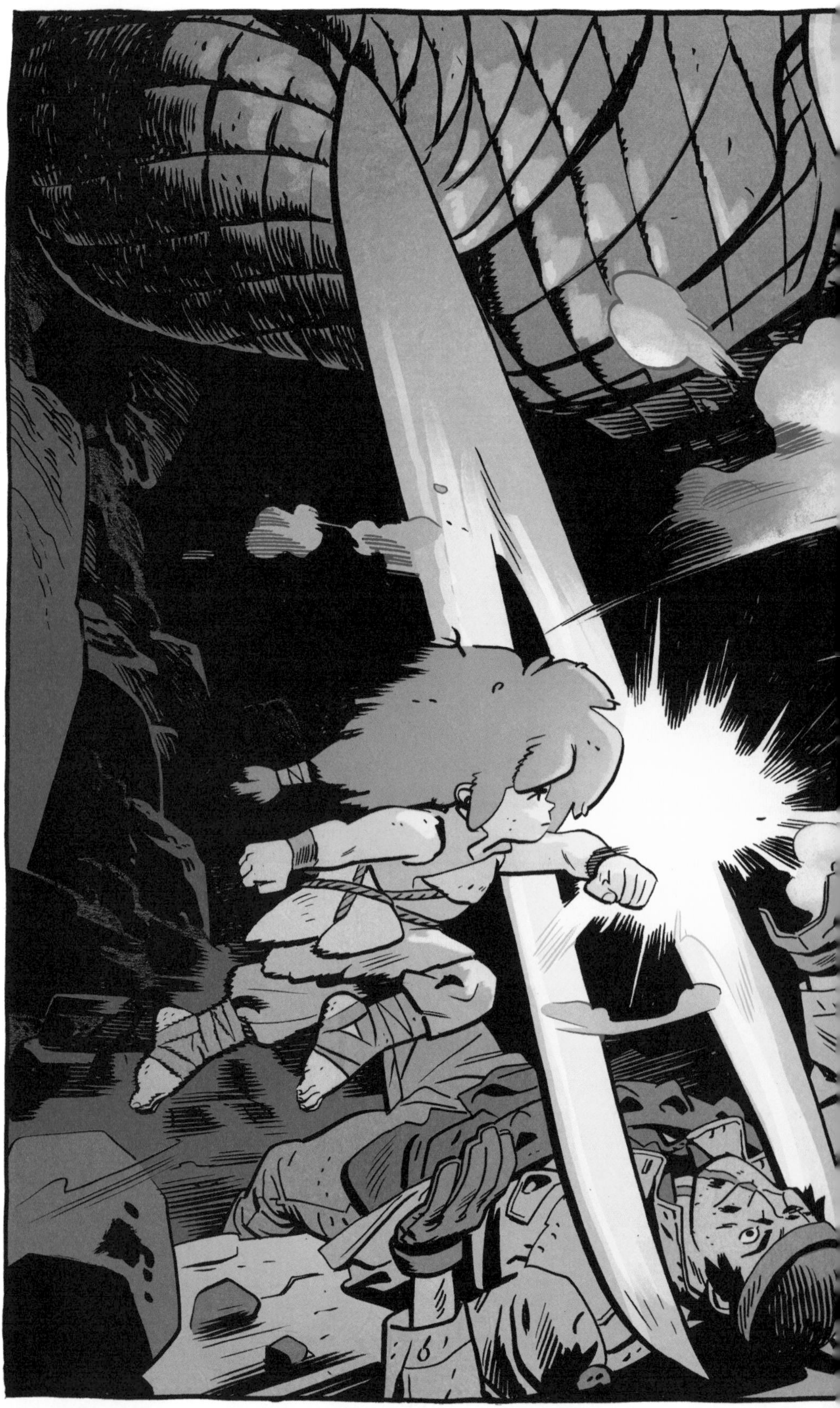

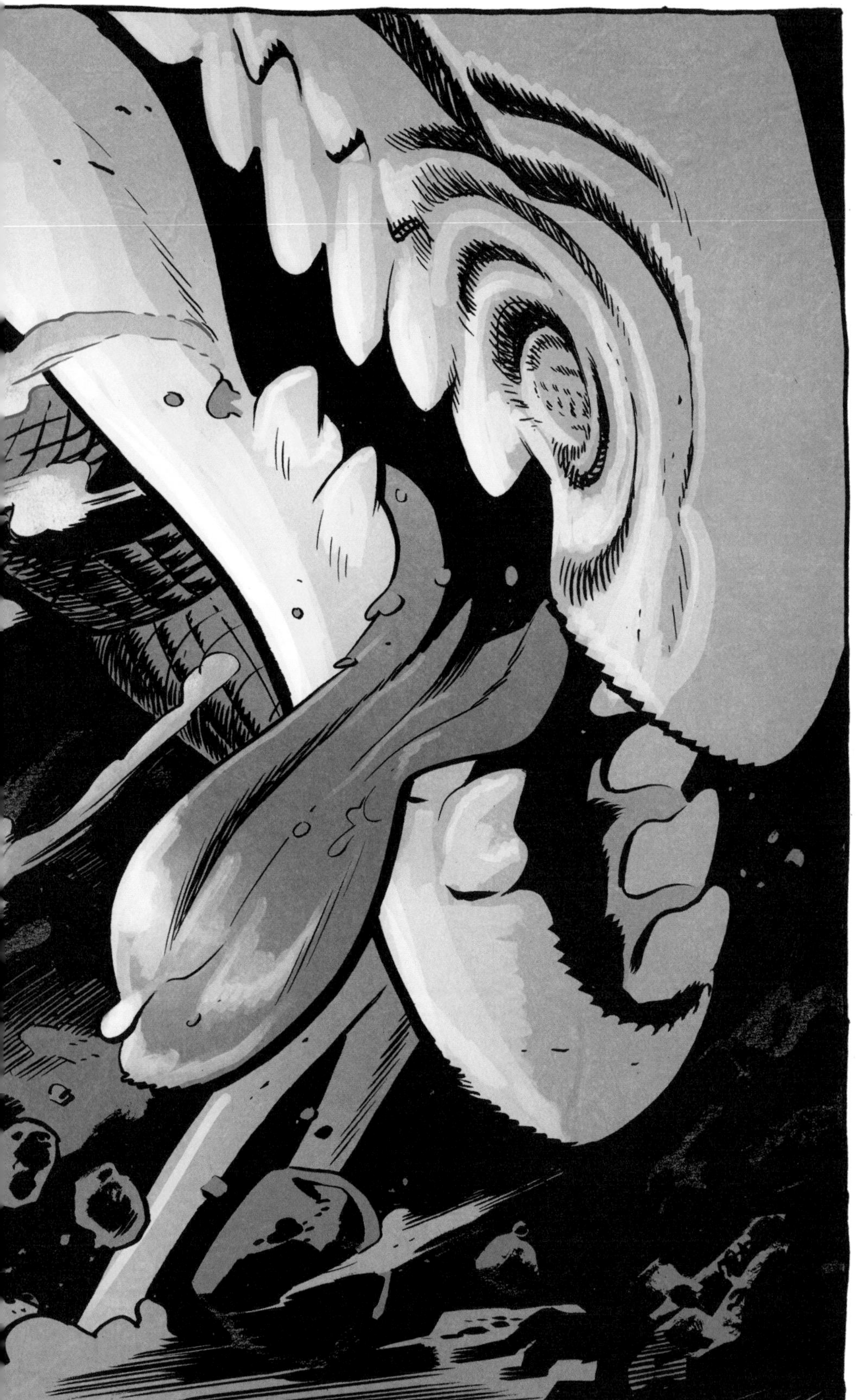

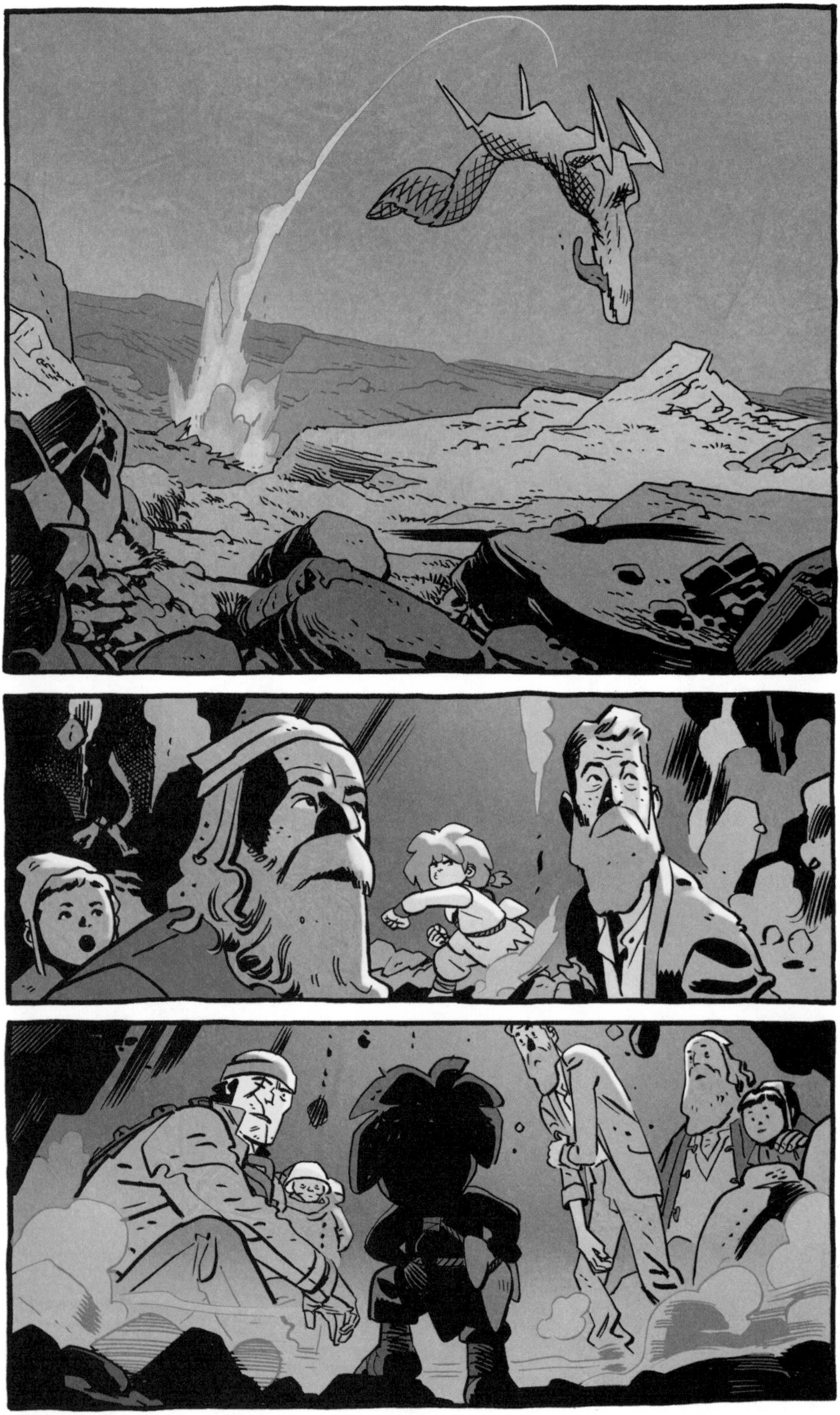

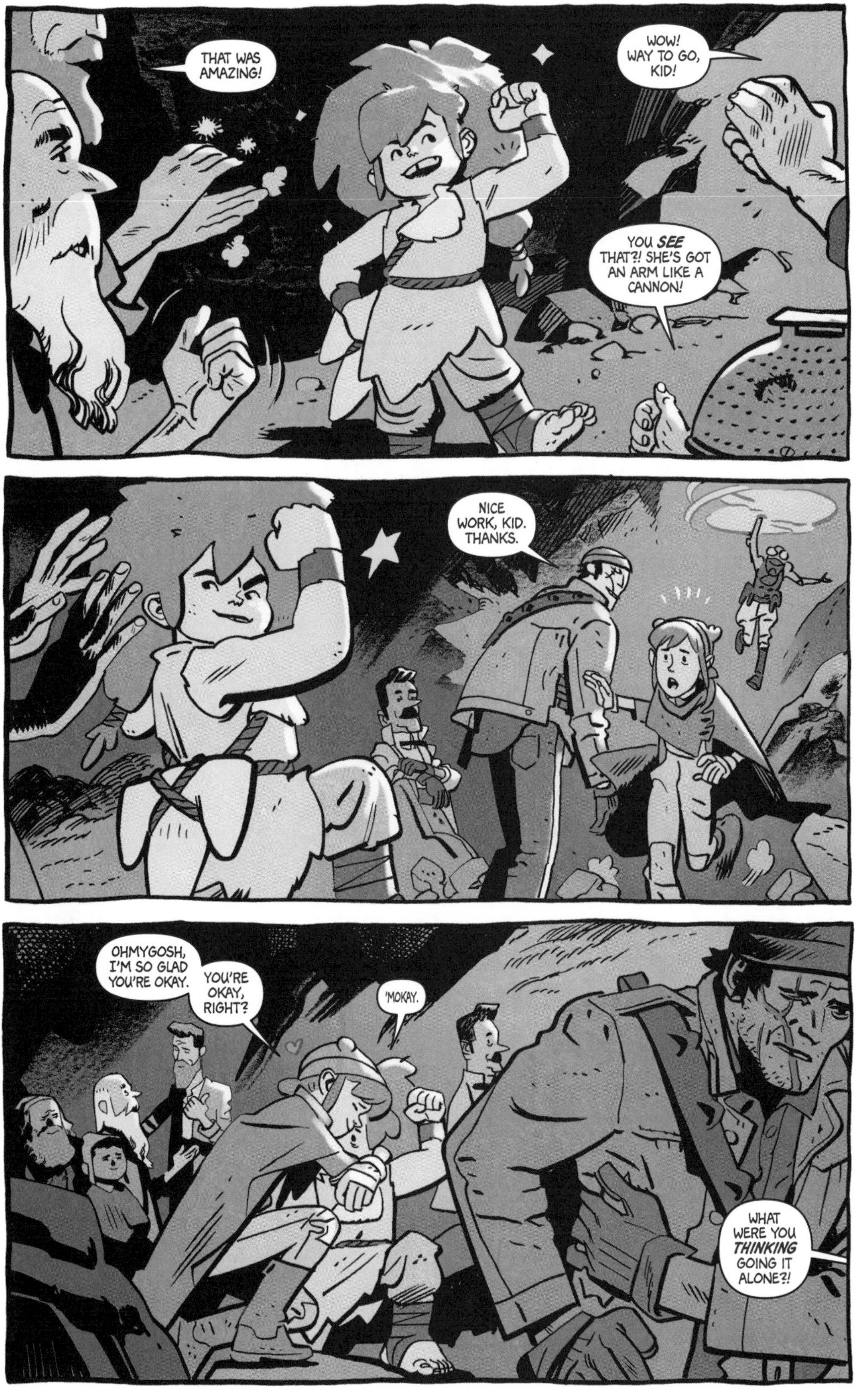
THAT WAS AMAZING!
WOW! WAY TO GO, KID!
YOU SEE THAT?! SHE'S GOT AN ARM LIKE A CANNON!
NICE WORK, KID. THANKS.
OHMYGOSH, I'M SO GLAD YOU'RE OKAY.
YOU'RE OKAY, RIGHT?
'MOKAY.
WHAT WERE YOU THINKING GOING IT ALONE?!

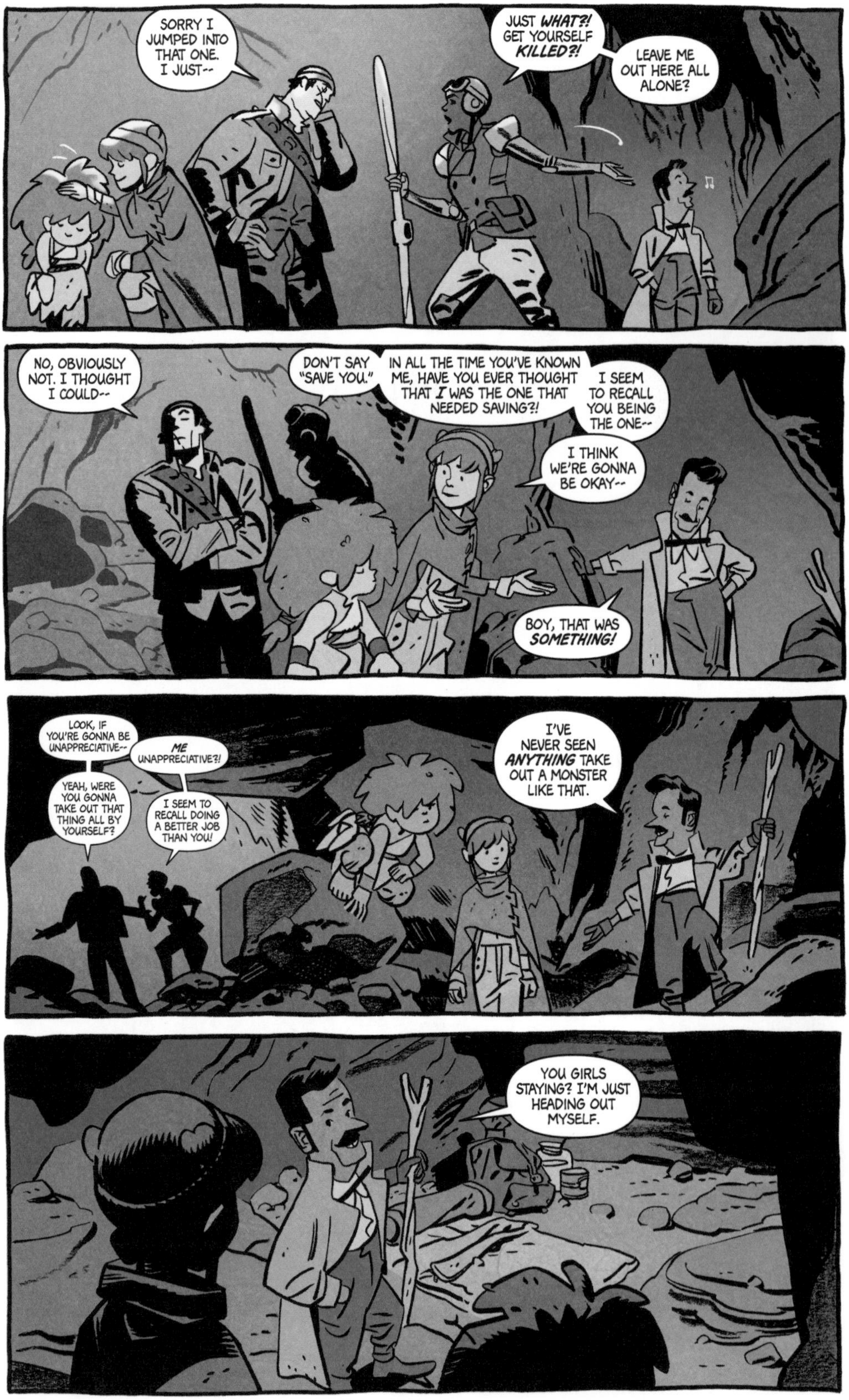

SORRY I JUMPED INTO THAT ONE. I JUST--
JUST *WHAT?!* GET YOURSELF *KILLED?!*
LEAVE ME OUT HERE ALL ALONE?
NO, OBVIOUSLY NOT. I THOUGHT I COULD--
DON'T SAY "SAVE YOU."
IN ALL THE TIME YOU'VE KNOWN ME, HAVE YOU EVER THOUGHT THAT *I* WAS THE ONE THAT NEEDED SAVING?!
I SEEM TO RECALL YOU BEING THE ONE--
I THINK WE'RE GONNA BE OKAY--
BOY, THAT WAS *SOMETHING!*
LOOK, IF YOU'RE GONNA BE UNAPPRECIATIVE--
ME UNAPPRECIATIVE?!
YEAH, WERE YOU GONNA TAKE OUT THAT THING ALL BY YOURSELF?
I SEEM TO RECALL DOING A BETTER JOB THAN YOU!
I'VE NEVER SEEN *ANYTHING* TAKE OUT A MONSTER LIKE THAT.
YOU GIRLS STAYING? I'M JUST HEADING OUT MYSELF.

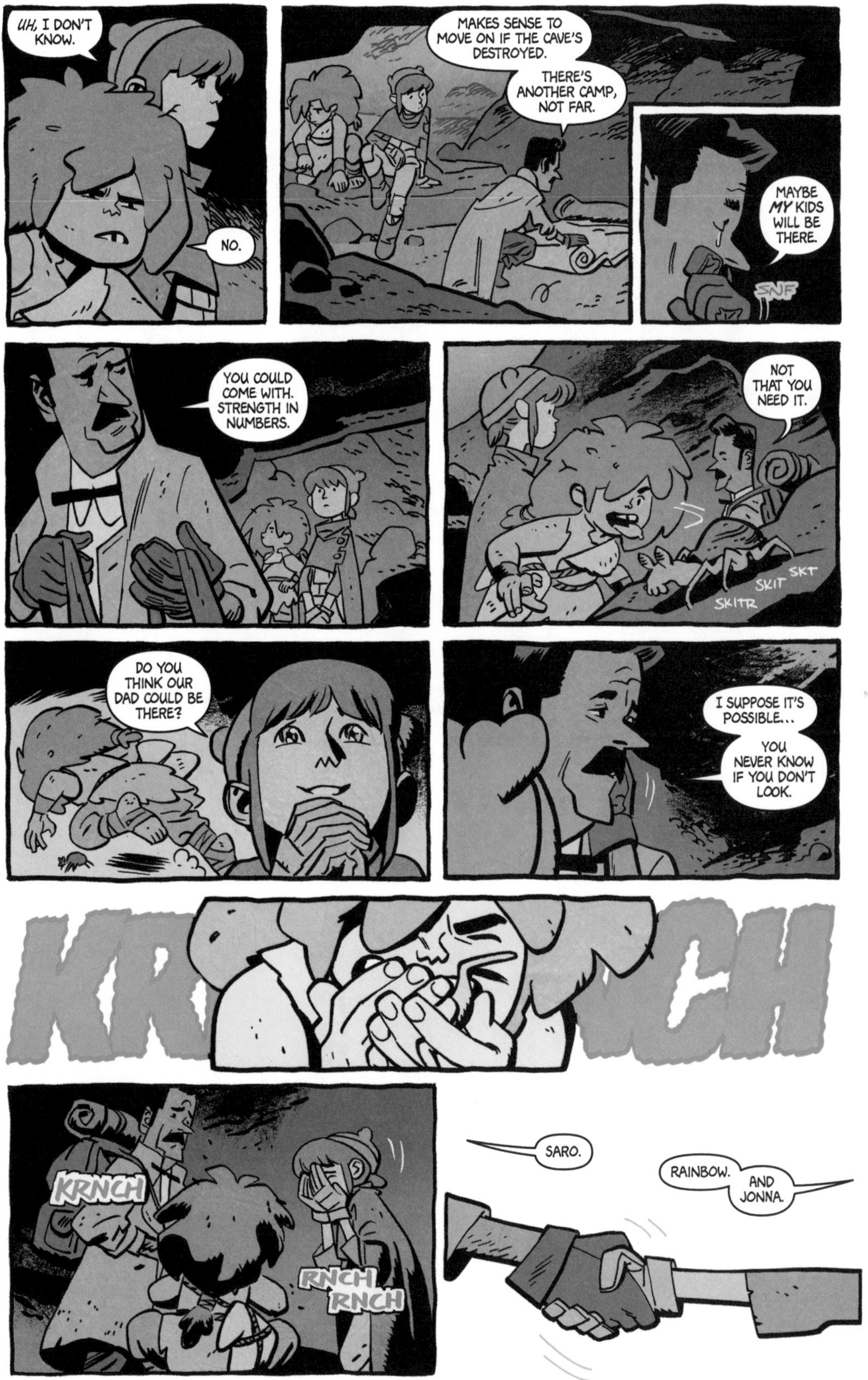

UH, I DON'T KNOW.
NO.
MAKES SENSE TO MOVE ON IF THE CAVE'S DESTROYED.
THERE'S ANOTHER CAMP, NOT FAR.
MAYBE *MY* KIDS WILL BE THERE.
SNF
YOU COULD COME WITH. STRENGTH IN NUMBERS.
NOT THAT YOU NEED IT.
SKT
SKIT
SKITR
DO YOU THINK OUR DAD COULD BE THERE?
I SUPPOSE IT'S POSSIBLE...
YOU NEVER KNOW IF YOU DON'T LOOK.
KR
CH
KRNCH
RNCH
RNCH
SARO.
RAINBOW.
AND JONNA.

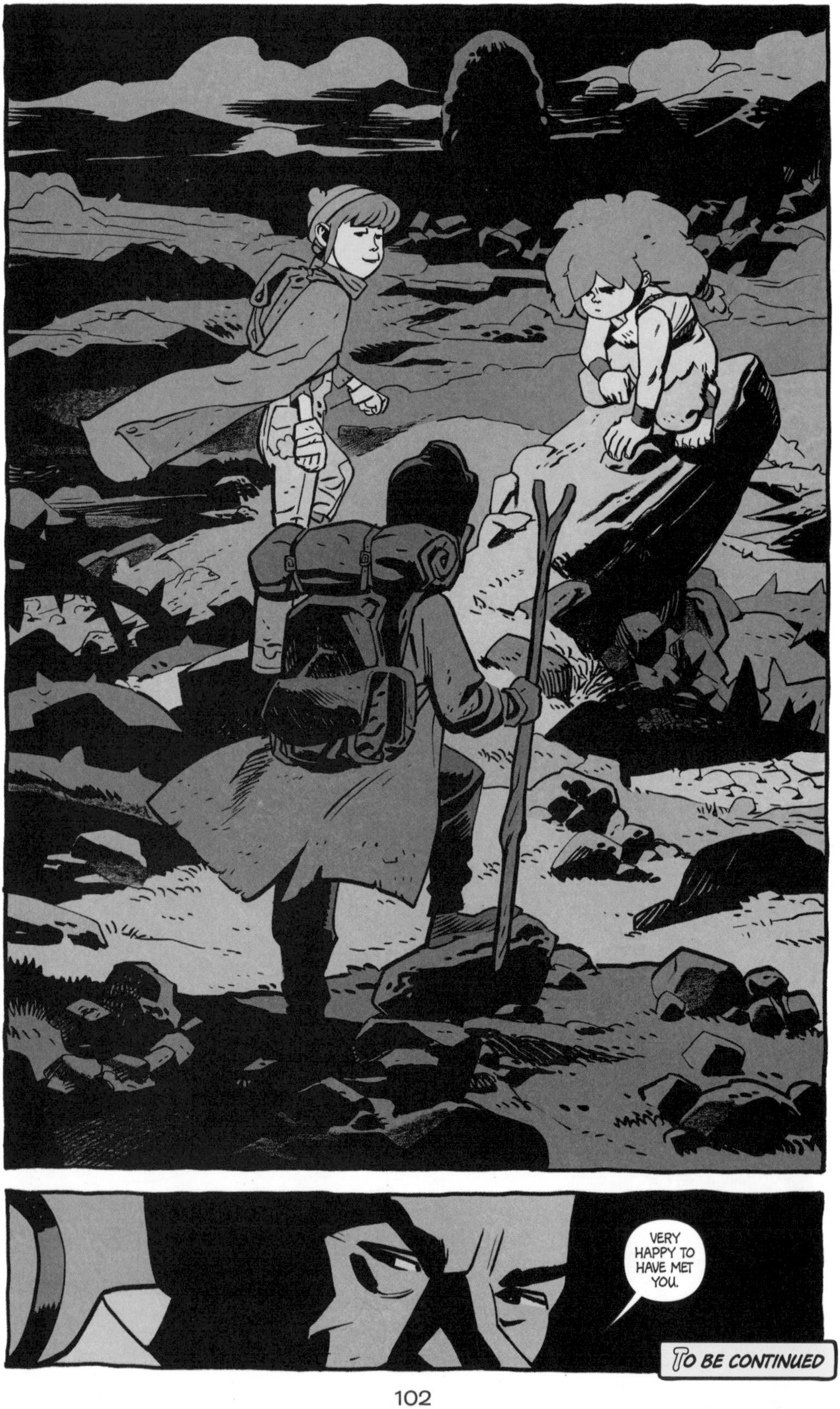
VERY HAPPY TO HAVE MET YOU.
TO BE CONTINUED

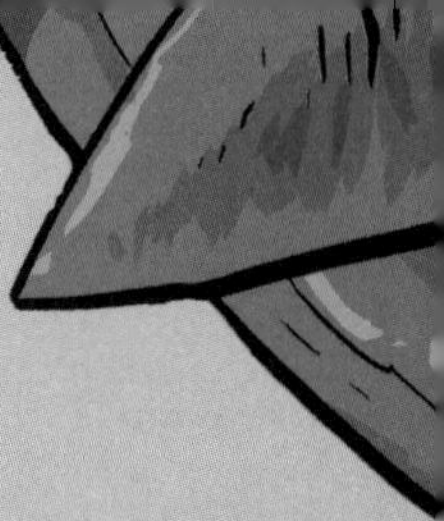

TO BE CONTINUED IN

JONNA
AND THE UNPOSSIBLE MONSTERS

VOLUME TWO:
out in Spring 2022

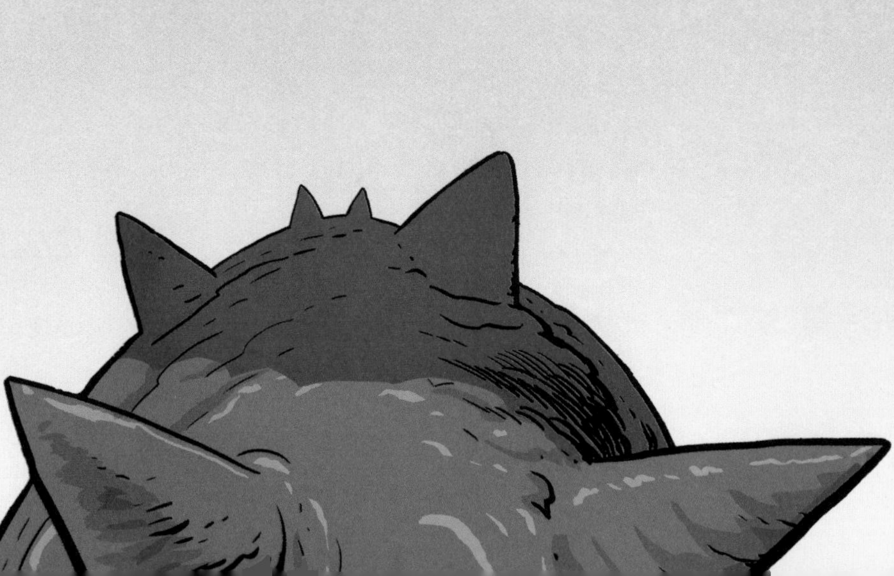

HELLO, READERS!

Our inspiration for creating *Jonna and the Unpossible Monsters* was to make something we could share with our three daughters. Not only were we inspired to create something *for* them, but we were inspired *by* them. The characters of Rainbow and Jonna were very much based on our two oldest daughters—one bossy, well-meaning older sister and one wild child who packs a mighty punch!

With this book, we wanted to tell a story about families and belonging—and, of course, monsters! After many years of drawing superheroes, Chris was excited to explore a world of monsters and rubble on his drawing table. He has always been a fan of the Japanese creatures known as kaiju, and knew that his first project as a writer/artist would include lots of monsters—the bigger the better!

We hope we've created a book that can be enjoyed by anyone—from the newest comic reader to the lifelong comic fan—and a book that would be enjoyed by both kids and their parents.

Thank you for joining Rainbow and Jonna on their adventure—we hope you enjoy the journey!

CHRIS & LAURA SAMNEE

JONNA
AND THE UNPOSSIBLE MONSTERS

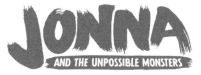

Activity Pages!

Break out your crayons, markers, colored pencils, or whatever you have at hand and color in our heroes! Draw right in the book or make a photocopy, it's up to you!

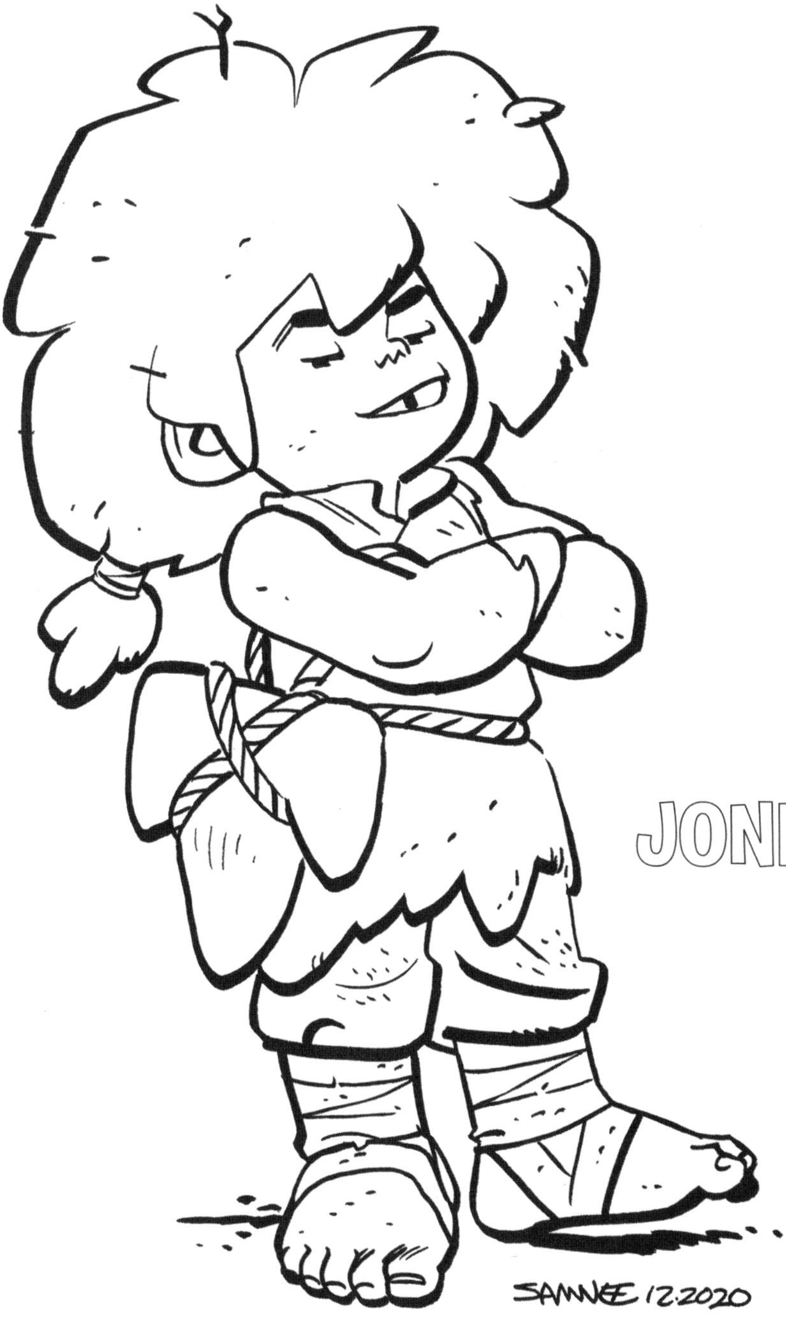
SAMNEE 12.2020

JONNA

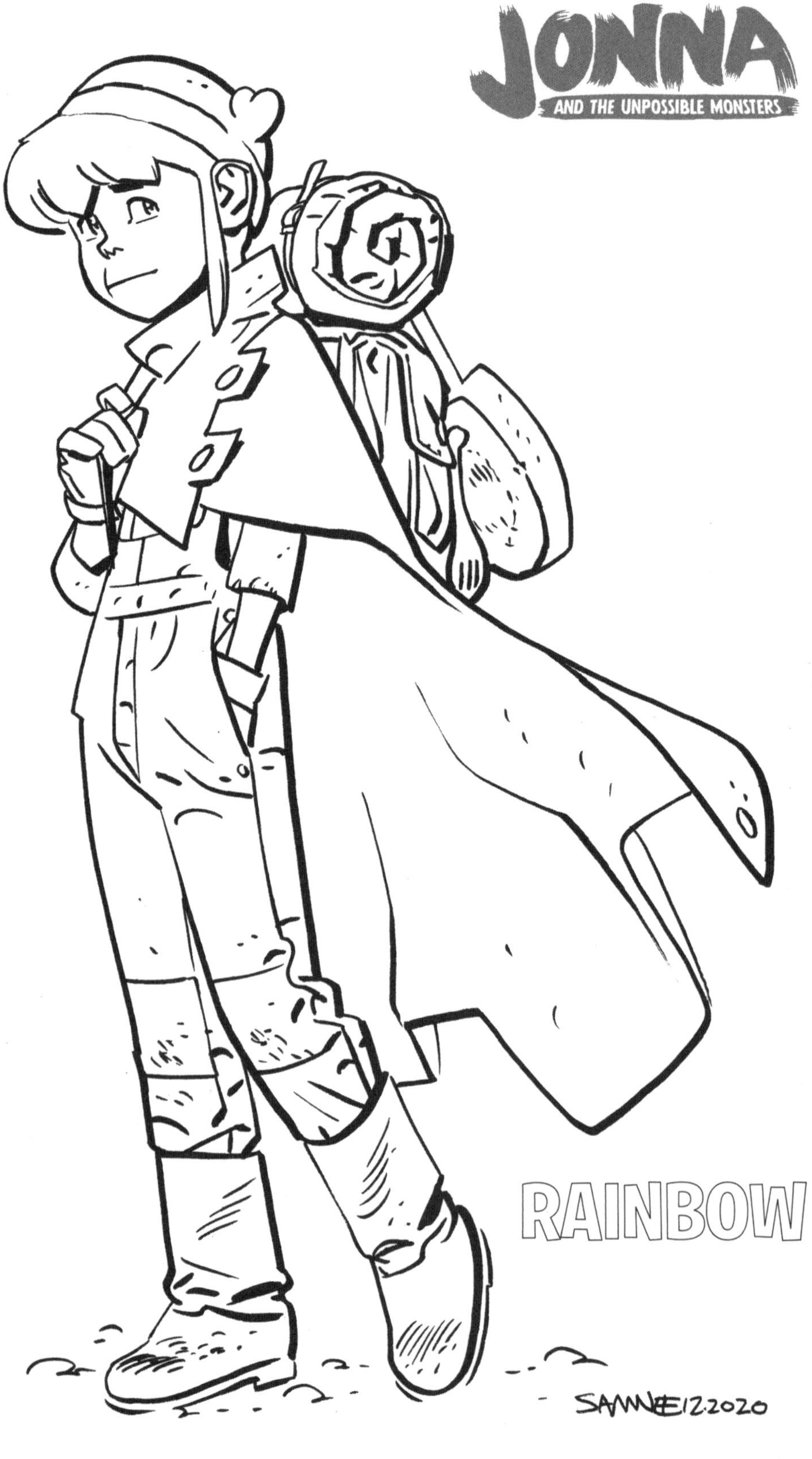
JONNA
AND THE UNPOSSIBLE MONSTERS
RAINBOW
SAMNEE 12.2020

JONNA AND THE UNPOSSIBLE MONSTERS

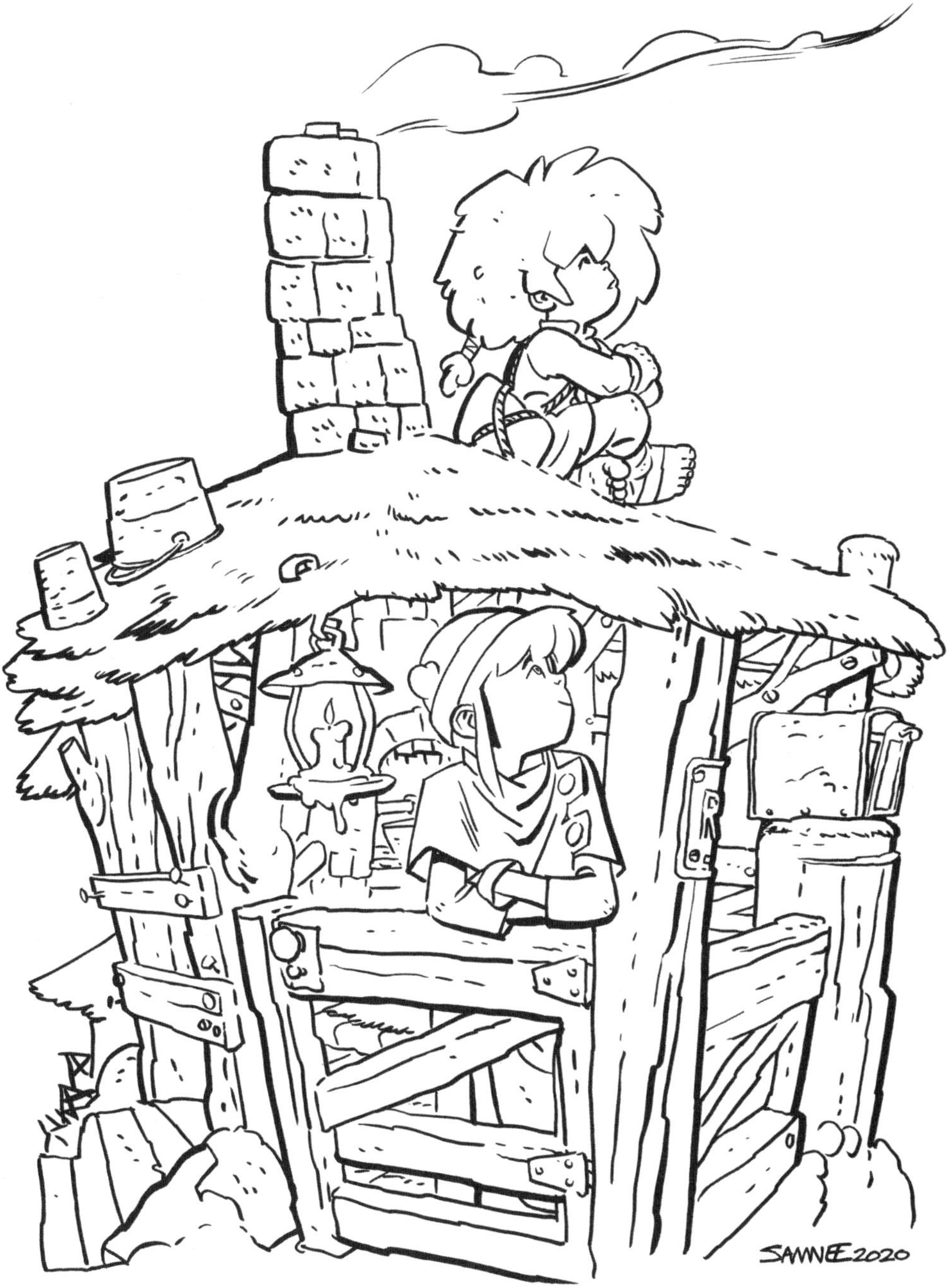
SAMNEE 2020

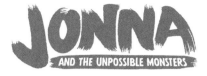

JONNA
AND THE UNPOSSIBLE MONSTERS

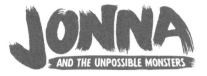

Help Rainbow find Jonna,
but be careful—there're MONSTERS out there!

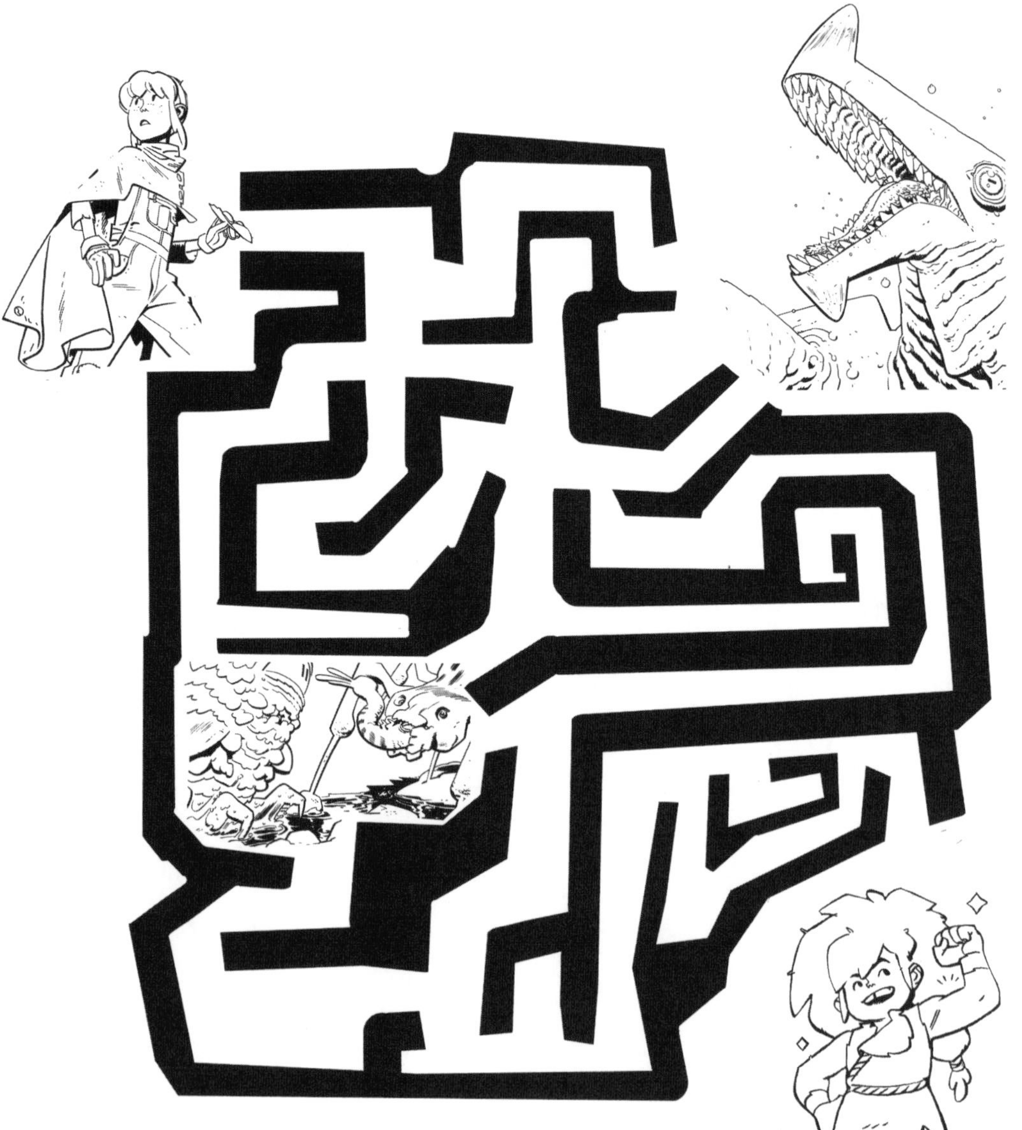

BIOGRAPHIES

CHRIS SAMNEE
is an Eisner and Harvey Award-winning cartoonist.
He's best known for his work on *Daredevil, Black Widow,* and *Thor: The Mighty Avenger.* He lives in St. Louis, Missouri, with his wife, Laura, and their three daughters.

LAURA SAMNEE
lives in St. Louis, Missouri, with her husband, Chris, and their three daughters. This is her first book.

MATTHEW WILSON
has been coloring comics since 2003. He's a two-time Eisner Award winner for Best Coloring and has collaborated with Chris Samnee on more projects than he can recall. When he's not coloring comics, he's out on a hike with his wife and two dogs.

CHRISTOPHER CRANK (CRANK!)
has lettered a bunch of books put out by Image, Dark Horse, Oni Press, Dynamite, and elsewhere. He also has a podcast with comic artist Mike Norton and members of Four Star Studios in Chicago (crankcast.com) and makes music (sonomorti.bandcamp.com).

Liked JONNA?
Check out these other g

PILU OF THE WOODS
by Mai K. Nguyen
ISBN: 978-1-62010-564-1

THE SUNKEN TOWER
by Tait Howard
ISBN: 978-1-62010-687-7

CRETACEOUS
by Tadd Galusha
ISBN: 978-1-62010-565-8

SCI-FU VOL. 1
by Yehudi Mercado
ISBN: 978-1-62010-472-9

COSTUME QUEST
by Zac Gorman
ISBN: 978-1-62010-559-7

THE TEA DRAGON SOCIETY
by K. O'Neill
ISBN: 978-1-62010-441-5